THE PIRATE

CAPTAINS & CANNONS
BOOK I

BY

GALEN SURLAK-RAMSEY

A TINY FOX PRESS BOOK

Tiny Fox Press LLC
North Port, Fl

For Dad,
You'd have liked this one

Chapter I
The Citadel

THE FRILLS BELOW the spearhead gave the weapon a nice finishing touch. This was something Sammy would've appreciated immensely, had the spear not shot from the ground and skewered him completely through the chest only moments before.

A few feet away, Zoey watched the life drain from him. Aside from her usual attire of dark breeches and an even darker linen shirt (the color of both helping to hide blood, as it was hard to be taken seriously as a dread corsair if people could see how many places you'd sprung a leak during a fight), she also wore a look of utter annoyance. It was a look she wore well, and sadly, had much practice with as of late.

"Where in the eleven seas did you find these guys?" she asked.

Stede, the grizzled leader of the expedition, shrugged as he ran an open hand over his bald head. "I don't know. Here and there."

"You don't know? Kraken spit. No wonder this has gone belly up."

"I know where, thank you," he said with an edge to his tone as he crossed his arms over his black leather vest. "I meant I'd have to think about the specifics. You want to know about Sammy or everyone else?"

"You can start with Sammy since he's the corpse we're staring at," Zoey said. She brought up her cutlass and poked the recently deceased in the side. "Let's hope he stays that way."

"Found Sammy in the tavern."

"Which?"

"*The* tavern."

"The Salty Dog? The one that's filled with fresh meat looking to be carried?"

Stede nodded. "Only one I know of. Slim pickings, though, lately."

"That's because they all end up like poor Sammy here and do something stupid, like step on a glowing portion of floor or a discolored tile and spring an obvious trap. I swear, no one respects hardcore anymore."

Zoey took a few deep breaths to calm herself, feeling her blood rising. While many people out there felt working under stressed conditions was far from ideal, Zoey took that to an entirely new level. One of her negative traits, *The Hunger*, was every bit as ominous as it sounded. When it grabbed her, she had to satiate her appetite, no matter where she was, lest she be wracked with tremendous pain and mental anguish. The more she was stressed, the hungrier she became. It could quickly send her into a downward spiral that had, on more than one occasion, only ended when someone died.

She tried not to think about that last part. "What about the others?" Zoey asked, blowing out one last puff of air. "Where did you get the twins?"

"Pete and Zachariah?"

"No, those two were just brothers," she said. "The twins were the ones crushed by the boulder right before we entered the catacombs."

"Oh. Where did we lose Pete and Zach then?"

"Monkey spiders."

"Right, the monkey spiders," Stede replied with a chuckle. "Found all four of them at the notice board, actually. They were putting up a sign. Privateers for hire, or something."

"What did you pay them?"

"Six nabloons up front, plus the usual half share," he said. "That's a bargain, I reckon."

"How's that?" Zoey asked. "They're all dead."

"Exactly. For six nabloons, we nullified four traps."

"One trap and one surprise attack."

"Eh, close enough."

Zoey furrowed her brow. "Okay, new rule. If you want me to join up next time, you're telling me who you're bringing, what you're paying them, and I get to approve each one. No more of this 'Meet us where X marks the spot' nonsense. God, I should've simply left the moment Rubio bought it."

"Come on, that's not fair," Stede said. "That troll had a killer ambush spot."

"First, he was under a bridge, where they always are," Zoey replied. "And second, that was Becca."

"Rubio was our voodoo doctor?"

"Yes. The one who couldn't be bothered to read the instructtions and turned himself into a pygmy-piggy-pegasus when his polymorph backfired."

"He did make a cute pig."

Zoey, against every fiber in her body, couldn't help but crack a smile. Stede wasn't wrong on that. The tiny, adorable little pink pig with a small horn coming out of his forehead and feathery wings would've made the perfect companion to cheer up any long sea voyage. Teaching it to ram enemies with its horn would've been handy, too. It was just too bad that hydra had shown up right after and treated itself to some pre-processed bacon.

"Regardless," she said. "They're dead, and I might not have much of a soul left here, but I've got some. I don't like the idea of suckering people to their untimely demise."

"No one put a pistol to their head."

Zoey raised an eyebrow.

"Okay, I put a pistol to Marcus's head, but that was only because I caught him cheating at Karnöffel." When Zoey didn't approve, or even say another word, Stede went on. "Look at it this way, more share for us."

"If we survive."

"Well, yeah, if we survive," he said. "Split between the three of us, you'll have a good chunk for that new ship you're wanting."

At that point in the conversation, Isabel, the third and final surviving member of the party showed up. She came from a side hall, strutting brazenly to such a degree that Zoey couldn't believe she hadn't been the one to set off the three dozen traps or ambushes they'd had to deal with. The reason why, Zoey knew, was all the luck points she'd invested in, plus the *Good Fortune* and *Flirter with Death* talents. Then there was the *Bribe Grimmy* perk that let her reroll any fatal damage or effect, not to mention the *Gambler's Luck* buff she always had on that let her make another two rerolls a day. Essentially, the woman had to be killed three times in a row for her to actually go down. Maybe more.

But one would never know all of that simply by looking at her. Isabel had wavy raven hair under a red band that vainly tried to keep it all tamed. Large gold earrings hung three on each ear, and she wore as many rings as she had fingers. The wealth she flaunted beckoned any foolish highwayman to make a try for her, but the double pistols tucked into her waistband and the cutlass that hung from her hip kept the more astute observers away. What she looked like, in short, was someone who didn't need luck at all, but as Isabel was always fond of saying, she'd rather be lucky than good.

Though Zoey couldn't deny such a strategy had kept the woman alive thus far, not to mention enriched, she hated such an attitude. Sure, it was good at keeping her own skin intact, but often at the expense of everyone else.

"Finally pried those silver scarabs loose," Isabel said in an accented, refined voice that belied her lawless look. "And you two wanted to pass them up." She stopped when her dark eyes saw Sammy. She cocked her head, smirked, and held out an open hand, palm up. "Pay up."

Stede grinned and slowly walked over to her. "I'm afraid my coin purse is empty. Can I work it off?"

"Mm-hm, and work you shall," she replied. Isabel wrapped her arms around his neck and pulled him close. She kissed him lightly a couple of times, at which point Stede pushed her up against the wall and kissed her neck as his hands found their way inside her clothes.

Zoey cleared her throat.

They kept at it, and a few seconds later, Isabel had her hand going for the inside of his pants.

Zoey cleared her throat again, and when they still ignored her, Zoey spoke. Loudly. "Alright. I don't care if you two are newlyweds. Get a room at the inn," she said. A couple of groans and a lot of necking later, she huffed. "Or don't. I don't care. I'm getting that gem with or without you."

"Stupid nympho trait," Zoey muttered, wishing she'd realized they both had it before she undertook this adventure. She'd barely pivoted on her heels when she heard the pair split apart. Stede said something, but she didn't pay it much heed since it was more complaint than anything else.

They followed the damp stone hall for another twenty yards, all the while taking care to avoid all the blatantly obvious tiles designed to skewer, smash, crush, fry, curse, and ruin the day of any hapless intruder who happened upon them. At that point, they reached a spiral staircase that, according to Stede's map (which had ended up being little more than a hastily drawn sketch based on tavern whispers from a drunkard), would take them up and into the throne room of an abandoned citadel.

And if the rumors of rumors were true—and so far, they certainly looked like they might be—the recently deceased necromancer who had once occupied this fortress had said throne room adorned in precious gems and priceless artifacts accumulated over the years, all ripe for the taking.

Assuming one could get to it without alerting the guards, that is—undead minions numbering in the hundreds, foul and deadly, with only one purpose left in this world: to protect their former master's estate.

Zoey was about to do what she did best, *Sneak* and scout ahead, when the hairs across her body stood on end. Without thinking, she grabbed Isabel, fearing the woman might decide to take the stairs before her.

"What?" Isabel asked, sounding both irritated and wary.

"Trap," Zoey answered, directing the woman's eyes not to the irregular stones that formed the dungeon floor, but to a single glyph faintly inscribed in the threshold between them and the stairs, about ankle high.

Stede grimaced. "That was close. What kind is it?"

Zoey knelt and examined it as best she could while staying far, far away. The rune had been etched long ago, and physically identifying it proved difficult. The power emanating from around it, however, felt weak. "Hex with one charge left, I think."

"You think?"

Zoey stood and crossed her arms over her chest. "Yes, I think," she said. "You're more than welcome to come take a look and offer your expert opinion, though. Oh, wait, you don't know a damn thing about traps, do you?"

Stede frowned and huffed. "Can you tell us anything else about it?"

Zoey let the situation diffuse on its own by not adding to the fire. "Only that it's Voodoo."

"Everything is Voodoo," Isabel said after a few muttered curses. "I miss the days when treasure was buried under six feet of dirt, and the most you had to deal with were scallywags trying to beat you to it. Can you counter it?"

Zoey shook her head. "No. Rubio maybe, but he's—"

"—a pygmy-piggy-unicorn," Stede finished. "Or was."

"Right."

"What about a sacrificial lamb?" Isabel asked.

Zoey grinned. "Are you volunteering?"

"No, but Sammy is."

Zoey glanced over her shoulder to where their former party member lay. His body was upright, more or less, but it had slid down the shaft about a foot. Blood still oozed from the giant wounds in his chest and back. When Zoey had first come to this world, such a sight would've made her stomach churn, but after seeing countless friends and foes mashed, shot, roasted, and gibbed—some in the most hilarious of ways—all she saw was a potential tool. "Worth a shot," she said. "I bet he's still fresh enough to trigger whatever magic is here."

"Good enough for me," Stede said. "Help me bring him over."

Isabel held up her hands and shook her head. "I'm not touching that."

Zoey rolled her eyes. "Shocker."

"Shut it."

Zoey ignored her and went to help Stede. Together, and with a great deal of effort, they freed the corpse formerly known as Sammy from the impaling device. At that point, they slung his arms across their backs and carefully brought him over to the threshold.

"How does this work? Just toss him through?"

"Sounds good to me," Zoey said.

"You sure nothing bad will happen?"

Zoey shook her head with a laugh. "I never said that."

Stede grunted and shook his head. "Fine. Whatever. On three. Ready?"

"Yup."

"One. Two. Three."

With a great heave, the two tossed the body through the threshold. The rune flared a dazzling purple as Sammy tumbled through. Wisps of putrid smoke rose from his skin, and his body twitched. At first, Zoey figured it was simply his muscles going into spasm from whatever unholy energy raced through him. But all that changed when Sammy rolled onto his stomach and pushed himself up.

Stede inched back. "Sammy?"

As a reply, Sammy snarled and drew his sword.

"Oh, that can't be good," Zoey said, pulling her black-powder pistol from her waistband.

Isabel followed suit, pulling both of her pistols free as well, but she didn't waste any time before firing. The shots hit Sammy square in the face, and when he didn't drop, Isabel cursed. "That really can't be good."

Chapter II
Lord Belmont

SAMMY LUNGED.

Zoey caught the blade on the strong part of her cutlass, easily trapping the attack against her handguard and deflecting it harmlessly to the side. She followed up with a counter-attack of her own, flicking her wrist first to send Sammy's sword flying to the side. Though he was wide open when she swung, and though she struck him directly across the collarbone, the attack did little other than produce a vicious gash across his body.

And when you're fighting the undead, vicious is all relative. Now that she thought about it, it was probably more of a tickling gash for the monster she was facing than anything else.

"Maybe he's not that fast," Stede said, edging away.

"He seems pretty fast to me," Zoey replied.

"Yeah, well, you keep him busy," he replied as he tried to dart around the reanimated corpse.

Sammy, however, was having none of that. He growled and jumped back with an agility that belied his broken, clearly dead frame and issued a wicked backhand that nearly took Stede's head from his shoulders.

"Cripes," Isabel said as she fumbled with her shot and powder to reload her pistols. "Keep him busy so I can blow his head off."

Sammy attacked again, forcing Stede to retreat, lest he be skewered like a pig on a spit. This left him open to a counterattack from Zoey, which she took advantage of. She hopped to the side, putting her directly behind him in order to maximize her backstab critical hits, and she stabbed for all she was worth.

The point of her cutlass drove through the back of Sammy's head and went all the way through so that the sword jutted out of his left eye. It ceased Sammy's attack on Stede, but much to Zoey's dismay, it didn't kill him. Well, kill him again. All it seemed to accomplish was to redirect his attention from Stede to Zoey.

Had she been the type built for deflecting and absorbing large amounts of damage, this would've been fine. A well-placed taunt, be it verbal or physical, had saved many a party in a dungeon or on a raid, numerous times. Garnering unwanted attention for someone less stout as she was, however, often had the opposite effect.

Sammy whipped around with such speed and power, Zoey lost the grip on her weapon. He swung his blade through the air, and the tip sliced through her left shoulder.

Zoey fell back, grabbing the wound. She was tempted to check to see how much damage had been done, but over the years since she'd first come here, she'd found that paying too much attention to the numbers meant less attention was paid to what was happening right then and there.

Sammy swung again, but this time, she wasn't caught off guard like she had been before. As such, she had no chance at failure, and the dodge was made automatically. When she recovered, she regained her footing next to Isabel, who had just finished reloading her pistols.

Thank the gods of the sea Isabel had opted to take *Fast Firing* four levels ago.

"Here you go, love," she said, bringing both flintlocks up. "Loaded these with something special for you."

Isabel pulled the triggers on both weapons. The pistols belched smoke and bright blue flames. The half-inch slugs from each weapon drilled through Sammy's head, causing it to explode in a shower of gore.

He dropped to the floor, and his body quickly dissolved into a puddle of black goo.

"Cripes, what did you use?" Zoey asked.

Isabel grinned, loading her weapons once again. "Silver bullets. You know, the usual standard against all things unholy or furry."

"Remind me to have this weapon blessed when we get back," Zoey said, picking her cutlass up and sighing with relief.

"When we get back, we'll each have enough money to bless an entire armory," said Stede. "Now, let's go."

The trio made their way up the ascending staircase. Once again, Zoey had the lead because neither of the other two were willing to walk point, especially since she was the only one who had managed to spy the Voodoo trap from before. By the time they reached the top of the stairs, they hadn't found or triggered anything else, which was just fine with Zoey.

Just fine indeed.

The staircase brought them into a small room clogged with cobwebs. There were so many, in fact, one could easily craft enough bandages for a small army, should one so desire. Zoey, however, didn't, and the thick webbing fell to her blade. After considerable effort on her part, she reached the door on the far side.

"Some throne room," Isabell grunted.

"Maybe it's through there," Stede replied. "Let's see."

Zoey spent a moment checking for traps and then two more rechecking and rechecking again. When she came up with nothing, she tried the handle, which turned easily enough, and pushed the door open.

It swung out, its rusty iron hinges groaning loudly in protest. What it revealed was, indeed, a large throne room, with them entering at the opposite end of where a king once sat. Large columns stood proudly on each side of the great hall, supporting a vaulted ceiling some thirty feet above. Immaculately cut marble tiles lined the floor, while tapestries, old as the sea on which the group had sailed to get there, hung from the walls.

Colored light poured in from the outside by way of stained glass windows set high, and while the evening sun only had an hour at best before dipping below the horizon, even at the low angle, it provided more than enough light to see.

Not that Zoey needed it. Again, character perk, *Night Vision*. Helped with her being a thief, among other things.

Cautiously, Zoey led the way forward, her eyes straining for any sign of a trap while her ears tried to pick up even the slightest hint of approaching guard. She saw neither. The former, she wasn't too surprised at, as practically speaking, it was a little stupid to trap one's own living space. The latter, however, concerned her.

Where were these hordes of undead they were supposed to be avoiding? The guardians of the isle seemed to be doing a pretty crappy job of guarding at this point. Were they elsewhere? Or had whatever magic that imbued them with life finally given out? She hoped that would be the case but feared it might not be. What if they'd never existed?

That last thought troubled her the most, and though she didn't have a concrete answer to what it would mean if that theory proved to be the case, she couldn't help but feel that it would be bad.

"Now that's a throne," Isabel said, her voice teeming with excitement.

Zoey snapped out of her thoughts and refocused on what lay ahead. Not even ten yards away sat an obsidian throne fit for a titan atop a platform with a half dozen steps leading up to it. Embedded along its sides were several diamonds and rubies, each easily worth the fortune of a small country. A single one could buy Zoey the ship she so desperately needed so she might finally be able to leave this world and go home.

"Hell yeah," Stede said, with a disbelieving laugh. "That's it. We made it."

"You suppose this is—er, was—the necromancer?" Isabel asked, nodding toward the skeletal figure with taut leathery skin who was slumped over in the throne.

"Probably," Zoey said, inching forward. "Stay back."

"Why?"

"Because I'd rather not set off one last trap since we're this close to getting what we came for," she explained.

Zoey went about her task as thoroughly and patiently as she could. Nothing on the floor stood out to her, nor the stairs, nor the throne. She even examined the corpse as best she could without touching it, fearing it might come to life as Sammy had.

It didn't.

But she did get a good look at the deceased. Whoever it was, he wore a fashionable navy longcoat embroidered with gold threads, as well as a white undercoat with matching trousers. On his head of stringy hair sat a bicorne hat, black, that appeared to be in remarkably good condition. One hand clutched an armrest, while the other tightly held a staff topped with a skull. A small ruby amulet hung around his neck, an impressive piece of jewelry, no doubt, but that gem paled compared to the ones actually set in the throne.

The very last thing that caught Zoey's eye was a pistol made of silver and dark wood that had been tucked into his belt. Across the butt of the weapon, Zoey could make out etchings—but etchings of what?

She leaned in for a better view. A spell? Enchantments?

She almost took it.

Stede's voice stayed her hand. "Hang on a second," he said. "What do you think you're doing?"

"Looking."

"More like taking," he said.

Though he was right on that part, Zoey argued against it. She wasn't intentionally being greedy, but there was an allure to the weapon, and curiosity demanded she at least pick the pistol up and see how it felt in her hands.

His objection did do something else other than keep her from taking the item. It allowed a thought to dawn on her.

"This isn't a necromancer," she said, backing away.

"Course it is," Isabel said, walking up to her. "Who else would it be?"

Zoey shook her head and retreated another step as gooseflesh appeared on her arms. "I don't know," she said. "But look at him. That's not the garb of a necromancer. An admiral is more like it."

The jewels on the throne suddenly faded away, revealing, Zoey immediately realized, that they were nothing more than illusions.

Before she could offer any sort of warning, withered fingers cracked as they flexed on throne and staff. The figure stood, body full of life despite its emaciated frame, and eye sockets full of fire.

"Allow me to introduce myself," the figure said before giving a sweeping bow. "Lord Belmont, at your service. Or perhaps I should say, you will soon be at mine."

CHAPTER III
ESCAPE

I SABEL DREW HER pistols before the breath had a chance to freeze in Zoey's lungs. "Think again," she said. "I've taken down worse than the likes of you."

Lord Belmont toyed with the top of his scepter without an ounce of concern for either the woman's threats or her weapons pointed at him. "And what are the likes of me, I wonder?"

"Skeleton. Weight. Revenant. Barrow fiend. Whichever, I don't care," Isabel said, narrowing her eyes.

As the two had their standoff, Stede came to his lover's side, sword drawn. Zoey, on the other hand, eased away. She needed options, either to look for a backstab or a way to beat a hasty retreat into the shadows.

"Going somewhere?" Lord Belmont said, turning his face toward the woman with a bemused look on his decrepit face.

Zoey froze, and she worried she hadn't a prayer to see tomorrow. She was fast, but the casualness at which this undead creature addressed them all told her she wasn't fast enough no matter what she tried. Or worse, even if she was, it wouldn't matter.

"A perceptive thing, aren't we?" Lord Belmont said as if reading her thoughts. He then gestured to a side hall with his scepter. "Could I interest the three of you in one last meal? I have so many questions regarding where you came from."

Isabel thrust her pistols forward, stretching her arms as far as they'd go. Her hands trembled, signaling the break of morale. "Shut up!" she yelled. "Get out of here while you still can, you mummified lobcock."

The amulet around Lord Belmont's neck picked up a soft glow, one that Zoey was certain only she noticed or understood. "He's not a mummy," she said, backing away a few more steps and voice trembling. "He's a lich."

"Right you are, my dear woman, and—"

Isabel fired both pistols, interrupting whatever else he had to say, screaming from the top of her lungs as she did. The bullets tore straight through whatever black heart still beat inside Lord Belmont's chest.

The lich didn't flinch. He didn't even snarl or seem mildly surprised for that matter. He simply raised his staff, and the skull's eye sockets briefly flared a deep orange before dark tendrils snaked out its mouth and wrapped themselves around Isabel.

The woman shrieked, her body contorting and aging a thousand years in the blink of an eye. Light poured out of her chest, but only for a moment. Those very same tendrils grabbed hold of it and pulled it back into the staff.

"Isabel!" The power behind Stede's yell was second only to the guttural war cry that followed it. He leaped through the air, sword high overhead, only to be met with a similar fate.

His withered corpse hit the floor next to Lord Belmont's feet, shattering into fragments of bone and dust.

Lord Belmont rubbed his now brightly glowing amulet, seemingly taking great pleasure in whatever sensation it gave him.

"This," the lich said, motioning to what little remained of Zoey's companions, "is why I'm the one to restore goodness to the world."

Zoey snorted, retreating further. "Yeah? How's that? You don't exactly seem to be the charitable type, seeing how you murdered my friends."

Lord Belmont snickered. "At least now I don't have to wonder about you."

"Come again?"

"By your own words, you're friends with thieves and brigands," he explained. "Those so brazen that they'd break into a man's home and rob him while he's still there."

"This place was supposed to be abandoned!"

"No, I believe you thought the necromancer who once lived here was now dead, which at best makes you a grave robber—a despicable sort, perhaps even more than those who rob the living," Lord Belmont corrected. "And for the record, the necromancer is indeed dead, by my hand, in fact. Resurrected to serve the greater cause by my hand as well. Which is exactly what's going to happen to you."

Zoey turned on the balls of her feet and ran, her legs pumping feverishly. She was fast, faster than most, but as she'd feared, she wasn't fast enough.

Lord Belmont whipped his scepter in line with her, and from his mouth, dark words of power flowed. Again, the tendrils came. They snaked around her arms and legs, burned her flesh, but Zoey pressed on, gritting her teeth and refusing to succumb.

Her legs gave out two strides later, and she crashed to the floor. Her head struck the ground, dazing her. She had enough presence of mind to keep scrambling for where she thought the exit lay, somewhere in the shadowy mess of darkness and shapes that now was her world.

Spidery fingers found the back of her neck and hoisted her off the ground. Her vision refocused right as Lord Belmont spun her around and slammed her back into one of the columns. He pinned her there, pressing his scepter against her neck, and eyed her as if she were some curiosity that had never graced this world before.

"What are you?" he asked, more to himself than her. A moment passed before recognition shone on his face. "I can't believe I didn't see it before," he said, laughing. "A kindred spirit, or maybe a distant cousin, all things considered."

"Let me go," she said, struggling against his grip, but she might as well have been struggling against a leviathan.

"I think not," he said, pushing a little harder. "But at the same time, I can't exactly kill you like the others, can I? What a waste of potential power."

Fear, in the most basic, primal sense, the sort of existential dread that only those who'd stood at the edge of the abyss and stared into its bottomless dark had ever experienced, took hold. Her strength left her, and she could feel the dark abilities she bore leave her body.

"You're...not...taking...me..." she croaked. Zoey's eyes rolled back as her spirit desperately tried to tap into one shred of her old self before Lord Belmont ripped it all away.

Her body dissolved into what was little more than a white mist, and Lord Belmont, caught completely unaware, stumbled into the column. When Zoey reformed, she was at the other end of the hall, running for the side room from which they'd originally entered.

Lord Belmont whipped out his pistol and fired. The bullet tore a chunk of stone out of the wall only an inch from her chest.

An instant later, she raced down the stairs, taking three or four at a time. She slammed into the curved wall more than once before she reached the bottom. Behind her, she could hear the lich bellowing, calling to someone, or someones, unseen.

She leaped over Sammy's fallen body, and after passing a T-junction, a hidden slab of rock dropped from the ceiling, blocking off her escape.

"Oh, come on," Zoey cried out. "That's not fair at all."

She backtracked and took the other hall, hoping, praying that this one would still lead to an exit. She ran for only the gods knew how long, down twisting passages, taking branches at random. Nearly a dozen times by her count, she spotted a pressure plate or a tripwire only a split second before setting it off, but her luck didn't hold forever.

She entered an L-shaped room full of wine barrels and was headed for the exit on the other end when she inadvertently stepped on a loose tile that sank a few inches when her foot struck it. Zoey tensed, expecting to be riddled with bolts or incinerated by fire.

None of that came, but what did was no less deadly. It started as a distant roar, some sort of sound she couldn't quite place. But a second later, she knew exactly what it was. It was the roar of a tsunami.

Zoey ran faster than before, throwing a glance over her shoulder to see a deluge of water rushing toward her.

She dashed through the lower levels of Lord Belmont's citadel at breakneck speeds. She bolted down a curved corridor that branched in three places near the end. She took the passage to the left and then up a flight of stairs, thinking going up might buy her some time against the flood behind her. These stairs dumped her into an octagonal chamber where two dozen skeletons lay strewn about along with the remains of one of their former party members.

She wouldn't have slowed here either if it hadn't been for the deep rumbling that came from practically every direction at once.

"What the—" was all she got out before a torrent of water came pouring at her from three different directions. Before she could even think about getting out of the way, the flood crashed into her and swept her away.

Underwater, Zoey rolled across the hard floor, twice striking her head. Thankfully, she had the wherewithal to hold her breath as she tumbled. Eventually, she struck something hard with her back, which kept her from rolling any further. Quickly, she pushed herself up and kicked toward the surface. When she broke through and gasped for air, she found herself in another part of the lower levels that she'd been in before, which meant she knew where the exit was.

"I swear, when I get out of here, I'm never playing this stupid game ever again," Zoey muttered as she went for a passage to her right.

She waded down it as fast as she could, and the water had risen to chest level by the time she'd almost reached a set of stairs she knew would lead her to safety.

A tentacle suddenly wrapped around her chest and dragged her under.

Zoey yelled in fright but managed to stop herself before completely expelling all of her air. The creature violently yanked her around. In the midst of the frenzy, she hacked away at it with her cutlass. The first couple of times she swung, she missed, but the third strike cut deeply into whatever had grabbed her. The tentacle instantly released its grip, and at the same time, whatever it was shot out a dark inky cloud that completely blinded her.

Sputtering, Zoey managed to reach the surface once again, but she had to swim for it. The water had risen so high at this point, there were only a couple feet between the surface and the dungeon ceiling. Worse, the current was strong and dragged her off.

Down the corridor she went, bouncing off of walls and columns until she managed to catch hold of an open doorway and pull herself onto some stairs. Tired, cold, and at her breaking point, Zoey stumbled up the flight until she reached a small square chamber that held only barrels.

"Come on," she said, glancing in each one. "There's got to be something I can use."

There was something. Wine. But at the moment, that didn't do her much good. Worse, the water had started to make its way into the room at this point. Giving up on finding some steampunk

SCUBA gear, or a potion that might temporarily transmute her into a mermaid, her eyes went to the walls.

There had to be a way out.

There just had to be. This place had been filled with secret passages practically from top to bottom. You could pretty much push bricks at random and find something eventually. And since the water rose here, that meant the air had to be getting out, too. As such, the odds of there not being one had to be astronomical. Or, well, maybe fifty-fifty if she was being honest. Ninety-ten, against, more like it.

Zoey shook her head, returning to the task at hand.

Each stone brick she saw appeared identical. Not a single deviation could be seen in any of it. They were all the same shape and color. Even the pattern of moss and how it branched in certain places was the same.

But then she saw it: a small gray mark in between the seams of one of the bricks, about chest high. Smiling broadly, she hurried over to it, her feet splashing loudly. Zoey threw herself at the mark, hitting it with an open palm.

The brick above it sank in a few inches, and she could hear a grinding noise somewhere. But then all was quiet, and nothing changed except for the rising water.

"No!" she screamed, hitting it again and again. "Work, damn you!"

The wall next to her slid into the floor. Once again, she was swept down the hall by a powerful current, which was fine with her if it got her away from Lord Belmont alive. The hall narrowed, and as it did, the speed at which she traveled picked up as well.

Soon, she found herself rocketing through a narrow passage, and then she was dragged under and into a pipe barely big enough to accommodate her slender frame. Her lungs burned as she held her breath far longer than she'd thought possible.

Right as the air hunger threatened to burn a hole through her lungs and she was about to suck in some water so she could drown and get it over with, she was shot out the side of a cliff.

Once more, Zoey yelled in fright as she sailed through the air and across a deep gorge. She smacked into a rocky wall, and after spending every bit of luck she had saved, she managed to grab onto some of the thick vines that had made their home there before falling to her doom.

It took her a good ten minutes to pull herself out of the gorge, and at least half of those were spent resting on a nearby ledge and trying not to look down. When she reached the top, she found herself on the other side of the Black Siren Mountains, the range that encircled much of Gibbon Isle.

"Well, Zoey, at least we're alive," she said to herself, laughing, but her celebration was short-lived. She turned her head over her shoulder and noted the golden sky and the sun starting to dip beneath the horizon.

"Damn. Damn," she said, realizing night would have long settled before she reached her ship. Possibly the next day would've come as well. Worse, she'd have to deal with whatever stark reputation loss she'd be hit with for returning sans party.

A wolf howled in the distance. It sounded large and hungry. So did all of his friends.

"Damn. Damn. Damn," said Zoey. She kicked a nearby rock and sent it sailing in the gorge just because she could.

"Damn."

With that, she took off running.

Chapter IV
The Fair

North Carolina State Fair
Circa Present Day

WITH AN ORANGE ticket in hand, Ethan pushed through the turnstiles and made his way into the state fair. He was going to meet one of his friends outside first, but since he'd gotten off work early and ended up beating Logan by an hour, he decided to head on in and see what there was to do. At the very least, he'd drop in on the arcade tent and put to good use the pocket full of quarters he'd brought.

Hopefully, he thought, they'd have Gauntlet again like they did last year. Given how maddening his tech support job had become the last couple of weeks ("No, ma'am, your computer doesn't have a cupholder. That's the DVD drive. You can't turn it on? What do you mean you can't tell if it's plugged in? It's dark? Well, turn on a light? You mean the power is out in the entire house?"), he could use some mindless fun running dungeons and slaying hordes of monsters.

As Ethan walked the fair, people bustled by, some bumping into him, even fewer apologizing for it, but he was too busy taking it all in to mind. A menagerie of brightly colored tents and even brighter neon lights assaulted his eyes while his ears took on the sounds of laughs, screams, and high-energy fun, and his nose relished the smell of funnel cakes and cotton candy.

Straight ahead, towering over everything like the eye of a giant cyclops, was a massive Ferris wheel adorned in lights and slowly spinning. Laughter, loud and joyous, came from it, which was to be expected, and to his right, beyond rows of stands filled with mouthwatering treats that ranged from funnel cakes, to bacon-wrapped corndogs, to apple pie, was the go-cart track Ethan wanted to hit before the night was up. He needed a rematch with Logan so he could redeem himself after being lapped their last run.

The line for the go-carts, however, had grown so large that it snaked out of the officially designated pathway and seemed to be longer than that great Norse serpent, Jörmungandr. And since Ethan decided he didn't want to be collecting Social Security before he got to drive one, he made a mental note that they should come back early the next day and get in on the action then. There was a visceral pleasure to be found there second to none when one got to ram another over and over again.

Ethan continued through the crowd and paused briefly at the ring toss. He watched as the guy manning the booth flipped ring after ring onto Coke bottles about ten feet away with ease.

"Step right up! Win yourself a prize!" the man shouted to no one in particular as he tossed three more red rings onto three more bottles. When the last one finished spinning around the neck of the bottle and settle down, the man looked at Ethan and smiled. "Hey, champ! Why don't you give it a go? Five dollars for five chances! You could win your girlfriend one of these cute plushies!"

Ethan eyed the stable of stuffed animals that were prominently displayed along the top of one of the counters. Each one stared back at him with big plastic eyes that looked straight out of an anime movie and could likely melt the heart of the Ice Queen herself.

"No, thanks," Ethan said, realizing that there was no way in pickled pig's feet this guy was in the business of just giving away prizes, and he didn't stand a chance at winning. As such, he concocted a painful, awkward truth to avoid embarrassing himself. "I'm kind of single right now. You know how it is."

"A handsome guy like yourself, single? I don't believe it," the man said with a hearty laugh. "Come on, give it a go. Tell you what. Usually, you need to land five for five, but if you ring four bottles with five throws, I'll let you take home Thurman."

Ethan's eyes drifted upward to where the man was pointing. Hanging on its own special hook was a mammoth teddy bear that was nearly five feet tall. Black, lustrous fur looked so soft and inviting that Ethan was sure he'd sleep for a week the moment he snuggled up to it. Moreover, while the other prizes looked like a step above a cheap knockoff and probably had seams that would bust after a gentle sneeze, this teddy bear looked like it had been made with an enchanted loom by the gods themselves. There was no telling how much this thing cost.

"Ah, see?" the booth operator said with a bright smile. "I know that confidence. This is something you can do. And if the ladies aren't flocking to your door already, I promise you this: you'll have the pick of the litter here if you walk through the rest of the fair holding Thurman here."

Against Ethan's better judgment, he seriously considered the man's words. He knew the booth operator was schmoozing him, playing up the idea that supermodels would somehow fight to be at Ethan's side just because he had a large furry animal in tow, but at the same time, Ethan couldn't help but wonder if Thurman wouldn't be a good conversation starter for at least one girl he knew.

"Where did you get that bear?" Melissa would say.

"Oh, this thing?" he'd reply as he leaned up against his beat-up Dodge Omni (in his fantasy, he wasn't delusional enough to think he'd be sporting a Porsche or a Ferrari). "I won it at the state fair last night. No biggie."

"That's amazing. At the ring toss?"

"Yeah, I think that was it."

"First try?" Her brown eyes would be bigger than the moon at this point. Her mouth would hang slightly open, and she'd be breathless obviously, with skin flushed.

Then he'd shrug as if the whole night was a blur of awesome. "I think so. Truth be told, I cleaned the guy out of all his prizes, so I don't remember when I won Thurman exactly. Of course, I had to donate all of the smaller plushies to the orphanage this morning, but I thought I'd keep Thurman here as a souvenir."

Her hand would cover her chest. "God, Ethan, you're incredible."

"I have my moments," he'd answer, and only barely at that. She'd jump into his arms and press her lips against his while her hands snaked around his neck.

Ethan's fantasy came to an abrupt end when the booth owner cut in once again. "Let's play," he said. "What do you have to lose?"

"Five dollars," Ethan said with a chuckle.

"And I wager a lot more than that if you don't give it a whirl, yes? I know that look in a person's eyes."

Ethan nodded. He dug in his pocket and pulled out a single wadded-up five-dollar bill. "Okay, let's play."

The booth owner plucked the bill from Ethan's hands like a hawk plucking a fish from the water. He then spread five rings out in front of Ethan and stepped to the side. "Have at it. And good luck!"

Ethan picked up the first ring and tossed it a few times in his hands, trying to get a feel for its weight. He was never the most skillful when it came to various athletic endeavors, but he could shoot wads of paper into a basket with ease from across the room. This couldn't be any harder than that, he reasoned. Besides, he did have one free throw, so it's not like everything was riding on the line with his first toss.

Exhaling slowly, Ethan began. He flicked his wrist and sent the ring flying to the lined-up soda bottles. To his dismay, the ring bounced off the top without having the slightest chance of hooking the bottle's neck.

"Oh, so close!" the man said with a snap of his fingers. "You'll get the next one, I'm sure."

Ethan did not get the next one. Nor did he get it on his third, fourth, or final attempt. What Ethan did get was a sinking sense that he had been swindled out of his five dollars. At first, he felt embarrassed and wanted nothing more than to slink away into the crowd. But then anger brewed inside, not at the booth owner—who Ethan reminded himself that he was only doing his job—but at himself for letting his concentration slip away. This game was like golf, where one only played against oneself. Getting too cocky, too frustrated, or any number of other things, led to failure. He would try again. And this time, he would win.

"Would you like to try again?" the man asked.

"Absolutely," Ethan replied, forking over another five dollars.

Round two went the same as his first attempt. Rounds number three and four didn't go any better. Some might have said afterward his situation couldn't get worse. Those people would've been dead wrong.

"Oh, this looks like fun," said a light, melodic voice from behind.

Ethan didn't have to turn around to know whose voice it was. It was Melissa's, the girl who lived in the apartment across from his own. The knockout redhead bounced next to him full of life and looked at all the prizes with glee.

"Win me that bear?" she asked.

Ethan turned to face her completely. He was about to pledge his service to the damsel in distress when a guy who looked like he negotiated billion-dollar contracts during breakfast and then spent the rest of the day lifting iron at his private gym in the Caribbean came up next to her.

"Whatever my girl wants, my girl gets," he said. He then flipped the booth owner twenty.

"Land three rings and get a plushy," the booth owner said as he spread the rings out on the counter. "Five will get you Thurman there."

The Incredible Corporate Hulk snatched up the rings. He weighed the first one carefully, just as Ethan had, before sending it arcing through air. It landed on the middle bottle without any trouble. After that, ring tosses number two through five were all met with equal success.

Ethan's shoulders fell as he watched Melissa leave with her date and her bear. His heart followed suit when he realized she hadn't seen him at all. He told himself she didn't want to be rude to her date, but that lie didn't last long.

"Maybe next time," the booth owner said, cutting into Ethan's self-pity. "Can't win them all, you know."

"Yeah, I know."

Ethan left the booth without another word, his soul feeling empty. He walked by a number of other games of skill, including a giant high striker. There was a modest line for that one, and the guy who manned the event was just as smooth as the ring toss guy when it came to selling attempts. Ethan didn't pay much attention to the man's words, but he did notice three even larger and more impressive stuffed animals that were prominently on display. Grand prizes, no doubt.

For a second, Ethan entertained the idea of winning one. But it didn't last. While he might have been able to kid himself into thinking he could win at ring toss, he knew he would never win at a game of strength. Muscles were not his strong suit, even if his grandma made him feel like he was Superman for opening a loose jar of pickles or moving a folding chair a few feet on the back porch.

Thus, Ethan sighed and kept moving. Maybe he needed something else to lift his mood. Maybe he needed a different game to play. Maybe he needed to go directly to the arcade and find some games there to play until Logan arrived. He could drop a few quarters into *Gauntlet*, be the hero, and slay minions of evil for the next half hour until—

His phone vibrated. Ethan fished it out of his pocket, looked at the text message splashed across its screen, and groaned.

Car's dead. Can't make it. Sry.

Ethan cursed his luck, and he wanted to curse Logan's car, too, but couldn't. Logan needed that car almost as much as he needed food and water, and since Logan's bank account had about half as much money as a four-year-old's piggy bank, buying a replacement was out of the question. Therefore, on the off chance curses were real, Ethan didn't want to risk further ruining his friend's already precarious position when it came to transportation.

So, he simply texted back a quick reply.

No worries. We'll go tomorrow or something.

Ethan pocketed his smartphone and was about to leave—but not before he picked up some funnel cake with his last few dollars— when he realized he was at the edge of the fair, and standing before him was an old covered wagon. There were no signs around it or lights attracting would-be customers. Ethan's initial reaction was that it was either simply for show or private property of one of the fair employees. Maybe whoever did the trapeze act lived here?

The gaudy wooden door opened, and an exotic woman with flowing brown hair covered by a red scarf appeared in the doorway. She flashed an enchanting smile at him, one that made him forget his previous encounter at the ring toss booth and, indeed, all his worries of life.

"Right on time," she cooed. "Come, darling, step inside, and let's see what your future holds."

Chapter V
Creation

INSIDE THE WAGON, two clay bowls of incense burned steadily, filling the tight space with a pungent aroma. Each bowl sat on a small wood table with the woman sitting behind. Flanking her on either side were shelves packed with trinkets and baubles, and Ethan wondered if perhaps these were prizes waiting to be won.

"Sit, sit," she said, motioning to a nearby stool. "What good is it to stand at the door when your future is but a few steps away?"

Ethan nodded and drew to her like a moth to a flame. He dropped onto the stool. At first, he folded his hands and rested them on the table as he waited for something to happen. But after a few moments spent in silence, anxiety grew, and he started idly tapping his fingers together.

"Relax, Ethan," she said as she sprinkled some brown powder into burning incense. "All is happening as it should."

"Have we—"

He cut himself off when blue flames erupted from the bowls with a crackling hiss, nearly sending him tumbling backward.

After a few seconds, the flames shrank, and colorful smoke began to rise. At that point, the woman finished the question he'd forgotten he'd asked. "Met?" she said. "No, my dear, but I'm pleased to meet you now."

The corner of Ethan's mouth drew back as a thought dawned on him. "Oh, I get it," he said. "I'm being set up, aren't I?"

"Yes and no, and not what you think, but all that and more, and all that at the same time," she said with the most delightful laugh. "But that is a talk for another time. We must begin your creation as time is short, and a good soul such as yourself is needed elsewhere."

"I'm needed at work? I already knew that," he said, thinking he wasn't very impressed with her fortune-telling abilities.

The woman reached across the table and took his hands in hers. "Darling, the work I speak of is far more important than what you do now. What I speak of will be life-changing, not only for yourself but for others as well."

Ethan pulled his hands away as curiosity got the better of him. "How life-changing are you talking?"

The woman ignored his question and instead took the conversation on a wild tangent. "Your neighbor owes your friend money, which he hasn't paid for a long time," she said. "One day, you see your neighbor drop his wallet that is flush with cash. Do you give it back to him with all the money inside, or do you first take a little out for your friend, knowing he needs to be repaid?"

"Why?" Ethan asked, looking around. "Am I on camera or something?"

The woman tilted her head with an amused look in her eyes. "Which do you choose?"

"I give the guy back his wallet with all his cash," he said. "I'm not a thief."

The woman nodded, and this time she sprinkled some red powder in each bowl. Again they flared, and again those flares died down and produced colored smoke.

"You've taken the oath of service to your country as a deep-cover operative. For years you've protected the innocent and combated horrors too ill to speak of for your country's sake. One day you learn that your superior is torturing a captive. He says he must protect the lives of thousands, yet he insists no one can know about this for reasons he cannot divulge. Do you honor your oaths and listen to your superior, or do you have compassion for the prisoner and report his deeds?"

"Well, you certainly know how to suck the fun out of the night, don't you?" Ethan said. When she didn't react to his comment at all, Ethan shrugged and answered. "I report him. If it's on the up and up, other people should be able to know, at least those with clearance or something. Right?"

To his surprise, she shrugged as well. "What is right and wrong? Even now, I can see you're questioning things. I suspect those questions will only increase from here on out."

"One day, a man threatens to attack you if you don't give him some food," she says. "Do you stand your ground and bravely fight him off, or do you give him what food you have and avoid the confrontation?"

"I give him—" Ethan stopped at this point. Would he give him his food? Perhaps in real life. But that's not what he would want to do. He'd want to say no. He'd want to fend off yet another bully who thought he could take from what was his without repercussions. Moreover, Melissa didn't date the weak. She wanted someone strong, brave. "I stand my ground."

The woman placed a small leather pouch in the middle of the table. She opened it with well-manicured fingers that were adorned with a half dozen rings. From it, she took two pinches of purple powder and carefully dropped each into the bowls. The flames burned with a fierceness that would have been the envy of any dragon and caused Ethan to shield his eyes momentarily.

"Holy crap. What are you making, thermite?"

"For years, you've hunted down your mortal enemy, and one day you finally reach him. The two of you engage in a mighty duel that taxes you both to the breaking point. In the end, however, you triumph, and he now lays helpless on the ground at the mercy of your sword, begging for his life and promising to never cross paths with you again. Do you show him compassion and allow him to yield, though this might not be wise, or do you take his life and grant him a valiant warrior's death, knowing this is the way?"

Ethan eased back as he thought about the question. How many assholes throughout his life in school would he have loved to run through because they found him easy prey? More than he'd like to admit. And that didn't count the couple of teachers whose only joy in life seemed to come from tormenting any student they could. But could he really do it?

"I allow him to yield," Ethan replied softly. "I can't murder someone."

On the game went, presenting Ethan with a dozen more scenarios, each one giving him increasingly more difficult choices where morality was murky at best.

It soon became clear to Ethan that the woman was after what he favored, or rather, what he wished he was: likeable, strong, and most of all, lucky. For even if he had the body of Adonis and the charisma of Christ Himself, unless he possessed the luck of the gods, Ethan felt he'd never have a snowball's chance in hell of catching Melissa's eye.

Then, before he knew it, the game was over.

"As you have spoken, your persona is made," the woman said after he gave his final answer.

He watched the fires wane for a few seconds before the woman reached under the table and pulled out a cedar box with an old ship-of-the-line etched into its lid. She gently lifted the brass latch on one side and opened the box. Inside, resting on a velvet lining, was a small booklet and a floppy disk within a paper sleeve. The disk, jet black, looked unremarkable, and the booklet merely had the words 'Captains & Cannons' written across its face in elegant calligraphy.

"Is that a five-and-a-quarter floppy?" he said, scarcely believing what his eyes were taking in. He was expecting a crown of gold with all the theatrics, not a relic from times long ago.

"It is."

Ethan chuckled. "Where did you get it? The Smithsonian?"

She shook her head and handed him the disk. "No," she replied. "You can donate it to them if you wish, but I think you would rather experience what's on it."

"Right," he said, eyeing it warily. "Look, I appreciate the show and everything, but my rig is top of the line. A dinosaur wouldn't even run this."

The woman curled her lips, and from somewhere in the dark, she produced one more item: an external disk drive, gray and slim. "Then I guess you'll need this."

Ethan picked it up and gave it a look. It had one slot where the disk was clearly meant to slide in, but it had nothing else. No spot for power. No slot for a USB. Nada.

"Assuming I take this," Ethan said. "How do I use it?"

"You mean when you take this."

"Fine, when I take this."

"Don't worry about the details, my dear," she said. "Put the disk in and start your computer. The rest will take care of itself."

"You really enjoy a mystery, don't you?"

"Mysteries are fun. Besides, a little mystery never hurt anyone." She stopped, chuckled, and put two delicate fingers against her lips before regaining her composure. "Well, maybe a little mystery hurt a few people, and some mysteries have hurt a lot of people. This mystery, however, will allow you to win prizes you never thought possible."

"What sort of prizes?"

The woman smiled as if the answer were plain to everyone but Ethan. Given it was only the two of them in the room, however, that was probably true.

"People probably don't like to be called prizes," she admitted. She pulled a small glass from a drawer nearby, and from that drawer, she also took a bottle of white wine and poured herself some. "Let me rephrase. With that game, you will be able to make yourself into whatever you like while saving lives—saving souls—from the clutches of Death. That sort of thing."

"You mean it's a role-playing game," Ethan said, eyeing the disk with some new respect. He wasn't sure how the woman had pegged him as a gamer, but then again, the cute little raccoon on his shirt with controllers in hand screaming "pew pew pew" probably offered all the hint she needed.

"It's more than a mere game," she went on. "It's an entirely new world offering the adventures you so crave."

"They all say that. Still, might be worth checking out."

"Then what are you waiting for?" she asked, nudging the disk and box toward him. "Give it a go, but don't forget to read the manual before you do."

Ethan hesitated but then took it all. After being reassured that he didn't have to pay her anything four times over, Ethan said his goodbyes and left. Once outside, he was shocked to find that the fair had closed. He went back to ask her what had happened, but when he got to the door and gave it a knock, no one answered. In fact, when he inspected said door, he discovered the wagon was nothing more than a stage prop.

"And I'm officially weirded out," he said to himself.

He hurried home, not bothering to answer any questions by the cleanup crew as to why he was still there.

Once he was in his car—a beat-up brown Dodge Omni—and had the engine cranked, his eyes locked on the game manual which he'd tossed onto the passenger seat. Curiosity grabbed him, and

Ethan picked it up while flipping on the interior light. He flipped through the manual, the pages feeling rough against his fingers as his eyes haphazardly scanned the text.

Sections detailed everything from character creation to bestiary with plenty of what he assumed was the game's world lore sprinkled throughout. Fatigue kept him from taking in much of anything in terms of specifics, but he felt as if he got the gist of it all: players made characters, did stuff, reaped rewards.

He could check out the specifics later, he told himself. With that in mind, he left the fair and headed home. Along the way, he pulled into a 7-Eleven and grabbed himself a cherry Slurpee. The waif of a girl who was the attendant that evening said something to him, but he couldn't remember what. His mind was still trying to understand all that had happened with the wagon.

He had gone inside. He didn't dream that up. After all, he had an old floppy disk and a game manual as proof. But he still couldn't shake the image of the wagon being nothing but an old stage prop either once he was done.

He must've gotten turned around somehow. The real wagon was off to the side that he hadn't seen. Yeah. That had to be it, he thought. It was dark. He was tired. Case closed.

But what was the bit about him saving people? She made it sound like he'd be saving actual people, not characters in the game. He hadn't seen anything about such a thing in the manual, but then again, he had flipped through it quickly. But how would that work? Did she maybe mean he'd save himself from boredom? Probably. Most definitely. What else could it be?

Ethan popped open the door to his car and put his Slurpee between his legs after getting in and taking one last sip. The sugary goodness helped him slip back into the mundane world where strange women in wooden wagons didn't fling ancient disks alongside promises of strange adventures.

"Maybe it's some sort of scam," he said to himself as he pulled out of the gas station. He then smirked at the next thought. "Or a way to try to sell me an extended car warranty."

The rest of the drive home flew by to the tunes of the Beastie Boys and Red Hot Chili Peppers. He'd gotten so caught up listening to the music, he almost missed his turn into his apartment complex and ended up fishtailing to such a degree that he left a good ten yards of tire marks on the asphalt. Thankfully, the roads were empty, the cops were elsewhere, and the only one who might have noticed was whoever was driving the pickup truck a quarter mile behind.

The car suddenly bounced upward as he hit a speedbump that had lost its yellow paint over the years. As his car slammed back down to the ground, his paltry shock absorbers did nothing but let the car make a loud bang. At the same time, his Slurpee left the warm confines of his legs, took a little solo trip through the air, and came crashing down so that its contents spilled all over his lap.

"Are you flipping kidding me?" he said with a huge groan. At least he was almost home, he told himself. At least he wasn't about to show up at work with a crotch full of melted ice. He didn't need to go through *that* again.

Ethan zipped into an empty parking space. He got out of the car, did his best to wipe himself down, and then decided how much he wanted to spend the next ten or fifteen minutes cleaning his car in the dark. He knew he had to, obviously. He couldn't let the Slurpee sit overnight. Not that the interior was the Sistine Chapel or anything. His seats had plenty of cracks, and the floor mats were as stained as the carpet in a dollar theater. The previous owner was to thank for that one, but no matter how much Ethan tried to clean them, the mats' fibers were forever soiled.

Right as he shut the driver's side door, the pickup truck that had been behind him earlier came into the lot. It parked in a nearby space. The driver left the truck running and didn't get out. From the looks of things, he was dealing with something inside the cab.

And since he didn't look like a psycho and all Ethan wanted to do was tend to the Slurpee and get to bed, he didn't stick around to see who it was.

Three minutes later, Ethan popped out of his small apartment, wearing a new pair of shorts. In his hands, he had two dirty towels to soak up as much Slurpee as possible, a roll of paper towels to get the remaining bit, and some generic liquid spray cleaner he'd picked up at the supermarket the other day.

Initially, his eyes were downcast as his energy reserves were depleting rapidly. A bit of movement caught his eye, however, and he turned and looked up to see a man standing near his neighbor's door.

The door in question belonged to Esther Williams, a spry, hilarious ninety-eight-year-old woman who went dancing every night, baked brownies for everyone in the hall, and loved telling stories about how she was one of the famous Rosie the Riveters from World War II. If she had a little too much red wine, which was more often than not, she'd also give Ethan advice that ranged from how to fold sheets properly to how to get over his nerves and ask Melissa out already.

But none of that was on Ethan's mind. What he was concerned about was why there was a guy right outside her home. He sported a gray, double-breasted pinstriped suit with a dark-pink tie and highly polished shoes, so he didn't look like someone who'd come to rob her. The man also had short, neatly cut brown hair on which a wide-brimmed fedora sat, as well as a face so cleanly shaven, it would've put any drill instructor to shame. So maybe he was a Fed? The fat, lit cigar held in the corner of his mouth and the clipboard with pen and paper in his hands would suggest that.

Then again, the guy looked more like he belonged in the 1940s than the 21st century.

The man looked up from the papers he was engrossed in. When his eyes met Ethan's, he straightened as if he thought he was the last man alive and had suddenly come across another human being.

"Can I help you?" Ethan asked.

The man didn't say anything initially. He turned around to see an empty hall behind him. He then faced Ethan once more and pointed to himself. "You're talking to me?" he asked, sounding like an overly exaggerated voiceover for a mobster cartoon.

"Yeah. Who else?"

The man shook his head and muttered some curses before striding up to Ethan. He came so fast, it was a small wonder that Ethan didn't bolt back inside his apartment, but something kept him rooted in place, something that felt unnatural enough that the hairs on the back of his neck stood.

The man took his cigar out of his mouth. "How you doing, kid? You here to do business or what?"

"No, I live here," Ethan replied, taking a half step back, not so much out of fear at this point, but because the man's cologne was overpowering and was making Ethan's allergies act up. "What are you doing here?"

"I'm here for Esther," he said, tipping his head toward her door. "Good gal. Thought she'd like it better if I came looking like her old days, you know?"

"Are you taking her out?"

"Yeah, you might say something like that," the man said, taking a long puff of his cigar before blowing a perfect smoke ring in Ethan's direction. "We haven't been formally introduced yet. So, it's more of a blind date at this point."

"A blind date at a quarter after one?"

"Is it that late already? Guess the traffic was worse than I thought." The man stuck his cigar back in his mouth. "You're busy. I'm busy. Let's get this done. What do you say?"

"Get what done?"

The man groaned and rolled his dark eyes. "That dame at the fair didn't tell you, did she? That figures. Broad like that wants to have her fun, too, and I don't mean rolling around in the sheets, you hear? That's one thing you don't ever want to do with her. She'll eat you alive, kid, and I'm not being figurative on that."

Ethan shook his head. He wasn't sure if it was the conversation or simply the fact that he was tired and his car still needed tending to, but whatever it was, all he wanted to do at this point was to clean the car and pass out on his bed. He did have the morning shift, too.

"Look, man," Ethan said. "I'm tired. The only thing I want to get done is mopping up the Slurpee I spilled."

The man perked. "You telling me you don't want to play for Esther?"

"Ah, no," Ethan said with a curt nod. "She's all yours, man. Just treat her right, you know?"

"Fantastic," the man said. He shoved the clipboard into Ethan's hands. On the clipboard was a piece of paper with a massive wall of legalese written in a font so small, Ethan would need an electron microscope just to read it. "Sign at the bottom, and we'll be done."

Ethan pushed the clipboard back. He may have been tired, but he wasn't stupid. "No way," he said. "I'm not signing anything."

The man took the clipboard and shrugged. He then scribbled something at the bottom of the page and spoke to himself. "Player refuses to sign, waives right to contest." Once he was done, he tipped his head to Ethan, gave an informal salute, and smiled. "Off you go, kid. Nice doing business with you."

"Whatever," Ethan said. He sidestepped the man and headed for his car. When he was about halfway down the hall, he stopped and briefly turned back around right as the man reached for Esther's door. "FYI, she packs. You go knocking on that door, and she might shoot first and ask questions never."

The man smiled brightly and winked. "Thanks, kid, but I've got it from here."

Ethan watched as he opened the door and stepped inside. He waited a few seconds, and when he didn't hear any bloodcurdling screams or the repeated shots from a .357 magnum, he figured that all was well, and whatever was going on was none of his business. Truthfully, he didn't want to know the details, either.

Over the course of the next ten minutes, Ethan cleaned the spill inside his Omni. Melissa happened to come home during that time. She even parked next to him as he worked, but she had her face stuck in her smartphone from the moment the car shut off—possibly even before that—and didn't seem to notice him before she disappeared inside the building.

Once he was finished, Ethan took small pride in the relatively small amount of paper towels he had to use. When he went back to his apartment, he noticed that Esther's door was open a few inches and light from her living room poured out into the hallway. He almost continued past, but a nagging feeling that something was amiss kept him from doing so.

"Ms. Williams?" he called out, cautiously approaching the door. "You left your door open."

Esther Williams did not answer. Neither did her mysterious guest.

"Ms. Williams?" Ethan knocked on the door this time, not hard, but it was enough that he accidentally caused it to swing open.

"Ms. Williams?" This last time he said it, however, his voice cracked as his eyes took in the scene.

Esther Williams lay sprawled across her entryway floor, dressed in her nightgown. Though she had a soft smile across her face and her eyes were closed, she didn't move a muscle. Not even those to make her breathe.

Esther Williams, the funny woman who lived by Ethan, had always been quite spry. Now she was anything but.

Chapter VI
The Police

"LOOK, THERE WAS a guy," Ethan said to the policeman. "I saw him. I spoke to him. He definitely went in her apartment before she died."

Officer Harper, a squat man of thirty-something years old with a high and tight haircut, broad shoulders, and a potbelly that would make any Vietnamese pig jealous, stood outside Esther's empty apartment. The paramedics had rushed her out the moment they'd arrived, but Ethan had overheard them saying she had no pulse and would likely be DOA once they got to the hospital. Officer Harper seemed to indicate the same. "Look, I need more than a guy was here. What was his name?"

"I don't know. I told you that."

"You still don't remember what he looked like?"

Anne started barking again before Ethan could answer. She'd been quiet for nearly thirty seconds now, giving Ethan a false sense of hope she'd given up on trying to be included on whatever was happening in the hall.

"Any chance you can get your dog to quiet?" Officer Harper asked. "Your neighbors would probably like to go back to sleep."

"I'm sure she'll settle down when I get in there."

The officer nodded with a resigned look on his face. "Fine. Let's try to get through this quickly, then. What did this man look like?"

Ethan rubbed his temples. He knew he had gotten a good look at whoever this guy was. After all, how could he not? Ethan had talked to him for a bit. He could remember everything about their conversation. But why the hell couldn't he remember what the man looked like? All Ethan could come up with to answer that was the unsettling feeling that something unnatural was keeping him from doing so. Or maybe magical? Like a spell of forget?

Ethan shook his head. That was ridiculous. Spell of forget. Yeah, right. Even the name sounded stupid.

"Well?" the officer pushed.

Ethan shrugged, wishing he didn't have to, and then wishing twice more that a mini-stroke wasn't the cause of it all. "Like I said, I can't remember. He was just a guy. I guess. Nothing weird about him."

"Hair color?"

Ethan shrugged again. "Brown, maybe? He was dressed nice. I remember that part."

"Height?"

"I don't know. Bigger than me."

"Fat guy? Skinny? Muscles? White? Black? Tan? Green? Had a beard? Clean shaven? Whistled Dixie as he walked around? You've got to give me something else."

Ethan shrugged a third and final time. "Look, it's late. I'm exhausted. I don't know what else I can say."

Officer Harper flipped his notebook closed and dropped his brow. "Have you been drinking tonight?"

"No."

"Done any drugs?"

"No," Ethan said with an exasperated sigh.

Anne's barks became more intense; so much so, they not only caused Ethan to worry something was wrong or that someone was in there with her, but they pulled Melissa out of her apartment. She stood a foot outside her doorway in soccer shorts and an oversized black T-shirt while wearing a scowl on her face. The moment her eyes spied the cop, her look of irritation vanished.

"What's going on, Evan?" she asked wearily. "Was there a break-in or something?"

"Uh, hi, Melissa," Ethan said, feeling dumb that she never got his name right. "No. Esther died. Anne's flipping out because the cops are here."

"That's horrible," she said. "Are you two at least going to be done soon?"

Officer Harper shook his head. "Not likely. This is being treated as a potential crime scene since there's a possible suspect we need to track down. In fact—"

Melissa's eyes widened. "What?"

"Ethan said you came home about the same time he did?"

"I don't know. Did I?"

Ethan nodded. "You did."

"I'll need you to come out here and answer some questions, too, then," Officer Harper said before giving her an extra up-down with his eyes.

Melissa shook her head and rolled her eyes as she muttered some curses. "Really?"

"Really."

"Can we quiet the dog first, at least?"

Harper glanced at Ethan. "Can we?"

"Give her some treats. She'll quiet for a bit."

Melissa, without a hint of warning, marched across the hall and into Ethan's apartment, giving him a minor heart attack. Not because Anne would attack her. Her only danger was that she'd lick a burglar to death. And he wasn't freaking out because the place was a total disaster, either. Far from it, actually. No, what his reaction was all about was the fact that since he had hopes of one day inviting her over, he desperately wanted to have more stuff inside, so it looked as if he was doing well for himself. Hell, that he was doing two steps below okay would be fine, too, as opposed to the "extreme minimalistic" motif he had going now.

"Where are they?" she called out, derailing his runaway thought train.

"Kitchen pantry," Ethan called back, trying to decide whether or not he should go in there with her. If he had more charisma, sure, or if his life had been spent climbing the Smooth Romantic talent tree, absolutely. But the only thing he'd invested on in life thus far outside of the basics was tackling games, which only went so far when trying to get to know the opposite sex while a cop stood outside your door, waiting to grill you both on a corpse that had been wheeled off less than ten minutes ago.

"Where? I don't—" Her voice cut off. The barking intensified tenfold for a few seconds and then silenced. "Found them! She's happy."

Ethan sighed with relief, and Officer Harper smiled as well.

For the next thirty minutes, the cop thoroughly questioned Ethan and Melissa. In reality, he questioned Melissa more, giving her easily five times as much attention as he did Ethan. Near the top of the hour, a radio call came in, and he had to excuse himself before promising to be in touch the next day to follow up.

Ethan had no expectations that that follow up would include him in any way.

"Wow, I can't believe she's dead," Melissa said, leaning against the wall with her shoulder, her eyes fixated on Esther's door.

"Me either. She was always so nice. Tell me stories about 'back in the day' and how to—" He caught himself before he flopped the 'and ask you out' blunder.

"How to what?"

"Fold sheets," he said.

"Sounds like her," she said. "I wish I would've seen her earlier. Maybe I could've done something, you know?"

Ethan nodded, feeling the same. "Yeah. Something."

"Well, g'nite, Evan," Melissa said with a yawn as she headed for her door. "I'm going to bed."

"It's Ethan," he replied, but it was so soft she didn't hear.

He watched her go back into her apartment and shut the door before he turned around and went into his. Anne nuzzled his leg and slobbered on his hand. He scratched her behind the ears before shuffling into his bedroom and collapsing on his mattress.

What a night, he thought.

He stared at the clock for about a minute before his thoughts settled, and exhaustion overtook him. His eyes closed, and then after what felt like five minutes at the most, he woke to his alarm blaring in his ears and sunlight assaulting his eyes.

"Seriously?" he said. "Maybe I should call in sick. Or take bereavement. Do I get bereavement for a neighbor? I should, right? A day or two?"

Ethan sat up, waiting for Anne to answer. Well, not answer, answer, but respond to his usual morning ramblings by barking at him, slobbering on him, or a combination of both until he got his butt up and let her outside.

"Anne?" he called out, shuffling into the living room. "Where are you, girl?"

Ethan cocked his head. She should've been barreling into him by now. He threw a glance at the front door as well as the sliding glass one that led out the back. Both were closed.

He was about to call out again when a sour smell hit his nose. He grimaced and forced himself to sniff the air to find the source of the offending odor. It was coming from the kitchen. Fearing Anne had gotten into the garbage again while he was sleeping and ended up yakking on the floor, Ethan hurried over, all the while reminding himself that owning such a cool yellow lab meant accidents would happen from time to time. Like when she had to be house trained for a year. Or like when she was five months old, and he left his sandals on the floor, and a whopping six seconds later, she'd turned them into an exciting trip to the vet to remove part of their strap she'd swallowed.

Ethan rounded the corner to his small kitchen, and his heart stopped. Lying on the cream vinyl floor, about a foot from his four-burner stove, was Anne. Her eyes were rolled back in her head, and her tongue flopped out of her mouth. Vomit coated most of the area, which was concerning enough, but her shaking and shallow, rapid breathing threw Ethan into a panic. This shot into full-blown terror when he saw an empty wrapper to one of his bars of imported dark chocolate lying on the kitchen counter.

"Anne!" Ethan cried out, bolting to his dog's side. "Anne, oh my god, wake up!"

Anne didn't move. In a flash, he scooped her up and stumbled out the door after grabbing his keys. Why the hell didn't they have 911 for dogs?

Once in the hall, Ethan readjusted his grip on his dog and lost his balance in the process. Though he didn't fall, he ended up slamming a shoulder into Melissa's door.

"Damn it!" he said, tears now welling in his eyes. He dared a glance at Anne. She looked even worse than before, if that were possible. Her breathing had all but stopped, and her gums had gone gray. "Hold on, girl! You're going to be fine."

Melissa opened her door wearing the same outfit he'd seen her in earlier, but this time her hair had been conquered by the almighty bed. "Evan? Oh my god, what happened to your dog?"

"Did you give her chocolate?" Ethan said, practically biting her head off.

"You said to give her a treat!"

"You can't give dogs chocolate! It's poisonous to them!" he shouted as he headed for the car again.

Melissa's hands went over her mouth, and her eyes went wide with fear. "I...I didn't know."

"Who the hell doesn't know that?" Ethan shook his head. "Never mind. Just grab my wallet from inside, okay? I'm going to need it."

Melissa nodded and darted into his apartment. Ethan sucked in a deep breath and shouldered his way out the door that led to the parking lot. Cold morning air kissed his skin, and colder pavement attacked his bare feet.

With only one hand semi-free, he managed to pop open the rear door to his Omni and put Anne in the backseat. He darted into the driver's seat and cranked the ignition.

All he was rewarded with was a *click, click, click, click* as the car tried in vain to turn over.

"No," Ethan whispered. He checked the dash. The voltage indicator for the battery was lower than his current outlook on life. "No! No! No!"

Ethan collapsed against the wheel, not knowing what to do. His mind clouded, and the world took on a surreal nature.

"Little too much booze last night, kiddo?" said a familiar voice. "You look like you need a few cups of joe."

Ethan jumped. There in the passenger seat, still dressed in his gray suit with the matching wide-brimmed fedora, was the guy he'd seen before. "What the hell are you doing here?"

The man motioned to the back seat with his cigar. "Came for her," he said. "Normally, animals are outside the scope of all this, but hey, you're in luck. Exceptions are always made for family."

"Look, I don't have time for this," Ethan said, shaking his head in disbelief. "Get out of my car."

The man shrugged. "Can't. Not without the dog."

"You touch my dog, and I'll kill you," Ethan said, surprised that the words came out of his mouth as strong as they did, especially since the last fight he'd been in was in third grade and in reality, it was more of him being used as a pinata than an equal, toe-to-toe match between dueling champions.

The man took a long puff from his cigar. "Alright, kid. You ready to do business this time or what? I've got to know, because if you're wasting my time like you did with Esther and you're just going to chicken out again, just do me the courtesy and tell me upfront. You want to play for your dog's soul or not?"

Ethan's face scrunched. "Play? You mean like you're Death or something?"

"Bingo, kid," the man said with a wink and a half grin. "Probably would've realized that sooner if you'd read the manual like you were supposed to."

"What manual?"

"The one that came with the game," Death replied. "I know she told you to read it. Part of the rules."

Ethan shook his head. "This is insane. You're not Death. You're flipping crazy, is what you are."

Death shrugged. "Think what you want, kid. But keep two things in mind: One, I'm the reason you couldn't give details to the cop, and two, this is your last chance to accept my challenge. If you don't, I take your dog by default, and then we can try this again some other time."

Something about the man's voice gave Ethan pause. There was an authority to it. Not one born from the appointment of man or government, but one born from the universe itself. Ethan tensed, but when he glanced back at his dying four-legged friend, he dared to believe. "Prove it."

"Here's your one and only demonstration," Death said. He stuck the cigar in his mouth, cracked his knuckles, and pointed at a pigeon on a nearby bench. "See that bird? He'll be dead in three. Two. One."

Right on cue, a hawk flashed through the air, snatching the bird in one swoop. Time seemed to crawl as Ethan watched the raptor sink all of its talons deep inside the pigeon's chest, no doubt killing it instantly, before flying off.

"Holy snort!" Ethan said, his hands gripping his steering wheel.

Death adjusted his fedora. "What can I say? I've had a little practice. So, what's it going to be? Play for your pooch or what?"

Ethan whipped his head around. "You're saying if we play a game and I win, I get my dog back?"

Death nodded.

"And if I lose?"

"Your pooch is mine. Pretty simple, no?"

Ethan paused, but only for a second. "And it's a fair game though, right? There's no catch or something, is there?"

"Of course, it's a fair game, kid. It's in the contract," Death said, producing the clipboard he'd had before. He stuck a finger near the top as he offered it to Ethan. "Says it right there. But if I were you, I'd read fast. Time's a ticking."

Ethan's eyes scanned the page. Sure enough, right at the top, the contest was clearly described as being a fair one. He tried to read the rest, but after a few seconds, he realized he'd never be able to without an hour to spare and hefty legal advice. "Fine. Let's do it."

Death produced a pen, and once Ethan had signed the bottom, he smiled broadly as he folded the contract in thirds and stuffed it inside his jacket. "That a boy. Word of advice, though."

"What's that?" asked Ethan.

"If I were you, I'd get to my computer in the next sixty seconds, because good old Anne here isn't going to last much more beyond that."

Ethan swore a dozen times over and dashed out of his car. He bounded up the three steps outside the apartment building and barreled through the door to the hall. He practically broke the sound barrier racing to his apartment and nearly took Melissa out as she popped out of his abode with his wallet in hand.

"Evan?" she called out as he raced by. "Evan, I've got your wallet!"

Now in his living room, Ethan jumped into his worn-out, slightly torn black leather chair at his desk. The computer was still sleeping, so the room was quiet, other than the music that drifted in from his neighbor's bedroom, and Melissa's repeated calls to him asking what was going on.

He whipped the 5.25" disk out of the box before sliding it into the drive it had come with and setting it next to his computer. What was supposed to happen next, he had no idea. The woman back at the fair hadn't told him, and for a brief second, he wondered if he should dig through the manual.

The monitor suddenly flickered to life, and then his wallpaper onscreen distorted and flashed. In a span of two seconds, the resolution he had previously set his computer to changed a dozen times, and all the while the pixels rotated through a variety of color palettes.

The screen faded, and music, if it could be called that, began to play through his PC's speaker. Not the 5.1 surround sound system he had going, but the actual speaker that was wired into the motherboard. The speaker that, as far as he knew, only gave the occasional beep during boot up or when, God forbid, something was wrong with the motherboard. It had never played a melody before, even a simple one like what was coming out now.

Two words formed across the screen, sapphire-blue and outlined in white flames. Two words that read:

Journey Onward?

Chapter VII
Welcome to Bartigua

ETHAN REMEMBERED PRESSING the 'y' key on his keyboard. He was sure of that much. What had transpired between that point and where he was now was a bit of a blur. All he could remember were the colorful swirls of light and feeling as if he had been stuck in a gigantic laundromat dryer that had been set to high. When everything settled, he found himself standing on the deck of an early 18th-century sloop that, to his utter dismay, happened to be in the middle of a brutal fight.

Smoke and wisps of flame filled the air as crew ran in all directions shouting, screaming, and fighting something out in the waters. Two cannons roared, their blasts thumping heavily against his chest and leaving a ringing in his ears. The scent of gunpowder assaulted his nose, and an acrid taste hung all around.

A tentacle as thick as Ethan was wide came up and over the rails. Two more followed. They smashed carriages, snapped lines, and grabbed sailors who tried in vain to fight them off.

"Oh god, this can't be happening," Ethan said, eyes wide as he backed away. He glanced left and right, hoping to find something, anything, that would see him to safety, but it was hard to see much of anything in the midst of all the chaos other than the broken ship he was on and the monster that was attacking it.

Pistols fired, and then a mast snapped. It crashed through the center of the deck, rocking the boat hard to port and sending Ethan tumbling. As he picked himself up, a new shout came, one that put the fear of God into Ethan.

"Fire in the magazine!"

Ethan ran as fast he could, his feet pounding the deck as he made for the railing. Two steps away from them, he launched himself into the air.

Cool, salty wind kissed his face as he sailed overboard, and then a monstrous explosion filled his ears. Debris flew in all directions, some of it wood, some of it crew. Ethan tried to pretend he didn't see the latter. He sucked in a deep breath right before he hit the sea. When he popped back to the surface, he swam as hard as he could until his arms and legs turned to jelly.

At that point, he'd thankfully put a few hundred yards between the battle and himself. Well, what was left of the battle. The sloop he was on had been reduced to nothing but large floating, burning chunks of wood that were surrounded by lots and lots of smaller chunks of wood. The monster, whatever it was, couldn't be seen anywhere, but since Ethan could see some survivors hanging onto driftwood, he hoped that meant the creature wasn't interested in snacking on anyone else, or at least, not him.

"Okay, Ethan, you got this. There's no need to panic," he said, using what was left of his strength to swim over to a few floating planks of wood. "We'll just get somewhere safe and figure out what to do."

Off in the distance, Ethan spied a shoreline of what hopefully was an island big enough that it meant people had settled there. Friendly people. People who didn't hang newcomers for fun or play games with ravenous sea monsters. He didn't know what he'd do if that turned out to be the case, but since his only options were either staying adrift in a monster-infested sea or making for shore regardless of what was there, his decision was easy.

At least the sun was out, so he wouldn't have to explore wherever he was in the dark.

After an hour of kicking on his makeshift raft and realizing that no, this wasn't a bizarre nightmare, he saw a coastal city not too far from where he was headed. This renewed his hope. After another hour, he made it into the harbor.

To be fair, calling it a harbor was being generous. The place wasn't much of a city either. Sure, it had a number of wood buildings, but each one of them barely looked like they could weather a strong sneeze, let alone any sort of storm. The wood they were constructed from appeared old and worn, and it looked like the the architect who'd built them had earned his degree from the back of a whiskey label. Not a single one stood upright. They all twisted and hunched in one direction or another. The worn-out roofs, which were missing more shingles than they had, were only the icing on the cake.

That said, the place did have a few noticeable attributes that kept Ethan's spirits from sinking completely. First, he could see several men and women walking the cobblestone streets, most with a drink in hand, all looking happy—aside from a few that appeared to be haggling over something at a vendor table. Second, several cannon emplacements had been built. Not only had they been built, but they were currently being manned, and since those who were stationed at each one hadn't raised the alarm or flat out sent a hail of grapeshot in his direction, he figured they might turn out to be helpful. Third, and most important, as he floated toward the harbor's sole pier, his eyes met those of a woman he hoped could help him out.

She sat at the edge of the dock, dressed in black leather, with tattoos all across her left arm. A large toucan—red and black of all colors—sat perched on her shoulder, eying him with suspicion. One of her hands had nothing but a slew of rings on its fingers, while the other clutched a large green bottle. Her hazel eyes regarded him with amusement from beneath her wide-brimmed hat, and she flashed a smile that looked as if it could capture any man's heart or break it just the same. She'd probably done both.

"Shame about your ship," she said. "It looked like a beauty from here, but at least you made it off alive. That's something."

"Yeah, thanks, but it wasn't mine," Ethan replied as he kicked his way closer.

"Even better."

Ethan brought himself to where some weathered thick rope hung from the docks, only a half pace away from where she was seated. He reached up and grabbed it, but before he could hoist himself up, she angled her foot and pressed her boot against his head. "No one's allowed on my docks without my permission."

"Your docks?"

The woman nodded and then nodded to the cutlass attached to her hip. "They're my docks, unless, of course, you can convince me otherwise."

Too tired for manners, but not enough to be completely crass, Ethan sighed. "Can I come aboard? I'm cold, wet, and just want a place to dry."

"Depends," she said. "Who are you?"

"Ethan," he replied.

"And why are you here, Ethan?" she said, still keeping her boot on his head. "Everyone with half a brain knows not to come here on anything less than a fourth-rate ship-of-the-line on account of Myriden."

"Myriden?"

"The monster who attacked you," she clarified. "Now, answer my question. Why are you here?"

"Hell if I know," he said. "Look, my fingers are going numb. Mind letting me up, or is this a lick-your-boot kind of thing?"

The woman smirked. "No, it's not. Not yet, at least. Why don't you start by telling me where you came from, and we'll go from there?"

Ethan muttered a few curses and huffed. "Fine. Whatever. All I know is that I was in my living room one minute, and the next—"

The woman straightened. "Living room?"

"Yeah, that's what I said. I was there and—"

"You're from outside?" she asked, interrupting yet again. Her boot lifted from his head, and her eyes looked at him with pity. "I mean, you're from where there are cars and computers and jets and rock bands?"

"Yes..."

"Welcome to Bartigua," she said. "Hope you at least got to enjoy the fair before coming here."

The woman then shifted in place before reaching down and offering him a hand. Once Ethan took it, she yanked him up with a grunt. He took a moment to shake himself dry and wring the water out of his blue shirt, but he soon realized it was pointless. "Hang on a second. How did you know about the fair?"

"That's where Madam Nataliya finds her 'contestants,'" she replied. She then folded her arms over her chest and snorted with disgust. "Someone should force her to play."

"I'm sorry, what's this about?"

"Nothing. Forget it," she said, shaking her head. The woman then extended her hand. "I'm Zoey, by the way. Used to live in Montana. Nice to meet you."

Ethan warily shook it. "Ethan, from North Carolina."

"I love North Carolina. Great peaches there."

"That's Georgia."

"Oh," she said with a hint of sadness. That sadness disappeared as her eyes lit up. "I guess I love Georgia, then. Don't suppose somehow you brought a peach with you here?"

"No. How would I?"

Zoey shrugged. "How would I know? I don't even know how getting here works, but I figured it wouldn't hurt to try. God, I'd make out with a sea hag for a nice juicy peach right now. There's not a single one in the whole land. Can you believe it?"

Ethan shook his head, not because he was answering her question, but because he was trying to shake the image of this young beauty in the deep throes of passion with a toothless old crone from his mind.

"You seem like you're a little lost here," she went on.

"Understatement of the year," he said. "Any chance you're willing to help me out a little?"

"Maybe."

"Maybe?"

"How would you feel about a quid pro quo, Ethan?" she asked with a beaming smile.

"Never was one for calamari," he replied. "But I could go for a nice burger."

Her brow dropped. "Are you serious?"

Ethan looked around, and realizing that they probably didn't have burgers in pirate land, he amended his statement. "I could do stew. That's got to be a thing here. Or chicken? Surely there's at least chicken."

"Quid pro quo," she repeated. "A favor for a favor."

"Oooh, right," Ethan said. He bit his lower lip as an uneasy feeling washed over him. He wasn't that much of a moron, he knew. Why the hell did he think that had anything to do with calamari?

"Is something the matter?" she asked.

Ethan nodded as his gaze drifted downward. "That wasn't right. I mean, I know that phrase. I did graduate middle school. High school, even."

"Oh boy," she said, taking in a sharp breath of air.

"What?"

"You probably didn't invest too much in intelligence, did you?"

"I have no idea what you're talking about."

"When you rolled your character, back at the fair."

"Um, sure I did," he said, completely making up the answer on the fly. Truthfully, he couldn't remember the details at this point, but what the hell did they matter? He'd always been one to appreciate the gray matter. Hadn't he? "When did I roll again?"

The woman shook her head. "The questions Madam Nataliya asked, remember those? Your answers dictate who you are and what you get while in game."

"They do?"

"Yeah. They do. God, I have no idea how you're going to win this," she said with a laugh.

"Why's that?"

Zoey raised an eyebrow and gave him an incredulous look. "You don't even know who you're playing against, do you?"

"Of course, I do," Ethan replied. "Death. Duh. I did meet him before I got sucked in here."

"Oh, right," she said. "Had to sign the contract. Forgot about that. But I've got twenty shillings that says you didn't even read it."

"Um, no," Ethan said, cringing. "Should I have?"

Zoey laughed and shook her head. "Yeah, genius. You should have."

"It's a fair game, though, right? I'll make it work."

"Fair? Ha! Is that what he told you?"

Ethan shook his head. "Yes, but it was on the contract. It said this was a fair game."

The woman shook her head. "Cripes, you're not going to last a day here."

"Why?"

"Of course, it's a fair game!"

Ethan stared at her blankly.

"A game from the fair!" Zoey said, her face full of irritation. "What else would you call it?"

"Oh. Oh, god."

The harshness in her face fell to sympathy. "Exactly. They're not exactly known for being rigged in the player's favor, are they?"

"Uh, no," Ethan said, now having flashbacks to his paltry attempt at winning a stuffed animal.

The woman sighed heavily. "Sorry. I know this sucks, and I know I just dumped a lot on you. I'm just tired of seeing people come here and die. I hope you're playing for a good prize, at least."

"My dog," Ethan said.

To his surprise, she seemed impressed. "Must be some dog."

"She is."

"So how does this work, exactly?" Ethan asked. "I mean, we're sucked into a game or something, right? Like in that movie... Gah! What was it called? With the rhinos and jungle and whatnot? Gemini? Jumanga? Mangione? Damnit. Whatever. Doesn't matter. You know what I mean. All I have to do is to beat Death at whatever."

"Yeah, well, that whatever was in your contract, which you didn't read. I doubt anyone is just going to run up to you and tell you what to do," she said. "Although..."

"Although what?" he asked as her voice trailed.

"A small, new building popped up not too long ago," she said. "A shack, really. Didn't think much of it, but it could be your starting room. Maybe whatever gear you'll get there will point you in the right direction."

"See? Everything is coming together already," Ethan said, saying such a thing to try and boost his dwindling morale. "I'll have Death defeated in no time."

The woman smiled, but it looked forced. "Good. That's a great attitude to have. Try not to lose it, but don't let it get to your head. That's when people get stupid, which is usually followed by getting dead."

"Why would I lose it?"

"You might when things get bad."

"Getting attacked by Myriden wasn't bad enough? Cripes, I about had a heart attack when he shot out of the water."

"Oh, there's plenty worse than Myriden in the open seas."

Ethan sighed. "Of course, there is."

"I should also point out, Myriden's the baby brother of sea monsters since he's basically a tiny kraken. Or maybe that makes him a distant cousin? I'm not really sure if those things have a family tree like we do."

The woman chuckled, and a small grin flashed across her face. "I mean, can you see that thing having sex? Or on its back in stirrups of the OB/GYN getting ready to shoot out a kid? Then again, he's probably straight out of your typical hentai cartoon, right? Maybe it does like getting laid after all."

"I can't believe you're joking after I nearly became its snack."

"Don't worry, if you live long enough, you'll have some pretty dark humor, too. Either that or you lose all your sanity. I've seen that happen as well. Just don't go screwing all the whores."

"Why not?" Ethan asked. Not that he had the immediate desire to, but it was a game, after all. Maybe he'd pick up some weird side quest or something.

Zoey threw up her hands in disbelief and gestured around them. "Look where we are. We're not exactly in the golden age of medicine. Whoever made this place also decided to include little things like disease, especially the STD kind."

Ethan grimaced. "Ew."

Zoey laughed and shook her head. "You don't even know. There's stuff out there that'll completely rot your little man in under an hour. Like seriously rot it right off. Won't even have a stub."

Ethan traded his grimace for nausea and couldn't help but tighten his legs together. "I take it you've seen a lot."

"More than you'll hopefully ever know," she said. "But don't worry. If you need to get your rocks off, there are ways to do it. Just got to be smart, is all. Having some holy water nearby probably wouldn't hurt, you know, to freshen up."

"Not on my bucket list at the moment, but holy water, got it," Ethan said.

Zoey nodded. "Now then, back to my deal, because that's what we really need to concentrate on. Work first. Play later."

"The squid pro go?"

"Quid pro quo," she corrected.

"Right."

"You help me get one little bitty gem, and I'll help you win whatever contest you've got going with Death here. How does that sound?"

Though Ethan appreciated having some help right off the bat, he was savvy enough to know a deal that was too good to be true when he came across it. "What's the catch?"

"No catch."

Ethan tilted his head to the side. "I'm not *that* dumb."

"Fine," Zoey said with a huff. "The catch is the gem is in an amulet tucked away in a fortress crawling with monsters, and we've got to hurry to nab it before someone else does. You can help with that, right? It'll be the easiest half share you've ever earned."

"A half? Why not a whole?"

"You're lucky you're getting that," she said. "It's not like I'm not helping you on top of that, not to mention keeping you alive in the process."

"I still say I should get a whole share."

"Half or nothing," she said, folding her arms over her chest. "Take it or leave it."

Ethan turned the offer over several times in his mind. He wanted to leave, but enough of him had the feeling that if he did, he'd be making a big mistake. So he opted for a more middle-of-the-road compromise. "Tell you what," he said. "How about you help me get my starting gear, and once I know what I've got, we'll take it from there?"

Zoey extended her hand. "Deal."

CHAPTER VIII
THE RACE

ZOEY LED ETHAN through the dilapidated buildings—and godawful smells—of shantytown. She was quiet for the most part, though would mutter the occasional curse when she had to bat away the hands of a would-be pickpocket. The dirt road they followed curved to the west before running up a small hill. It looked as if it would run into a small market area, but they never got that far, which was too bad, Ethan thought, as something delicious in the air wafted down from it and into his nose.

Thoughts of delectable food, however, vanished the moment she pulled him down a narrow alley that probably had more diseases in it than all of medieval Europe. At least, that's what the putrid odor of it said.

"Try not to touch anything," Zoey said.

"I'm trying not to even think about touching anything," Ethan said, gagging. "What died back here?"

"That guy," she replied as she pointed to a skeleton slumped against the wall.

Ethan grunted at the sight. "Seriously? Doesn't anyone bury the dead?"

"Sometimes," Zoey replied with a shrug. "Kind of pointless when they simply dig themselves out, though."

Ethan slowed his pace.

"Relax, I'm just messing with you," she said, drawing the corners of her mouth back. "If you want to bury him when we're done, be my guest. But as for me, I'd like to just get through this place and see what's in your shack."

"Yeah, let's," Ethan said. He picked up the pace, which sent a half dozen rats scampering for cover, squeaking as they did. Realizing he needed something to take his mind off the here and now, Ethan thought about his situation in general. "I have a question," he said. "This is like a game, game. I mean, like an RPG with characters and classes and whatnot, right?"

"In a manner of speaking, yes," she replied.

"Does that mean I'll get powers?"

"Maybe."

"So, yes," he said, deciding that a maybe was as good as a definitely for him. He wondered what those would be, but before he had a definitive answer, they broke free of the alley and ended up on the outskirts of town. A little bit away, maybe another forty yards, was a solitary wooden shack.

"Come on," she said, waving him on. "We're here."

Ethan didn't. He was still trying to guess what skills he'd been gifted with. He had to start with something, right?

Ethan looked himself over. He did have some more muscle in his arms than usual, but he wouldn't be a ringer in an Ironman competition anytime soon. Still, it was a nice start. Maybe he was superfast, or super smart, despite the quid-pro-quo flop. He'd probably made a critical failure on some crucial roll. Yes, that was it, he decided. Even the greatest minds flub stuff now and again.

With that thought set firm, Ethan tried to recite pi. He got as far as "3.14 something, something, something," before deciding that no, he hadn't been gifted with an IQ higher than Mount Everest. Then again, maybe he was an eclectic genius, the sort who forgot the mundane all the time but came up with observations that even Sherlock Holmes would be envious of.

Zoey, clearly irritated at this point, stood a few paces away with her hands on her hips. "What are you doing?"

"One second," Ethan said, squinting his eyes. "I'm onto something."

"This better be good."

Ethan held up a finger and studied her every facet. She had a simple chain around her neck from which hung a teardrop pendant. On her right hand were three rings, two silver and one gold. Several others adorned her left. Her attire looked well-kept, but there was a bit of dirt on it near the top of her thigh as well as on her knee. The full sleeve of tattoos on her left arm felt as if they were random and probably had no overall purpose other than to show off cheap artwork.

"You got that front pendant from your mother," he said. "Family heirloom?"

Zoey's face scrunched, but before she could say anything, Ethan expanded. "You wear it close to your heart, but it's not magical because it doesn't glow, and it's made out of material too common. It seems more at home than out in the wilds, so you got it before you became an adventurer, ergo, a family heirloom. The rings on your hand, however, are magical. I can see little burn marks where they've scorched your skin from repeated use, and since you don't seem to mind them hurting you, they must be powerful indeed. Perhaps they take a toll on you mentally as well when you use them. That would explain the dirt on your knee, because you had to drop to it after casting such powerful magic. Fighting a dragon, maybe? No, you'd at least have soot on you from its breath and probably have a donkey laden with gold in tow."

Zoey held up her hand and cut him off. "I have no idea what you're doing."

"Testing my intellectual prowess," he said. "Seems like it's pretty good. I nailed your backstory, didn't I?"

"No," she said with a laugh somewhere between amusement and annoyance. "You couldn't be further from the truth if you tried. I picked this necklace up at a carnival last week. I bought the rings a long time ago and wear them in case I ever need to sell them for a crown or two. They're an investment, nothing more. The dark skin you see around them is dirt because I haven't had a bath in a while, rain aside, as clean bathwater is a rarity. As for the dirt on my knee, what can I say? Again, there's not exactly a hot tub every ten steps to soak in, and the sea is dangerous, savvy?"

Ethan twisted his mouth. Maybe he needed to develop his sleuthing skills more, but that didn't mean he wasn't gifted elsewhere. Seeing how games let you play who you wanted to be, not necessarily who you were, he ran another, hopefully more successful, skill test. "So," he said, dropping his head a little and giving her the best swoon-worthy, panty-dropping grin. "How you doing?"

Zoey took a quick step back. "Are you hitting on me already?"

Ethan felt his face flush with embarrassment as he realized he was as smooth as a cactus. "No, sorry. I mean. I was trying to, you know, see how much charisma I had. I'm really not like this. Quite the opposite, actually. Oh, hell, shoot me now."

"Alright, Casanova, you're not that hideous," Zoey said as Ethan buried his face in his hands. "Don't fumble a fast talk with me and give yourself a coronary. I don't need that kind of emotional baggage."

"Sorry," Ethan said as his shoulders fell. "I was hoping for some starting skills or talents or whatever you get around here. I mean, I don't even seem to have a character sheet to go by."

"Assuming that's your shack, your sheet will be in there," she said. "As for skills, we can see what you've started with and the rest will come with time. You've got to think of yourself as coming fresh from the creation screen, so to speak, and this is all intro—or even better, this is a cutscene. However you want to think of it. That said, the only thing you're good at right now is being a meat shield, which honestly, I won't be surprised if that's all you become."

"Wow, thanks."

Zoey grimaced. "Sorry, that came out bad," she said. "I only meant you need to be careful, and if you want to survive and get better, you need to be realistic. You're not slaying any dragons right now—thankfully, we don't have many of those, but we do have their nasty cousins swimming about, the sea serpent."

"Got it. No sea serpents."

"Or leviathans."

"None of those, obviously," Ethan said. "I mean, who tries to tackle a leviathan?"

"And no harpies, werewolves, or demons—"

"Okay."

"Or phantoms, or drowned folk, or ahuizotls—"

Ethan cocked his head. "A what?"

"An ahuizotl," she said. "Like a giant dog crossed with a panther, with human hands and a wicked set of claws that drip with poison. Oh, and its tail can shred you in the blink of an eye, too. Best to simply stay away from it at all costs."

"Can do."

"But that might be hard, now I that I think about it."

Ethan cringed. "How's that?"

"They're masters at manipulation," she explained. "Illusionists, some say. But whatever they are, they can make their prey disconnect from reality, even when they're eating them alive."

"Lovely."

"Oh, and definitely avoid the luscas, sirens, cyclopes, anacondas—"

Ethan held up a hand. "This sounds like a long list. Is there anything I shouldn't run away from?"

"Maybe a bilge rat," she said after some thought. "You could probably kill one of them. Well, a baby rat, that is. But then you'd have to deal with its three hundred brothers and sisters as well as the momma rat."

"Okay, guess I'll need to be careful," Ethan said with a heavy sigh.

The two made their way up to the shack, and once there, Zoey made a sweeping motion with her hand, as if inviting him to enter. "Your turn," she said. "I got you here. You get to open it."

Ethan, looking at the large iron lock on the door, tilted his head. "Should I kick it down or something?"

"Check your pockets," she said. "You ought to have a key."

Ethan, realizing he had pockets for the first time since he got there, shoved a hand in one. Much to his surprise, he found a small brass key in one. He stuck it in the lock, and the tumblers turned easily. It was only a matter of a simple push after that to get the door to swing inside. "That was convenient."

Zoey smiled knowingly. "Don't get used to it," she said. "This shack is your one and only freebie."

The two stepped inside, and Ethan spent a moment taking it all in. The interior was dimly lit by a couple of burning oil lamps that hung on opposite sides of the single-room building. In the very center was a red-and-orange woven rug that had probably looked nice once, but now was caked in dirt and had frayed in more places than it had stayed together. The walls looked even more pathetic than from the outside if that were possible, and a glance upward to the rotted, web-covered rafters had him wondering if the only thing holding it all together was the spider silk.

"Talk about a fixer-upper," he said. "I hope I'm not supposed to have to build this up."

"It's not that kind of game here," she said.

"Could you maybe tell me what kind of game it is?" he asked.

"The best way I can describe it is we're in a cross between a giant sandbox and an old-school RPG game," she said as she made her way to a chair and plopped herself onto it. "Not like modern ones or MMOs—we still have MMOs, right?"

"Uh, yeah. Why?"

Zoey bit her lower lip, and it was clear she was struggling with a lot that she wasn't sharing. "It's hard to tell how much time passes back home compared to what passes here."

Ethan felt his gut tighten. "How long have you been here?"

The moment those words left his mouth, he knew he didn't want to hear the answer. Fortunately, Zoey was all too eager to oblige his unspoken request. "I don't want to think about it, and honestly, I'm not going to ask you any questions in that regard, so please don't talk about the real world too much. Well, our world. It's really depressing, and I need to save my rum for things that don't involve me drowning out my sorrows."

"Can do," he said, knowing full well he probably wouldn't be able to keep that promise. When he got nervous, he liked to chat about anything and everything except for what was going on, and he had a gnawing feeling that the anxiety he was experiencing right this moment was just the start.

"Actually, I do have a sort of question to that," he said. Zoey raised a wary eyebrow, and he held up his hands before going on. "Nothing bad, I don't think, but why are you here?"

"Same as you," she said. "Playing for a couple of unfortunate souls."

"What do you have to do for them?"

"Right now? Nothing," she said. "My contest with Death hasn't officially started—or resumed, rather. In the meantime, I'm looking to build skills, wealth, and gear."

"I feel like you're being intentionally cryptic."

Zoey sighed and shook her head. "Trying not to be," she said. "The short, short version is I tricked him into a game of chess when I realized the duel we were in the middle of was going to end badly for me."

"How'd the chess game go?"

"Forced a draw," she said. "Once that happened, per my contract with him, I'm able to stall for time until I'm ready for a rematch."

"A rematch in chess?"

"That part is still up in the air," she said. "Hoping it's not going to be another duel."

"Ah. Got it," Ethan said.

"Anything else?"

"Yeah, actually, there is," he said. "How many other players are there around here?"

Zoey's eyes went up and to the right as her mouth twisted left. "From our world? I'm not sure," she finally said. "Our numbers have been dwindling for a long time now. Not sure why."

"Are the rest NPCs?"

Zoey shook her head. "No. They're real as far as I can tell. They're just part of this world."

Ethan nodded. "Speaking of the world, what sort of RPG are we in? One with pirates, obviously, but what else? Gothic fantasy? Steampunk? Horror?"

"Mostly pirates, but a little bit of the others, too," she said. "Some pretty funny things happen from time to time. And some weird stuff, as well. But I think all that's because nothing is scripted from what I've seen. This place is what we make of it for the most part, which is why I said it's like a giant sandbox game. Think something like Minecraft crossed with the old Ultima games but steeped in the Age of Sail."

"Oh, I liked that series," Ethan said, perking.

"That's good because you're essentially in it now."

"Next question: since this is a sandbox, how will I know how I'm supposed to beat Death if I don't have my contract? You said something here might help."

Zoey's eyes scanned the room for a moment before they lit up and she pointed to a small end table tucked in the corner. On it was a solitary envelope. "There," she said. "Give it a look. That might have something."

Dear Master Ethan,

It is with great pleasure that I write you and it is with my sincerest hopes that this letter finds you well. I hope you will forgive my absence in personally meeting you at Bartigua for a proper welcome, and I would wager that you are full of fears being in an unknown world; however, Madam Nataliya has taken it upon herself to see you fit for your journey ahead.

Thus, I will bid you good fortune and favor so that you might find your way to this year's Grand Regatta where the winner will be awarded high honors in front of the king himself, as well as be granted the soul of one canine companion, commonly known by mortal tongues as Anne.

Your ever-dutiful competitor in good faith,

-Azrael

"I have to get to a regatta?" Ethan asked. "Is that it?"

"Looks like it," Zoey said with a horrid cringe.

"What?"

"What, what?"

"You made a face."

"That regatta is in two weeks," she said. "That doesn't leave you a lot of time to get a ship, hire a crew, and be there when the race starts."

Ethan cursed under his breath, and he dreaded asking his next question. "What's the rest of it?"

Zoey hesitated; her face filled with sympathy. "Azrael is undefeated."

"But that's only because he's never raced before, right?" Ethan said, ever hopeful.

"No, he's been the reigning champion since its inception," she said. "And the race has been going on for a few hundred years, as far as I know."

Now it was Ethan's turn to cringe. As he stood there in silence, two thoughts crashed together. First, that was one hell of a track record. Second, his dog, Anne, was counting on him. He wasn't about to let her down and give her up. "Okay," he said, taking in a deep breath. "I can do this. I can do this."

The look in Zoey's eyes, however, disagreed.

CHAPTER IX
GEAR

I'M GLAD YOU'RE not letting this get you down," Zoey said, obviously trying to sound upbeat for his sanity. "As long as you don't act like a complete noob, we can get that gem, and then at least you'll have a good start on getting a ship." The moment she finished her sentence, her eyes widened, and a look of dread washed over her face. "For the love of all, please tell me you guys still say noob."

Ethan laughed uneasily. "Yeah, we still say noob."

"Oh, thank god," she said, falling back in her chair. "For a moment there, I thought you were going to look at me like the only person you'd ever heard say that was your great-great-grandfather."

"No, you don't have to worry about that," Ethan said with a chuckle. "What happens when you die here? Is this where I respawn?"

Zoey laughed, and the notes she hit when she did made Ethan wish she hadn't found whatever he'd said disturbingly funny. "Respawn. Oh, wouldn't that be nice? If there's only one thing you remember at all, remember this: we're in hardcore mode. Got it?"

"Hardcore like no saves?"

"Mm-hm."

"Limited gear?"

"Yep."

Ethan felt his throat tighten. "And no respawn?"

"One life, kiddo. Enjoy it."

"Okay," Ethan said, taking it all in. "But what *does* happen if you die here?"

Zoey shrugged. "I don't know. All I know for certain is no one ever comes back, which means at the very least, you lose whoever you're playing for."

"And at the worst, you die in the real world, too," Ethan finished.

"Exactly."

Ethan drummed his fingers on his side for a few moments. "Does Death have to play by the same rules?"

"He does."

"So if he dies here, he doesn't get to come back, either?"

Zoey shrugged. "I would assume."

Ethan nodded with purpose. "Then, I guess if I can't outrace him, I'll just have to kill him."

"Remember when I said don't act like a noob?" she asked. "That's acting like a noob. Aside from the fact that he easily beat me in a duel, he also has a massively loyal and deadly crew. And that's not counting the fact that his ship is brimming with so many cannons he could level a small country."

Ethan frowned. This hardly seemed like a fair game, and not even in the sense that he had a fair chance at winning. Even the games at the fair gave the illusion one had some hope. This seemed to be anything but. "I thought you were going to help?" he finally said. "This doesn't feel helpful."

"Being realistic is helpful," she replied. "Besides, you're the one who came up with the 'Let's kill Death' plan. As if that hasn't been tried. What you're forgetting already is that you don't have to kill him. You only have to win a race."

"Right," his voice trailed, but then he repeated what he'd said one more time a little more forcefully. "Right. Right. Okay. I can do that. And this gem is going to get me the fastest ship on the high seas."

"Ah, well," she said with hesitation. "Your share will get you a ship. Or part of one. It all depends on what we can get for it. But you know, there's probably plenty of other treasure where we're going. We could come back with enough gold for a king's ransom if we do it right."

Ethan perked, liking the sounds of that. However, reality blunted his dreams right after. "If this place is so loaded, why haven't people taken it all already?"

"First off, I presume others are trying, or will again shortly, which is why we need to hurry," Zoey replied. "Second, the fortress itself wasn't loaded with anything until Lord William Belmont recently decided to make it his home. So there hasn't been a lot of time for people to learn about it, let alone raid it."

"Hang on a second," Ethan said, holding up a hand. "You never said we were stealing from a noble."

"He's more of a lich than a noble," she said. "The lord part is a self-appointed title from what I've gathered."

"Now he's a lich?"

Zoey nodded. "I take it you know what that is?"

"An insanely powerful undead wizard?"

Zoey nodded again. "Pretty much. But don't worry. I don't plan on fighting him or his hordes of undead minions. There are some old tunnels that he doesn't know about we can use. All you have to do is help me slip inside, and I'll steal the gem, and we'll both be set."

"This is insane," Ethan said, shaking his head. "There's no way it's that easy."

"Honestly, it's not."

"I figured that. Details."

"Lord Belmont loves finding trespassers," she said. "He sets up all sorts of traps to capture them, and when he does..."

"Let me guess, he tortures and kills them."

Zoey laughed and shook her head. "No, he's a lich, remember? He turns them into undead servants. Last I checked, over the past month or so, those servants have tripled in size."

Ethan's shoulders fell. "Please tell me you've got a plan that will let us not end up like the others."

"I'm putting together a raiding party that will get the job done, yes," she said.

Despite her affirmation, Ethan looking at her warily. "By raiding party, do you mean a massive army that can storm any citadel?"

"Not exactly."

"Powerful guild with a vault overflowing with enchanted items?"

"Afraid not."

"A full company of veteran wyrm slayers? Temple full of ninjas? An orbiting battlecruiser that's locked on and ready to bombard our foe with the fury of a thousand suns?"

Zoey pressed her two forefingers together as her lips tightened. "Let's just say adding you has significantly increased our ranks after some minor setbacks."

"How significant are we talking?"

"Well, you might have doubled the numbers I was fielding as of this morning."

"Doubled! It's only you? You said you were putting together a raiding party!"

"I did! And I am!"

"Then when and where are we getting everyone else?"

Zoey tried to stay upbeat, but her body deflated, and she shook her head. "Okay, I should be upfront," she said. "You deserve that.

My reputation around here isn't too hot, which is going to complicate things when it comes to getting help."

"What do you mean?"

"My previous party was the last formal group to go in," she said. "I'm the only one who made it out—penniless, but alive, obviously. No one is going to join us with me as a failed party leader, especially when there's a high risk of being turned into a skeleton, zombie, or ghoul."

"I could be the party leader," Ethan said, thinking the answer obvious. "Then we could get a lot more help."

Zoey cracked a half grin. "You can barely lead a group to scrape barnacles off a rowboat. No one is joining with you at the helm."

"Are you saying it's going to be the two of us, no matter what?"

"Most likely."

"Going into certain death. Or eternal, undead servitude."

"Possibly, but it's not a certainty," she said. "Look, we both need that gem, and we can make it work."

"Why do you need it?"

"I need my reputation back," she said. "And honestly, the crowns from the sale will go a long way to lifting my spirits."

"There has to be a better way to get money for a ship," Ethan replied.

"In less than two weeks? I seriously doubt it," Zoey said. "I know this sounds scary, and it is, but don't forget, I'm going to be doing this with you. If I didn't think we could pull it off, even with you being here less than a day, I wouldn't push it at all. Do you honestly think I want to get caught and turned into an undead minion?"

"No, I don't think you'd want that at all," he said. He then went back to drumming his fingers on his side. He hated every bit of this plan, and he had no idea how they'd pull this off, but at the same time, he felt like the payoff if they succeeded was more than enough to at least explore the risk.

"Okay, I'm tentatively in," he said. "What's our first step?"

"First, we get your gear and check out your character sheet," she said. "Then we'll have a better idea of what we're working with when it comes to your skills. After that, we need to head to a town called Weynock. There, we can pay for a ferry to take us to the southern side of the island, provided there's one available sporting at least a dozen eighteen-pounders."

"Eighteen-pounders?"

"Cannons," she explained. "Ships that don't have big enough guns tend to wind up as snacks for Myriden."

Ethan cringed as he had flashbacks to his intro to this world. "I'd rather avoid him again if I could."

"We will. Don't worry," she said. "Anyway, let's see what you've got."

"Great. How do we do that?"

Zoey motioned toward a small wooden chest tucked in the corner. "That's where all your stuff will be," she said. "It won't be much, but it'll be something. Also, it'll be based on whatever your answers were with Madam Nataliya. So good god, I hope you answered well and didn't get stuck with a shepherd hook like the last guy."

"Me too," he said, thinking it best not to ask what had happened to whoever she'd come across last. Probably retired to a nice estate in a coastal town after finding a lost idol inside a forgotten, goblin-filled dungeon and was now sipping mead while watching the sailboats come and go. Yeah, that was it. Definitely.

With that, Ethan walked over to the chest and opened it. Inside he found a bound scroll along with a leather cuirass that would be lucky to stop a butter knife. There were also two vials containing red liquid, a coin purse the size of his palm, a small backpack, and a worn cutlass that looked duller than a five-volume series on the historical significance of table lint. Despite being greeted with such items, all Ethan could do was chuckle and shrug.

"Guess as a starting character I can't expect much more than this, huh?"

"Nope," she said, taking to her feet. "Get your stuff, so we can go."

Ethan grabbed the sword.

You have taken the cutlass.

"What?"

"What, what?" Zoey said, tilting her head.

"You said I picked up the cutlass," he said.

Zoey stifled a laugh and then recomposed herself. "Sorry, forgot to mention that. That's Narrator. You'll notice him from time to time."

"Narrator?"

"Well, I don't know what else to call it, but yeah," she said. "He tells you what your character is doing. I guess you could call it a console but more for your mind? Anyway, I like calling it Narrator more. Feels more likeable, you know?"

"Ugh. Why do I have the feeling this is going to get incredibly annoying, incredibly fast?" Ethan said as he took the rest of the items from the chest. When he did, the voice inside his head sounded four more times:

You have picked up the leather cuirass.
You have picked up two vials of red liquid.
You have picked up the coin purse.
You have picked up the backpack.

When his face soured, Zoey laughed. "Don't worry. You can learn to tune him out if you want. But if you want some extra fun, try taking the mirror in the corner."

Ethan eyed it suspiciously. "Why?"

"Just do it. You'll see."

"If this turns me into a frog, I'm jumping in your hand and peeing all over you."

"Not if I step on you first."

"Rude."

"Says the one trying to pee on me," Zoey said. "Now, take the stupid mirror already."

Ethan shrugged and reached for the mirror, vowing to out hop any stomps she might send his way. But as he went to take it, he pulled back as a thought struck him.

You don't feel the need to take that right now.

"Say what?" he said, straightening. "The hell I don't."

Ethan tried again. And again, he pulled back.

You don't feel the need to take that right now.

Ethan sighed and shook his head. "You've got to be kidding me. I'm a total puppet to this narrator?"

"No, but he will get in the way from time to time, sorry. Game limitations, I guess. I told you, sometimes this place is like an old-school RPG. As a word of advice, when that happens, all you can do is roll with it."

Ethan grumbled. "As if I have much of a choice."

"Exactly," she said. "How are your stats?"

Ethan opened the scroll and immediately wished he hadn't. There was a lot of writing on it, the flowery kind that looked nice but made it hard to read. "I know cal...cali...califly..."

"Calligraphy?" she offered.

"Yeah, that," he said. "I know it's supposed to be fancy and make things all pretty, but for the record, I'm not a fan of it."

"Why's that?"

"I like things simple," he said with a shrug. His eyes scanned the parchment. "What are these stats out of? Nine? Ten?"

"Twenty."

"Aw, man," Ethan said. "I was hoping to have giant strength."

Zoey grinned. "Yeah, don't we all wish for that. Now then, what do you have?"

"Strength, twelve. Reflex, eleven," he said, reading. "Charisma, fourteen—told you I was cute."

"No, you tried to hit on me the first chance you could and failed miserably," she said. "You're not that cute."

"I try to date up, what can I say?" Ethan said, unapologetically shrugging his shoulders. Zoey drew back the corner of her mouth in genuine amusement, and Ethan mentally gave himself one point before continuing with his reading of the stats. "Let's see what else I have," he said. "A big fat fifteen on the intelligence, yeah, baby. Oh! Oh! And super lucky. I have eighteen points of that."

Zoey raised an eyebrow as surprise splashed across her face. "You've got two high stats?"

"I guess. Why?"

"Are you sure?"

"I'm sure I can read," Ethan said, looking it over again. "Maybe."

Ethan cocked his head as her voice trailed. "Maybe?"

"Keep going," she said. "Maybe something else will make sense of it all."

Ethan shrugged and did as she asked, but most of the rest went right over his head. Most, that is, except for a couple of lines on the right. "Says my class is *Gambler*."

Zoey sucked in a breath and bit her lip. "That could be handy. Maybe. Or completely disastrous, to be honest. What starting skills did you end up with? That's going to tell us what you can and can't do more than anything."

"Where are they?" he asked. "Ah, never mind. At the bottom. Give me a second. Skills: pistol, novice; swordplay, novice; cooking, novice; gambling, proficient; sailing, novice; swimming, competent; sleight of hand, competent; Hobby: card tricks, competent."

"Typical group. Just so you know, any skill you're not at least novice at, you take severe penalties for when trying to use."

A thought popped into his head, and Ethan scanned his sheet, hoping to find the answer. "Where are my hit points?" he asked once he gave up searching. "I have those, right? All it says is 'healthy.'"

"A lot of damage and health is under the hood, so to speak," she said. She then went on to explain, using her fingers to illustrate each point. "Aside from being healthy, you can be lightly, moderately, seriously, critically, and gravely wounded. After that, you're dead."

"Simple enough."

"Only in what Narrator and your sheet tells," she said. "Like I said, there's a lot under the hood. We can talk about the details later. What about your other traits?"

"Traits...traits...traits, ah. Traits," he said, running his finger down the sheet. "Sweet. I'm exceptional."

Zoey's face soured. "Ugh."

"What? Don't be jealous."

"Believe me. I'm not," she said with a snort. "That's not a good thing."

Ethan shook his head. "I don't see how it isn't."

"It's covering up for a negative trait. Or two. Or three. You think you're awesome, but you're not, even if you did get a slight bonus to other base stats."

"Or maybe you're jealous."

Zoey folded her arms over her chest. "And what would that get me?"

"I don't know, but that doesn't mean you aren't."

Zoey shook her head and sighed. "Look, you're going to have to trust me on this. You could be anything from harebrained to overconfident."

"I doubt I'm the latter, but the former seems pretty good," Ethan said. "You know, probably a good thing to think quick like a rabbit."

"It means you're rash and foolhardy."

"Oh," Ethan said, slumping. "Are you sure?"

"Quite, and I'm starting to think your INT isn't near fifteen at all."

Ethan frowned before he glanced at his character sheet once more, specifically his primary stats. "Well, according to this, I'm not as dumb as a box of rocks. So maybe this negative trait of mine is something else, like adorably forgetful."

"That's not a thing."

"Could be."

"It's not."

"First time for everything, you know."

Zoey furrowed her brow. "You're quickly sailing into mildly annoying."

"Sorry," Ethan said with a sheepish grin. "We'll figure it out. I can always fix it later, though, right?"

"Yeah, you can," she said, visibly relaxing a little. "It's not easy to buff out a negative trait, but it can be done with a lot of work once you know what it is."

Ethan grinned. "Perfect. We'll do that, then. What say we get moving?"

"I say that's a pretty good idea. We've spent enough time here as it is."

Chapter X
Mail

THE TWO HAD been on the road for nearly an hour, traveling down a wide dirt path through a forest lightly populated by pines and the occasional scrub. The terrain was a little hilly, and the path they were on at times was broken and rocky, but the track wasn't anything Ethan couldn't handle, even if the most he usually hiked was from the far side of the parking lot to his front door when all the spaces were taken.

Since they had left Ethan's shack, he'd been practicing swinging his cutlass. It felt as normal as any other sword as he swung, not that he was a master dueler back home by any stretch of the imagination. In fact, the last sword he'd ever used was a little wooden one he'd gotten at the medieval fair when he was seven. Its expert forging had lasted precisely three blows against the neighbor's bush before the blade snapped at the handle. Ethan prayed the cutlass he now possessed would last a touch longer, especially if he were to fight with it.

"This is really doing a number on my shoulder," he said, taking a break from practicing and sliding the weapon back into the sheath on his belt. "Don't suppose we'll find some aspirin later? I think I'm going to pay for this tomorrow."

Zoey paused in the middle of the dirt road and shook her head. "The game's not that detailed," she said. "You won't be sore from a little exercise."

She was going to say something else but stopped when the sounds of a distant argument drifted through the air. She held up a finger and then began to creep into the forest.

"Who's yelling, and is this something we want to get mixed up in?" Ethan whispered, trying his best to stay quiet as he hurried up next to her. "I thought you said this place was dangerous."

"It is for the most part, but the stuff around here isn't too bad," she said. "Besides, someone might need our help."

"Well, if we run into a two-headed giant arguing with himself, I vote we leave him alone."

The corners of Zoey's mouth drew back. "If we run into an ettin, you'll be voting by yourself, because I won't be around to form the committee. Those guys are way more trouble than they're worth."

They pressed on a little deeper into the woods, and soon they found themselves at the edge of a campsite where three little creatures with hunched backs and gnarled skin covered in warts argued amongst themselves. They were dressed in baggy clothes that looked like they'd been tossed away from a beggar's wardrobe on account that they weren't fine enough. Each one had a black pipe stuck in its mouth, and as they would argue their points, they each would take their pipes out and wag them at one another. Next to the arguing trio, a few feet away from the campfire, sat a wooden cage with iron bars. Inside said cage was a small canine-like pup, with wet, dirt-covered fur and a look of resignation upon its face.

"What are those things?" Ethan asked. "Goblins?"

"No, they're kobolds—goblins' weaker reptilian cousins."

"What are they doing with that dog?" Ethan asked.

"I think it's a jackal," Zoey said. "And I'm not sure, but I imagine that's what they're arguing about. We should go."

"Why? We can take them."

"I'm sure we could, but I'm not one for random slaughter, and that's all this will be. They're not hurting anyone."

"I probably need the combat practice, though, right?"

"Yes, but still," Zoey said with hesitation. "I don't feel like this is the right time."

Ethan didn't know what to make of her wariness, but at that point in the conversation, the three kobolds took note of them both. They whipped around to face them and drew daggers from their waistband. In prompt response, Zoey grunted and pulled her pistols.

"What you humanses wants?" the one in the middle asked, shaking his weapon at the two of them. "This is our find. Our goat!"

"Goat? What goat?" Ethan said, readying his cutlass. Though he was squaring off against three kobolds, and in every game he had ever played these little guys were nothing more than cannon fodder, somehow staring down these creatures as they held very real and very sharp-looking daggers pointed at him made things a little different than when he was in front of his computer.

"What goat? What goat! You leaves our goatses alone!" it shrieked right before it charged.

The kobold was faster than Ethan anticipated, and when it swung at him with his dagger, he barely managed to jump back in time before he had a good look at his entrails. Still, he didn't escape unscathed. The point of the dagger drew across his leather cuirass, but thankfully it didn't manage to cut through.

A kobold grazed you.

Not expecting Narrator to, well, narrate, Ethan jumped back again, nearly losing his footing as he did. The kobold pressed the attack, but this time Ethan was ready enough to knock the blow aside with his blade.

You parried the kobold's attack.

"Yes, I figured that part out, thank you!" he yelled. "I don't need a play-by-play account right now."

Ethan's attacker stopped his assault, probably trying to figure out why he was screaming at an unseen someone. Ethan seized the opportunity and swung with his weapon. The blade neatly loped off the kobold's head, and the body fell to the ground with a quiet thump.

Kobold killed!
You feel slightly more experienced.

Narrator sounded thrilled when he made that first announcement, though since it was all playing in Ethan's head, Ethan wondered if maybe he had some effect on how it came out since he, too, was ecstatic that he'd made his first kill.

Ethan spun around, expecting that at least one, if not both, of the remaining kobolds would be coming at him. Instead of staring at flashing steel, he saw one kobold flat on its back with a hole in its head, and the other staring down the barrel of Zoey's second pistol, which had yet to be fired.

"Last chance to run along," she said. "I won't miss."

The kobold didn't reply, but it definitely understood. It spun around and darted off, wailing in a high-pitched voice the entire time. Once it was finally gone, she stuffed the weapon back in her belt and reloaded her other gun.

"Nicely done," she said while working. "I would've been embarrassed otherwise. Not sure I could even admit having known you had you died on your first encounter."

"Thanks," Ethan said. He then pointed to her outside forearm where a fine red line ran across it. "Looks like he grazed you, too."

Zoey looked down, and she sighed heavily. "Damn it to hell and back," she muttered, shaking her head.

"What? It's not that bad. It's barely bleeding."

"Don't tell me what's bad and what's not," she snapped. Zoey held up a hand and sighed before shaking her head. "I'm sorry," she said in a much more controlled manner. "I shouldn't have bitten your head off like that. It's a little embarrassing he got me at all, you know? I mean, damn, I saw that knife throw coming a mile away, and it still nicked me."

Ethan scratched his head, unsure of how to respond. He felt there was more to it than what she was saying, but at the same time, he didn't feel it was worth pursuing, either—or perhaps wise, for that matter. There was something dark right behind the liveliness in the pirate's eyes, something he didn't want to know about.

As such, he decided to search the body of the kobold he'd killed. "Wonder if he's got anything."

"A farthing or two, I'd wager," Zoey said as she sifted through the pockets of the kobold she'd dropped. Her eyes lit up as she pulled forth a copper coin. "Oh, look! A penny! Holy snort, that's a lot of coin for one of these guys."

"Don't spend it all in one place," Ethan said with a grin.

"With three more, I could buy everything you own."

Ethan unapologetically threw up his hands. He might have currently been sporting "economy gear" for the "budget-friendly" swashbuckler, but that wouldn't last, especially if this was a land ripe with pirates, because much like dragons, where there were pirates, there were hordes' treasure, only without the promise of a fiery death or tied-up damsels in distress.

"Let's see what sort of loot awaits," he said, rifling through the dead kobold's pockets. "Piece of string. A halfpenny. And a ring."

Two of the three he took. One of the two he used. Narrator narrated accordingly.

You have taken the halfpenny!
You have taken the ring!
You've put on the ring!
New trait gained!

"New trait gained?" Ethan repeated, looking himself over.

"Trait?" Zoey tilted her head to the side, but then her eyes went wide as she dashed over to him. "Oh, god, no!"

"Wait, what?"

Zoey sighed and shook her head as she looked at the thin bronze band Ethan now wore on his right hand. "Ethan! Why the hell did you do that?"

"Do what?" he asked. "Take the ring?"

"Yes. I mean, no. I mean, please, God, tell me you can take it off," she said.

Ethan tried. Though it had slipped on easily enough, the little piece of circular metal wouldn't budge in the least when he sought to remove it. "Cripes, that's a tight fit," he said. "Hope that doesn't mean we have to cut it off later."

"No, it means someone will have to cut you in two if they want it," Zoey replied.

"Come again?"

"Or shoot you, or stab you through the heart, or take your head off," she went on, enumerating on her fingertips.

"Hey, now, I don't want it that badly."

"Well, you should've thought of that before you stuck it on your hand," she said with a huff.

"Could you fill me in on the rest," he said. "Because clearly, I'm not following what you're telling me."

"Some magical items around here don't like being passed around," she replied. "So when they find a new owner, they stick to him like glue. Hopefully, this isn't one of those that's cursed, too."

Ethan felt queasy. "Cursed? With what?"

Zoey sucked in a breath through clenched teeth. "No telling. Do you feel different?"

"No?" Ethan patted himself down a few times to be extra sure. "I feel pretty good, to be honest."

"That's something, at least," she said. "Still, we'll need to get it identified by someone soon, assuming we can't figure it out on our own."

"Can we? That would make things a lot easier if we did."

Zoey shrugged. "Maybe. People have before. But with all the endless possibilities and ways of tapping into that magic, it's pretty hard. See what your character sheet says. Maybe it will help."

Ethan took out the paper. Under his main stats, which hadn't changed, much to his disappointment, was a new line beneath the traits section. It read:

Ring Bearer (unique trait): Be they in sunken wrecks or misplaced chests, ye have the uncanny knack to find lost bands of metal. But ye best batten down the hatches, lad. Everyone from scallywags to sea dogs will want ye precious!

Ethan inspected the ring as creases formed in his brow. He had a new respect for the tiny piece of metal, and he wondered what mystical powers it might hold. "Wonder if it turns me invisible. That seems pretty standard."

"Given I can still see you, I'm going with no."

"Obviously," Ethan said, sticking out his tongue. "I meant, maybe I have to activate it in some way." He then held up his hand, ring pointed to the sky, and intoned a magical incantation. "Klaatu...Barada...Neck...tie? Nectar! Nickle..."

"Going to try noodle next?" Zoey said with a smirk.

"I'm working on it," Ethan said, trying to stay focused on the task at hand. "I can feel the energy flowing, and what's next is an 'N' word. It's definitely an 'N' word."

"If you say so," Zoey said with a raise of the shoulders. "Look, there's no telling what the ring does or how it works. It could be anything at this point. I've heard of rings that ranged from granting extra strength, to bestowing the ability to fly, to quieting the wearer when he's snoring."

"Bah. Who would ever want that last one?"

"Someone who's tired of sleeping next to a noisy partner."

"So where can we go to get it looked at?"

"There are a few practitioners of Voodoo in Weynock if you know where to look," she said. "And Hagitha still lives there, too. She's a witch. Well, she's a witch to those in the know. She keeps it pretty low-key."

"With a name like that? Never would've guessed," Ethan said as he walked over to the cage. He knelt at its side and studied the jackal inside. The jackal, in turn, appeared to study Ethan, too, and not in a good way. He couldn't help but feel how he imagined a rat might feel being dangled in front of a python who might not be hungry, but occasionally went for a mid-week snack.

Ethan shook his head, ridding himself of such nonsense. If the kobolds had him caged, the jackal had to be harmless—relatively speaking.

"Should we let him go?" he asked. "Or do you think I could turn him into a pet?"

"A pet?" Zoey chuckled. "Do you want to drop by the store and get him a chew toy, too?"

"No, I didn't mean like that. I mean like a battle companion or something. It's a standard trope in fantasy and RPGs. You know, like you might have a familiar or something, but since I'm not a magic wielder, I get a 'pet.'"

Zoey nodded. "I know. I'm just busting your balls. I'm not sure he's that type, though."

"Well, whatever. We'll see. At the very least, I'll feel good about rescuing him," Ethan said as he undid the latch to the cage and swung open the door.

The jackal tilted his head and went into a downward dog to stretch for a moment while giving a big yawn. He then moseyed out of the cage, but he didn't run off, nor did he do anything affectionate such as bathe Ethan's hands with his tongue, rub up against him, or wag his tail so fast that it might break the sound barrier.

Instead, the jackal huffed, sat on his haunches, and looked Ethan directly in the eyes. "The next time you want to play hero," he said, "maybe you should make sure that your 'damsel in distress' actually needs saving, or fellow in this case."

Ethan's jaw dropped. "You can talk?"

"And you can hear," the jackal replied without losing a beat. "I guess that means we both deserve a parade."

"Oh, I like him," Zoey said. "He's got spunk."

"I can't believe you're being like this," Ethan said, shaking his head, and then shaking it again when he realized he was still talking to a jackal. "We just saved you from being skinned alive and eaten."

"Skinned alive? You think that's what was going on?"

Ethan shrugged. "You were in a cage. Are you trying to tell us you liked that thing? It wasn't exactly a grand palace. At the very least, they were going to sell you to someone who would've skinned you."

"*They* weren't doing anything but being my playthings," the jackal said, giving one of his forelegs a tongue bath. "There were eight of them originally, and over the last week, I'd eaten five. I was so looking forward to another few days of relaxed dining, but you had to come along and bollix that up."

"I seriously doubt that," Ethan said. "How did you eat kobolds from inside a cage?"

"Did you miss the part where they thought I was a goat?" he said.

"I heard them say something about a goat, but there's no way they thought you were one. Even kobolds aren't that stupid, are they?"

"Who are you talking to?" asked a voice from behind.

Ethan spun around to find the jackal perched on a log, grinning from ear to ear. He then turned back around and realized he'd been staring at a moss-covered rock moments ago. "How did you do that?"

"Do what?"

"Teleport."

"I didn't."

"Or blink. Or whatever you call it." Ethan turned back around, only to find the jackal had disappeared completely. "Now, knock it off."

"Knock what off?" the animal asked, this time his voice coming from the side.

Ethan spun again, and the creature was now scratching his back against a small pine tree, looking ever so happy. "I suppose you knew he was like this," Ethan said to Zoey.

The woman shook her head and chuckled. "No, at least not before he talked. I'm just glad he's picking on you and not me."

"Since you decided to ruin my fun, I suppose I'll tag along for a bit," the jackal said. "I could use the entertainment, not to mention a meal or two."

Maii has joined the party.

"That was odd," Ethan said, straightening at the sound of Narrator's voice. The hairs across his body rose, and his ring finger warmed. "What's going on?"

"I am accompanying you on your journey," Maii replied.

"And what aren't you telling me?"

The jackal's lips pressed together, and he sat his haunches on the ground as if he'd been whacked across the nose with a belaying pin. "You have my former master's ring," he murmured.

Ethan's eyes lit up, and he held up his hand. "This?"

"Yes."

"You have to follow who wears this?"

The jackal nodded. "Yes."

"Obey, too?"

"For now," Maii said with a growl. "But that might change one day. So, if I were you, I'd be nice."

Zoey laughed, though it sounded more nervous than amused. "I don't like the sound of that."

"It'll be fine," Ethan said, giving her a dismissive wave. "Don't worry, my furry little guy. I promise I won't do anything to humiliate you, but I am going to make you stop messing with my head. Got it?"

The jackal turned his head to the side as he eyed him. After a few moments, he broke the silence that had settled. "I understand, but I'll also make you a separate deal, newcomer," he said. "Keep me fed and happy, and I'll make it worth your while one day."

"What makes you think I'm a newcomer?" Ethan asked, feeling put off that it was obvious to even a pet, regardless of how magical it may or may not be.

"You have a look of adventure in your eyes," he replied. "And foolish naiveté." The jackal paused before he darted on top of a boulder near Ethan so he could stick his face into Ethan's. He sniffed around both of Ethan's cheeks and then under his chin before backing off a half pace. "Ah, that explains it. You're Death's newest fresh-meat challenger."

"I am not fresh meat," Ethan said, puffing his chest and folding his arms across it.

"That's what the last two I came across said," the jackal replied with a wry grin. "For your sake, I hope you're right. But if you aren't, at least it looks like I'll have a sizeable meal after you die."

"After I die?" Ethan stammered as he worked out what the jackal was insinuating. "What exactly happened to your old master?"

"Such a long, boring story, I doubt you'd want to hear the details," Maii casually replied. "The short version is he crossed the wrong people. They found his antics infuriating, and I found his body delicious."

Ethan cringed. "You're right. I don't want to know."

"You could always free me from servitude if such thoughts bother you," the jackal said, eyes sparkling with a touch of hope.

"That might not be a bad idea," Zoey chimed in. "Not sure I like the idea of having a party member around who's eaten others."

Ethan shook his head. "I will later," he said. "I have a feeling we'll need him, and if there's one thing I know, it's to trust your gut."

Maii, surprisingly, nodded and flashed a sharp smile. "And if there's one thing I know, it's you're going to want to keep me fed. Always."

Chapter XI
A Rough Night

THE GROUP HAD traveled almost to sunset before they stopped to make camp. Though there was still a little bit of golden light filtering through the trees' hunter-green leaves, and Ethan wanted to press on, the shadows of the forest were long, and the likelihood of them finding a better spot before darkness engulfed everything was slim.

Immediately after coming to a group consensus that this was where they'd rest for the night, Zoey started to build a fire. She did so in a slightly peculiar way, gathering hefty branches that looked a little wet, which she carefully arranged in a cleared-out section of the forest floor.

At that point, she didn't bother to look for or make any kindling. She simply took a leather pouch from inside her pack, poured a tablespoon's worth of rusty-clay-colored powder from it on the wood, and then topped the stuff off with a little gunpowder.

"What's that?" Ethan asked

"Dragon's breath," she said. "Burns through pretty much anything. Handy for starting fires."

Ethan didn't say anything at first. He simply watched her set the powder alight with a fuse. The gunpowder flared up, and then a split second later, the dragon's breath ignited with all the fury of a fifty-ton flying, fire-breathing lizard.

"Hot damn," Ethan said, whistling. "That is handy. Where do you get it?"

"You can make it with a basic skill set in *Chemistry* as it's no harder to craft than gunpowder," she explained. "There's usually a few people you can pay to do it as well in a decent-sized town. It's hardly a technological secret."

"Gunpowder isn't that hard to make, right?" Ethan asked. "Can you teach me both?"

Zoey grimaced. "I better not."

"Why?"

"Not until you're at least a novice in *Chemistry*," she said. "And I can't help you there."

"Oh, right, penalties and critical failures," Ethan said as his body hunched.

"Exactly," she said. "You'll probably end up grabbing the wrong reagents on your first go and nuking half the world when you mix them together."

"I don't think they have nukes here."

"No, but there's a first time for everything," she said.

Ethan conceded the point, and when his stomach rumbled, he changed the subject. "Maii went hunting?" he asked, noting the jackal still wasn't around.

"That's what he said."

"Wonder if he'll get a rabbit," Ethan said. "They make a good stew, I think."

"Usually. But he might get something else. So, don't pin your hopes on anything in particular."

Ethan grunted, but when her words sank into his mind, his face soured. "God, I hope he doesn't come back with a rat. Or worse, half a rat."

Zoey laughed and shook her head. "You'll survive."

"Maybe not," Ethan said. "In fact, I'm going to go tell him right now we don't want rat."

Ethan wandered off in the direction he'd last seen Maii go. He didn't get very far before his stomach rumbled again, and he decided that his time might better be spent foraging for food on his own. With that in mind, he started a search of the area for something, *anything*, delicious that was definitely not a rodent.

His quest for food ended up not taking him far. Near the base of some sort of leafy tree (a pine, oak, or palm tree, Ethan knew) that stood fifty yards from camp, greenish mushrooms with white stalks and gills grew. Ethan, though, realized he didn't have much (if any) skill in the game when it came to wilderness survival; it seemed as if that didn't matter at least for today, thanks to the insane amount of luck he possessed. Hopefully, Zoey would know what they were, too, as he wasn't keen on taking his chances ingesting an unknown fungus.

"A dozen ought to do it," Ethan said, picking twelve of the largest caps before heading back.

When he returned, Zoey had already put some more wood on the fire and was currently using the flames to warm her hands. "We should reach Weynock tomorrow," she said, stretching her arms. "Maybe by midafternoon."

"That's not bad," Ethan replied. "Found some stuff for the stew. Do you want to eat now or later?"

"I'm not hungry," Zoey said. "You two can eat whenever."

"Not at all?"

"Nope."

"How come?"

"I'm just not, okay?" Zoey snapped.

Ethan straightened, unsure what he'd said or done to elicit such a reaction. "I didn't mean anything by it," he finally said as he sat down on a large flat stone across from her.

Zoey took a deep breath and sighed heavily, her shoulders falling in the process. "Sorry," she said. "Haven't eaten in a while. It makes me cranky."

"But—" Ethan cut himself off when Zoey looked up at him and shot him a glare. "Alright, I get it," he said before rummaging in his pack for the mushrooms he picked. "But if you change your mind, you can have some of these, assuming they're the edible kind."

Terror gripped the woman's face. Faster than Ethan thought possible, Zoey dashed toward him and knocked the mushroom caps out of his hand. "Holy crap, Ethan," she said, frantically whipping out her wineskin and dousing his hands with the water. "What the hell are you doing with those?"

"Apparently, I'm staying far, far away from them," he said, eyes fixated on the spot where they'd landed.

"Yeah, good idea," she said, shaking her head. "Those were death caps."

Ethan felt his stomach go in knots and his legs weaken. "I take it they're a little poisonous?"

"Yeah, in the same way a bite from a black mamba carries a little bit of venom," she said, laughing and shaking her head. "Cripes, Ethan, you can't just go eating stuff around here—especially stuff that you don't know what it is."

"I wasn't going to eat it without showing you first," he said.

"Glad to hear, but don't go picking stuff without my consent, either. What if you'd decided to lick your fingers?"

"I'm guessing I'd be dead."

"Very," Zoey said with a definitive nod. "Look, I told you, if you're not at least a novice in something, you could royally screw it up, and if you're unsuccessful when you're untrained, you've got double the chance at a critical failure. Case in point, what you brought back on your foraging attempt. A single bite from even a small death cap would kill you in under a minute."

"God, I wish I wasn't so dumb and useless," he said, plopping to the ground and crossing his legs in front of him.

"You're not useless," Zoey said. "Or dumb."

"I did just try and kill us with mushrooms. Hell, I couldn't even do that right."

Zoey laughed, which instantly melted the worry from both their faces. "You won't be like this forever, I promise. Enjoy the training wheels while you can. This world gets really scary, really fast once they come off."

"Right, well, I guess in the meantime, I'll have to wait for Maii to bring back dinner," Ethan replied.

Zoey shook her head, likely out of pity, going by the look in her eyes. "I don't think he's hunting for anyone but himself."

"Does that mean I get to starve?"

Zoey shook her head one more time before she went into her own pack, reached inside, and tossed him a large, hefty biscuit. "Here. Eat this," she said. "You can buy me another one when we get to Weynock. They're cheap."

"What is it?" Ethan said, inspecting it.

"Hardtack."

"Hard what?"

"Hardtack," she repeated. "Pretty much flour and salt. Tastes like crap, but it'll fill your belly and takes forever to go bad."

Ethan hesitated, but when a stab of hunger ran through his gut, he decided something was better than nothing, and he gave it a bite. Bad, as far as describing its taste went, was an understatement. Aside from being jaw-breaking in terms of hardness, the biscuit tasted like pressed sawdust, and Ethan had to take two swigs of water to get the first mouthful down. A few bites later, Ethan gave up and handed it back to her.

"I'm good now, thanks," he said. "If I go to sleep, I'll be fine."

"You do that," she replied, cozying up to the fire. After a few moments, her eyes found his, and the ones she had stared a little too hard with a little too much annoyance for his likes. "You're not sleeping."

"Yeah, sorry," he said before turning his pack into a makeshift pillow. "Where are you going to sleep?"

"Don't know yet," she said, surveying the campsite. "Now, seriously. Get some rest. I'll take first watch."

Ethan nodded, quietly scolding himself for thinking she might snuggle up next to him on her own. He thought about inviting her to join him, but given how hard she'd shot him down when they first met, he figured another attempt at wooing her wouldn't amount to much at best and would completely backfire at worst.

Thus, Ethan spent the next thirty minutes or so practicing his sleight of hand skills with the halfpenny he'd looted off the kobold. He only did so because his body told him that although he was tired, he wasn't quite ready to close his eyes for the night. But by the time he finally decided to call it a night, he felt like he could keep the coin palmed with no one noticing, or even "magically" make it disappear with a simple wave of his hand.

Ready to pass out, Ethan pocketed the coin and looked for Zoey once last time. He saw her at the edge of the campfire's light with her back turned. She had her hands on her hips for a moment before they reached up and started fixing her hair. As she did, she turned halfway, presenting him with a side view of her body. His eyes followed every curve she had, from the top of her head, across her button nose, down her slender neck, across the rise in her full chest before sliding across a flat midriff and down the gentle curves of her legs.

Ethan took in a long, deep breath and wished he was the kind of guy who knew how to go up to a woman as gorgeous as she was and have something clever to say. Or at least not utterly stupid. However, he did seem to have genuinely made her smile a couple of times. Maybe as they spent some time together, things would change. Who knew?

And if he was lucky, maybe she'd visit him in his dreams that night where anything could truly happen.

He smirked at himself at that last thought. Little lame. Little stupid, but whatever. It was what it was.

His eyes closed, and he fell asleep a moment later.

Someone straddled his waist.

That was Ethan's first conscious thought when he opened his eyes. A dark female silhouette loomed above, leaning back and studying him as a panther might a recently caught rabbit, trying to decide whether or not it wanted to play first or get right down to eating.

Ethan's face scrunched as he tried to make sense of it all and decide whether or not he was still dreaming. He had to be.

"Zoey?" he whispered. "Is that you?"

"Shhh," she whispered back in a sultry tone. "It's late, and you're tired."

Her voice echoed in his ears and sent him into a trance, one that he both struggled to break free of and longed to stay forever in its blissful state.

"What are you doing?" he asked. He tried to sit up, but she placed both hands on his chest and gently pushed him to the ground.

Zoey leaned close, her dark hair covering her face even more than the shadows were. "Do you want me to leave you alone?" she asked, her hands now rubbing across his body.

Ethan felt his groin stir. "No. No, that's not it at all."

"Good," she said, leaning back. She rocked her hips a little before trailing an unusually sharp nail down the side of his face and across his neck. "Ethan, can I be honest for a moment?"

"Of course."

"You look absolutely delicious."

Ethan cocked his head, not sure what to make of it, or even if he should care. The clouds overhead parted at that point, and light from a full moon swept the campsite. Zoey stretched her arms up over her head before brushing her hair over her ears and out of her face.

And when the light struck her, Ethan's heart skipped a beat.

His eyes hadn't found Zoey's hazel ones as he'd expected. What he found were eyes as black as the abyss looking back at him, eyes filled with excitement and hunger, eyes whose devilish nature came second only to the predatory grin Zoey flashed him a moment later.

Ethan's mind reeled, and he shook his head, hoping to God that what he was seeing was a trick of the light. His fright, however, only lasted a few seconds. The more he stared at her, the more he was drawn into her hypnotic gaze. A tantalizing scent wafted from her skin, one that eased him back into a docile state where both mind and body relaxed.

Without warning, Zoey threw herself forward, eyes gleaming in the moonlight, fangs glistening. She used one hand to drive his head to the side, and with the other, she pinned his left arm to the ground. Her open mouth found his exposed neck where pain exploded a moment later.

Ethan gasped as he arched his back. Euphoria washed through him as he felt her go to work. His vision dimmed while goosebumps ran across his skin. He didn't know what to make of it all, but he could still see the top of Zoey's head and feel her attached to his neck. Somewhere in all of that, he realized his blood was flowing.

Did he care?

Not in the least.

After what had to be hours, Zoey rose to her full height while still keeping him straddled. Soulless eyes casually regarded him as she wiped the bottom of her lip with her finger. "Delicious," she said. "Exactly as I thought."

Ethan nodded stupidly. "Thanks?"

"You're welcome," she replied, patting the top of his head. "I still want a peach, though. Now go back to sleep. You're going to need the rest. I promise."

Chapter XII
Weynock

ETHAN WOKE, BARELY, to rays of sunshine on his face and a throbbing skull. Fleeting images of the night before ran through his mind, images of Zoey on top of him, images that felt far more dreamlike than real, much to his utter confusion.

"Time to rise, Master Ethan," Maii said, sounding amused when Ethan prodded his neck with his fingers.

Ethan sat up, instantly regretting the act as a sharp pain shot through his head, and then an even sharper one as he turned his head to look at the jackal. The animal sat on the other side of a pile of blackened coals with a freshly killed rabbit at his feet and a grin on his face.

Ethan narrowed his eyes as a thought—no, a certainty—as to where the source of his dreams was. "You better not have."

"I better not have what? Killed a rabbit?"

"Messed with my head. I told you not to. Ever."

Maii's eyes lit up with delight as he flashed his lips pulled back. "I'm not 'messing with you' as you like to say."

"I don't believe you."

"I don't care what you believe," Maii said before taking a bite of his breakfast. Once he finished chewing and had swallowed, he licked his chops with an air of satisfaction about him. "Delicious. Care for some? I'm getting full."

Ethan was barely paying him attention as he was desperately trying to make sense of the fragmented images still floating in his head. Zoey had...had what, last night? Grabbed him? Kissed him? Scratched him? No. None of that seemed to be it.

Then what was it? She'd had fangs, hadn't she? Actual fangs, which meant she did what? Bite him? Was that why his neck hurt?

No. No way.

Ethan frowned and shook his head as he wrestled with an image that wouldn't leave: Zoey, framed by the moonlight, looking down at him with gleaming canines and eyes darker than a demon's heart.

"Oh, damn," he muttered.

Ethan snapped his head up, and he scanned the area for her. She wasn't anywhere to be found, but he did see her pack lying on the ground nearby.

"Something the matter?" Maii asked.

"That wasn't a dream," he said, as much to himself as the jackal. "Was it?"

"Maybe this is a conversation best had with her," he offered. He then shrugged. "Or not, given its perilous nature. Sometimes ignorance not only provides bliss but a little bit of safety, too, albeit temporarily."

"Tell me what happened."

"I can't."

"Can't? Or won't?" Ethan said. He then held up his ring. "You have to obey me, you know."

"Only to a degree," Maii coolly replied. "I don't have to speculate, and truth be told, I honestly have no idea what she'll say.

I don't think I've met anyone quite like her before. However, I'd wager you have an inkling of what she might tell you."

Goosebumps formed on Ethan's arms and quickly spread across his body as more and more of his encounter with Zoey crystallized in his mind. "What is she?"

"A recent companion?" Maii replied. "An intriguing female of uncharacteristic beauty complemented by no small amount of wit and reflex?"

"You know what I mean. Is she human?"

"Is who human?" asked a voice from behind.

Ethan spun around to find Zoey stepping into camp with a small sack filled with something in hand. If recent events proved true, he hoped it wasn't a severed head.

"Well?" she asked, drumming a set of fingers on her hip.

Ethan almost played it off. Almost. He'd never been one for confrontation in the real world, but since this was a chance to reinvent himself, he opted for the straightforward approach. "You."

"Oh," she said as if they were shooting the breeze. Even though a good half dozen paces separated them both, Ethan caught a glimpse of fire in her eyes. "What do you think?"

"That depends," he replied. "What happened last night?"

Zoey's brow dropped, and she shot him a lighthearted, pained look. "Ooooh, last night," she said. "Given that you're asking and Maii is now shying away from me, I'm going to venture to say that what happened last night is precisely what you think happened."

Not ready for her bluntness, Ethan didn't know what to do. The air caught in his chest until he forced it out. Part of him wanted to run for Weynock as fast as he could, but the other part, the part that refused to stay stuck in the mindset of the old Ethan, the Ethan who rarely stood his ground, rooted him in place and took over. "How could you do that?"

"It's quite easy," Zoey replied nonchalantly. She then made a half snarl. "Though, I'm annoyed my charms seem to be failing. You shouldn't have remembered any of it."

"I can't believe you ate me," Ethan said.

Zoey held up a finger. "Correction: I nibbled you," she said. "And technically speaking, you wouldn't be talking to me right now if I'd eaten you."

"Well, not unless you only ate part of him," Maii interjected. Zoey shot him a glare, and the jackal inched to the side. "What?" the jackal asked. "It's true."

Zoey stuck out her tongue. "Shush. You're going to scare him off or make him do something dumb like attack me."

Ethan shook his head and probed his neck once again. It was still sore, but now that he had the memory fresh in his head and her confession ringing in his ears, finding a pair of rough, round patches of skin ended up being easy.

"I gave you a little bit of a healing potion," she said. "In case you were wondering. Figured it was better than letting you be bedridden for a week after I drained you."

With a huff, Ethan folded his arms over his chest and shook his head yet again. "I still can't believe you ate me."

"No, Ethan, I nibbled." She then flashed him a wry smile. "And sucked. Most guys like that part."

"Not like that on the neck, they don't."

"Would you rather my fangs go down there?" she asked, pointing below his belt.

Ethan grimaced. "No, I'd rather them not find me at all. I didn't agree to this whole gem thing only to become your blood doll."

"Beggars can't be choosers," she said with a shrug. "Did you know you taste like a full-bodied merlot? To me, at least. It's quite nice."

"No, I can honestly say I had no idea whatsoever that's what I'd taste like."

Zoey rolled her eyes with amusement. "Look, we don't have to dwell on this for the rest of the day. Everything is quite simple when you get down to it. You help me. I help you. Before you know it, you've won your race, and you're back in the real world, happy."

Ethan groaned with frustration. What choice did he have? None, at the moment, despite his wishes to the contrary. He needed a ship, and for that, he needed money. And as best he knew, the only way to get that much coin in such a short time was to get that gem. Maybe she'd come in handy down the road, anyway.

"Fine," he said. "But no more sucking my blood. I happen to like it inside of me."

"If you say so."

Ethan pressed his lips together into a tight line, unsure if she was actually making a promise or merely being patronizing. "Mind at least telling me what you are? Demon? Succubus? Blood witch? I know you're not a vampire."

"You do, huh? How's that?"

Ethan pointed a finger at the sky. "The sun's out. Duh."

"Lovely day, isn't it?" she said, amused. "But to your point, you're wrong. I'm very much a vampire."

Ethan furrowed his brow and pointed at the sky again. "But the sun..."

"You do realize that there are like a hundred different versions of vampires throughout the world's history, right? Only a few of those die from sunlight."

"Yeah, but you're not even sparkling."

"I'd rather burn at the stake than be one of those," Zoey said with a scoff.

"Then what do you do?"

Zoey's mouth twisted to the side as she thought, and then she started enumerating on her fingertips as she explained. "You know, the usual. Suck blood. Charm victims. Move fast. Resist curses. Regenerate grievous wounds. Talk to rats and wolves. Working on the shapeshifting now, but I still need more experience to make that happen—at least, for anything fun other than turning to mist for a few moments. All of that seems to be a fantastic package for you to have in a traveling companion."

"Except for the whole feeding off me at the end."

"A small price to pay at best," she said. "Look, if it makes you feel better, hunger pangs from this whole blood lust deal are terrible. Imagine the most severe cramps during your period and then make them a hundred times worse. That's about what it's like when I haven't had a snack in a bit."

"Uh, right. Cramps."

Zoey rolled her eyes. "Try. Anyway, I usually don't end up killing my meals. You'll be fine."

Ethan straightened and felt the color drain from his face. "Usually?"

"Well, if I get really hungry." When Ethan started to inch back, Zoey titled her head. "Now, Ethan, you're not getting cold feet around me, are you?"

"I think anyone else would call it being smart," Ethan replied as he was reconsidering his decision to stay. "I need to win this race and save my dog. Haven't you ever heard the phrase 'never stick your dick in crazy' before? This is all kinds of crazy, and we're not even having sex."

"You're looking at this all wrong," she said. "I didn't have to spare you, and I certainly didn't have to give up some of my healing potion, either. I'm clearly looking out for your interests as well as mine."

"Why do I feel like this is a horror movie then, and this is the one part everyone in the audience is screaming 'Run, you fool!' yet the hero does anything but?"

Zoey sighed and folded her arms over her chest. "Why don't you try looking at it from a different possible future instead?"

"Such as?"

"How unstoppable you'll be with a vampire at your side," she said. "Seems to me, that's a surprisingly good thing to have, especially in a world as dangerous as this place is. No? Besides, I'll admit, there's something adorkably cute about you that I'm a sucker for, no pun intended," she went on. "We might be friends soon enough, or more, if you play your cards right."

A flutter went through Ethan's stomach, her words planting fantasies in his head faster than his heart pounded in his chest. "You want us to be a couple?" Ethan asked, scarcely believing the words.

"Want? No," she said. "Against? Also, no, but if I'm being perfectly honest, Ethan, I'm simply not looking, but as I said, who knows, right? Don't be so quick to write our story one way or another. Just go with the flow. It'll be better for both of us that way."

Ethan tapped his fingertips on his thumb. He wanted more with her, for certain. Well, he'd definitely wanted more before he found out she was a bloodsucking fiend from beyond the grave. Now? Well, he probably still wanted more, assuming they could work around this little feeding problem they were having. But all couples had their issues, didn't they? Or future couples, as the case may be. "For my own clarity, then, what are we, again?"

"A pair of people whose interests happen to be in alignment: i.e., we both need that gem," she said. "And in the process of getting that gem, if you do and say things that I like, one day, maybe we'll be more. Right now, though, all I'm focused on is succeeding in this quest of ours."

"In other words, you're using me."

"If you want to be pessimistic about it, fine. I'm using you," she said. "The glass can be half full, you know."

"I know."

"Then act like it and let's keep our team together," she said. Zoey bit on her lower lip, letting a fang show in the process, and shrugged. "Or you could go your own way, and eventually, when I get hungry again, I'll have to go hunting. Who knows who I'll find? Probably someone isolated, not sure of where they are or how to protect themselves."

Zoey's thinly veiled threat wasn't lost on Ethan. That said, he still wanted some extra input and reassurance, so he turned to Maii. "What do you think?"

"I like her," Maii replied. "Stock up on healing potions. Problem solved."

Zoey flashed a smile. "See? He knows what's what. This is all going to work out. I promise."

Ethan spent the next several moments turning it all over in his head. Could he do this? Should he? He wasn't certain on either point, but he did know he was short on time, and thus far, she was the only one willing to help him.

"Alright," he said with a short nod. "Let's do this."

They reached Weynock a little before noon. The town sat atop a small hill, surrounded by stone walls with guards at the top and a few more posted at each of the gatehouses. According to Zoey's history lesson along the way, Weynock was one of the larger ones in the area and was famous for its wine distillery and silver mine, both of which provided a great boost to the town's local economy. There would've been an even bigger boost had Myriden not taken a liking to sinking nearly everything that dared try and make port, as well as the occasional disappearance of young men and women who Zoey swore she knew nothing about—despite the look of guilty pleasure on her face.

As they neared, Ethan's feet went from sore to throbbing. Apparently, his traveler's boots weren't made so much for traveling. Either that, or much more likely, his feet weren't made for traveling. The trio paused about fifty yards away from the southern entrance so that Ethan could sit for a minute, pull off his boots, and inspect his aching feet.

"No blisters, at least," he said, massaging his right foot for a few moments before slipping the boot back on. "That's something."

Zoey nudged him with her elbow. "Then up and at it," she said before giving a slight nod to the guards ahead. "They're starting to look at us."

"Isn't that what guards do?"

"Yes, but these guards love to take advantage of the weak, too," she said. "Which means unless you want to give up all you have and then some for 'protection,' I suggest you treat this seriously."

"I will. Don't worry," he said, taking to his feet. "Besides, can't you hypnotize them or something?"

"One person at a time," she said. "And since I'm not a thousand years old, the more alert someone is, the less chance I have for success. Believe me, if they caught wind of what I am, we'd all be used as kindling before sunset."

Ethan soured his face. "Ugh."

"Exactly, now move it."

"I will! Give me a second."

"We don't have a second."

"Look, I get you're worried, but you're overthinking this too much. There's barely any line. We'll be inside in no time. You'll see."

Zoey shook her head. "That's what worries me. They won't be in a hurry to push people through and might have a few extra questions for us. Do you still remember your story?"

"Of course," Ethan said, a little perturbed. "We've only been practicing it for the last three hours."

"And for two of those, you kept calling yourself three different names," Maii said with a chuckle. "Is your plan to confuse them so much that they'll let you through? I've got to be honest: That's a bold strategy. Might not be the brightest, but I have to respect your bravery."

Ethan ignored the jackal and started toward the town. Zoey jogged a few paces to catch up, and soon the three of them reached the gate.

The guards, dressed in dingy uniforms of quilted green-and-yellow checkerboard fabric, carried muskets with bayonets in their hands and weariness on their faces. They also had the unmistakable air around them of those who hadn't seen a bath in six months, and when that air assaulted Ethan's nostrils, it was all he could do not to empty his stomach.

"All right, one at a time," the lead guard said, lazily pointing to Zoey. "Come forward and state your name, goods, and purpose for being here."

Zoey took a few quick steps forward and answered, "Zoey Becker. Carrying food and personal items. Came looking to see what work's available or to put together a group."

The guard raised an eyebrow. "Group for what?"

"Temple run, hopefully," she said. "We're under the impression there's still treasure there."

The guard chuckled. "And a lot of dead adventurers."

"Only adds to the treasure," Ethan chimed in.

Zoey shot him a glare as the guard directed his attention to him. "You," the guard said, beckoning Ethan forward. "That's awfully glib of you."

Ethan shrugged. "Only stating the obvious. I'd think anyone that's been around these parts for more than a day would know that."

Zoey gave a slight, approving nod that the guard didn't see and which helped to boost Ethan's confidence. Not that he needed it, of course. He was going to blow through this even easier than she had. All he had to do was not be a total noob.

"Fine," the guard said. "Let's have a look at you, yes? State your name, goods, and purpose for being here."

"Ethan Silverhawk," he replied, immediately cringing afterward. It was supposed to be Sparrowhawk. Hopefully, it wouldn't matter, or they wouldn't notice. What the hell was a Silverhawk anyway? The name sounded like it was for a guy who flew around space jamming to old 80s rock that was heavy on the synthesizer and light on the lyrics.

"Silverhawk, eh?" the guard said, arching an eyebrow. "That's a different one."

"Tell me about it," Ethan said, re-composing himself as quickly and as bestly as he could. Bestly? Ethan felt his stomach tighten again. That's what he called it? Bestly? God, he couldn't even be a non-noob when it came to the English language. How was he going to get through this one intact?

To Ethan's relief, the guard, while still more alert than he was with Zoey, didn't seem to care about Ethan's internal reactions regarding his mental abuse of grammar. "Out with the rest. Goods. Purpose."

"No goods," Ethan said. "Same as Zoey's. Looking for work or a group."

"Not with that paltry set of gear," the guard scoffed. "I've seen better from a trash pile in a goblin's nest."

"Looks can be deceiving," Ethan replied. "Why do you think I was hired to protect her?"

The bluff was on, and from the skeptical looks of the guards, the life expectancy of the bluff was being measured in heartbeats of the single-digit nature. "*You* are protecting *her*?" The guard said. "What are you protecting her from, being taken seriously?"

"He's very—" Zoey began, but she was cut off in a flash.

"Stand back!" the guard commanded. "He can and will answer for himself, understand? You speak out again, and I'm throwing the lot of you in a cell."

Ethan felt his throat tighten, but then realized he was behaving exactly how he should be. He needed to be strong, confident, and absolutely, positively not new. He sucked in a quick breath and held it to refocus his thoughts and to get in character. And that's all he was doing, he told himself, playing a character like he would in any other game.

Tapping into a deep reservoir of swagger that he made up on the spot, Ethan crossed his arms and leaned forward ever so slightly with a knowing grin on his face. "That's what the ettins thought."

The guard eyed Ethan. There was still a lot of suspicion in his face, but there were hints of respect as well. Or at least the potential for it. "You have to give me more than that to believe you."

Ethan slowly drew his cutlass and nodded to the bit of dried blood still on it. "That's the blood of two ettins. It gushed out of them when I split their skulls in two."

"Nice try. Ettin blood dries green, not brown."

"Not when it comes in contact with Glamborleg, the giant cleaver," Ethan replied, not losing a beat and making up the name on the spot.

The guard opened his mouth, apparently wanting to argue, but he didn't. Perhaps he didn't know the answer as to whether or not giant blood changed color if it touched magical items, which was what Ethan was obviously insinuating, or maybe the guard simply wanted to believe. Whichever it was, doubts remained. "Still," he said, "that armor is paltry. A giant killer would have better."

"Keeps my opponents off guard," Ethan said. "Take you fine gentlemen as an example. None of you think I'm dangerous. How much less dangerous do you think an ettin would find me, before I ended its life, that is."

"You're serious? You actually killed an ettin?" the guard said, relaxing.

Ethan nodded. "I have."

"That's impressive," the guard replied with a whistle. "I've seen one get bored of fighting a dozen men with halberds and wipe them all out with one well-placed swing of a tree."

Ethan smiled and felt the warmth of pseudo-pride fill his soul, making him feel like he could take on anything. "It was two ettins, but who's counting?"

"Perfect," the guard said, waving him forward. "I have someone who needs to hear this."

"I'd be happy to recount my tale over a hearty stein of ale and some juicy mutton," Ethan said, enjoying his momentary fame. "Perhaps you and your comrades in arms could join us at the tavern tonight, and I could also speak to whoever you need me to."

The guard shook his head and turned to one of the men on his right. "Fetch the Sergeant at Arms. Tell him we have a solution to our giant problem."

Chapter XIII
The Ettin

"**W**AY TO STICK to the script," Zoey whispered the moment they were no longer within earshot of the guards. "What the hell were you thinking?"

"I don't know!" Ethan whispered back. "I was caught up in the moment, okay? It's not like we came up with a contingency plan if they didn't believe I was your bodyguard. Besides, what were the chances they had a flipping ettin problem? I thought this was the world of pirates, not all things mythical."

"It is a world of pirates, but it's also a world with plenty of monsters and creatures of all sorts, most of which aren't too friendly? So I'd say those odds were pretty damn good! Why do you think towns are always so small?"

"I have no idea what the town size is around here," Ethan shot back. "This is my first time visiting. If you are so keen on me knowing every little thing about the places we go, you need to do a better job at playing Tour Guide Barbie—or Count Barbie as the case may be."

"Gah!" Zoey shook her head in disgust. "Okay, listen up. Here's a friendly little hint: the reason every town, city, or castle has such a ridiculously small population compared to what it should be isn't because the population around here has an unnatural fetish for birth control. It's because there's always something eating them. Always. They're lucky to keep their numbers even, let alone experience any sort of growth."

"I guess you should be glad I didn't say was a dragon slayer," Ethan said with a sheepish grin.

"Well, I hope you have a plan for talking a way out of this because you are in no way, shape, or form ready to tackle a two-headed giant."

"I am keenly aware of that," Ethan admitted. "If you have any suggestions on how to get out of this, I'm all ears."

Zoey didn't get a chance to reply. The guards, who had gone off a few paces to confer with themselves in private, returned, this time with the sergeant at arms in the lead. He was dressed in a similar uniform as those who were posted at the gates; however, he was a half foot taller than the rest, with broad shoulders and a battle-weathered face covered with stubble. "Geoff," he said, offering a huge hand.

Ethan gave it a shake and tried not to cringe as the man practically crushed his hand in his viselike grip. "Ethan."

"A pleasure and an honor if what they say about you is true," the Sergeant at Arms said. "We've got a two-headed bastard running loose out in the forest, having its fun ambushing caravans and seeing how far it can punt the pack animals—those it doesn't straight up eat, that is. Ought to be right up your alley for a giant slayer like you. It's not even fully grown yet. Barely seven feet tall."

"Seven feet, huh?"

"No more than eight."

"Now it's eight?"

"A few inches shy of ten, I'd say. Eight was a guess."

Ethan threw a nervous glance at Zoey who couldn't reply much more than a noncommittal shrug. "Well, that does sound interesting," he said, desperately trying to figure out a way out of this mess without exposing himself as a total fraud. "But my services are already being employed."

"Doesn't matter," the sergeant said. "I'll conscript you for the job if I must, but I'd like to keep this cordial if we could. Easier that way, and by the gods, if there's one thing I hate more than ettins, it's doing paperwork in triplicate. I mean, at least ettin killing might land you some nice treasure after. What's paperwork going to land you? A cramped hand, that's it."

"But at least not a crushed skull," said Ethan.

"Unless you botch one of the pages, and the judge is in a bad mood," he replied. "I swear, I've seen him throw his gavel harder than a titan throws bolts of lightning."

"Point taken," said Ethan. "If you want to keep things cordial, you best know I'm not cheap. What's the pay?"

"Twenty crowns when you bring me back either of the ettin's heads as proof of the deed," the sergeant replied. "You also get to keep whatever loot he's got lying around, assuming there is any."

Ethan had no idea on whether or not he was getting a fair deal out of this, assuming he could do it, but judging on the looks of Zoey's and Maii's faces, they both seemed impressed at the bounty. Ecstatic, even, if he didn't know better.

Still, Ethan had seen enough movies, played enough games, and read enough books to know that the highly sought-after monster slayer never settled for the first offering. "Okay, I'll consider it," he said. "But I have questions first, and maybe a counteroffer of my own. If it's so small, why haven't you killed it?"

"We have enough issues of our own in town, and I can't spare the men to go out on a search party," the sergeant said. "Not to mention, it's small, but it's not stupid. Well, not that stupid. It's all relative, you know? Ettins are dumb. But it won't get anywhere near a warband. That said, it'll likely take a jump at the two of you and your dog the moment it picks up your scent."

"Fair enough. What sort of town problems do you have going on here?"

"I've got a nasty infestation of all sorts of horrid creatures in the sewers. They're bubbling out like a boiling brew from a witch's cauldron. Do you have any idea how hard it is to keep that in check?"

Ethan nodded and chuckled. "I've never had to tackle that personally, but I can imagine. Why do city engineers always build these sewers so big, anyway? Maybe if they weren't big enough for a dragon to squeeze through, the tunnels wouldn't be a hotbed for monsters to breed in."

"Exactly!" the sergeant said, throwing up his hands. "The town proper has less than a thousand people, and yet the idiot designer planned a sewer system for a hundred times that. With such an extensive network, it's no wonder they keep coming back no matter how many we kill. And don't get me started on the mines, either."

"What's with the mines?"

"I said, don't get me started. The short, short version: same problem as the sewers, only worse."

"At least it keeps your skills up."

"Not really," the sergeant said. "You can only kill so many rats before you stop getting anything out of it. But that's nothing you don't already know. Any other questions, or are you ready to earn your crowns?"

Ethan nodded. "I think that's all I need."

After a moment's silence, the guard cocked his head. "Well, what you waiting for? Get moving and get me an ettin head."

"Right, sorry," Ethan said, not wanting to admit why he hadn't moved. "I was planning my tactics and strategy and stuff."

Before he could fumble any further, Zoey pulled his arm and led him out of the gatehouse and back toward the forest. "Get our crowns ready," she said over her shoulder as they left. "We're going to have an ettin head for you before you know it."

They traveled a few dozen paces before she elbowed him in the side. "What were you waiting for back there?" she asked. "We both know you weren't channeling Sun Tzu."

"I was expecting a little more from accepting my first quest."

"Huh? Like what?"

Ethan shrugged. "Something. Anything. You know, like a drum roll accompanied by a giant floating question mark."

"I told you before, this isn't that kind of game," Zoey said. "And we're in hardcore mode, remember? Even if there were such things in normal mode, they wouldn't be here now. There's no handholding, so forget about massive, glowing punctuation marks telling you where to go and what to do and—" She stopped in the middle of her mini-lecture and tilted her head, face full of confusion. "What?"

Ethan's gaze dropped a foot and a half, so it was no longer staring above her head but now ensured that his eyes met with hers. "You've got an exclamation mark over your head right now."

"No, I don't."

"Yes, you do. Look!"

Zoey folded her arms, and her brow furrowed. "I've been here a hell of a lot longer than you have, Ethan. There are no quest markers here."

"Well, there are now," he said. His eyes lit up. "Oh! What if you can't see it?"

"I can't see it because it's not there."

Ethan gasped. "What if you're an NPC? That would explain a lot."

"I'm not an NPC. I'd know if I were."

"Would you?" Ethan challenged. "I mean, guys running around telling the same old story about taking an arrow to the knee probably have no idea they're NPCs, repeating the same useless garbage. Why would you?"

Zoey folded her arms over her chest. "You think I'm giving you the same useless advice?"

"No, but who knows? Maybe you've got a more complex dialogue tree," he replied. "Also, how would a player get to be a vampire then? That seems a little OP."

"How would an NPC talk about the real world?"

Ethan paused as her comment sucked the wind right out of his sails. "Okay, well, yeah," he stammered. "But what about the vampire bit? I didn't get that option."

"I got that option because I negotiated it in my contract before getting drawn into the game," she said, sounding annoyed. "You're allowed to do that. I took vampire because I thought I'd be in and out in a flash and not have to deal with the whole blood-cravings part or feeding-off-others-to-stay-alive bit. But that didn't happen, and now I'm stuck here with an insatiable lust for blood."

Ethan nodded, and though he was mostly convinced that she was right and he was wrong, he did want to test one last thing. "Hey, I have an idea. Why don't you try giving me a quest? Surely there's something bothering you that I could take care of for a handsome reward."

Zoey's gaze dropped. She bit her lower lip and toyed with her hair. "There is something," she said softly. "Something I need someone big and strong for, someone I can trust explicitly with."

"What?" Ethan said, feeling his heart jump into his throat. Before she answered, however, he shook his head with a heavy sigh. He then briefly shut his eyes, and when he opened them again, Maii was sitting a few feet in front of him while Zoey was several paces down the trail, smirking and shaking her head.

"So close," the jackal said with some disappointment. "I was too over the top, wasn't I?"

"I thought I told you not to mess with me," Ethan said.

"You did," Maii replied. "I was messing with her. You were inadvertently caught in the fun."

"Okay, new rule: no messing with either of us."

"Fine, but you should know, the less happy I am, the less useful, too," Maii said.

As they continued to walk, Ethan's brain turned to the task of ettin slaying. "How hard is it to kill a baby ettin?"

"Ten feet tall is hardly a baby," Zoey said. "Their skin is thick, too, making shots from pistol and musket mostly useless. And even with you wielding your Dramgorleg, we'll need a better plan than 'tank and spank' since your tanking experience amounts to precisely one kobold."

"It's Glamborleg," Ethan replied, patting his cutlass.

"Sorry, I didn't jot your pseudo-artifact's name down in my journal."

"Well, you're a vampire," Ethan pointed out, thinking where he was headed with it all was pretty obvious. "Can't you do super vampire things and kill it quickly?"

"I'm not *that* powerful," she admitted. "My charms won't work on him, and I might be able to move fast, but he'll knock my head off with one hit just the same as you."

"Speaking of losing heads," Maii said. "The two of you are making this much harder than it needs to be."

Ethan turned and saw his own disembodied head lying on the ground, staring back up at him with a bloody smile. He jumped back with a yelp, driving into Zoey as he did. The two tumbled to the ground in a messy heap.

Maii suddenly appeared on Ethan's chest, grinning from ear to ear. He leaned his head in close so that his nose was only a few inches from Ethan's. "Need another demonstration?"

"No," Ethan growled. "Again, stop messing with me."

"Messing? No. Demonstrating, yes."

"Demonstrating what, exactly?" Zoey asked as she squirmed out from underneath Ethan.

"I can drive the stupid insane with an illusion of death," he said. "And ettins are very, very stupid, as the guard said."

Ethan's eyes lit up at the possibilities. "That's handy. Can you do it whenever you want?"

Maii's ears dropped an inch as he jumped off Ethan's chest. "No. Not yet. Once per day, and only when I'm rested. It takes a lot out of me to keep it up long enough for someone to go crazy. Also, I have to watch my prey for a while, see how it interacts with the world and others, and most importantly, find out what it fears the most. If I don't know what it's afraid of, I can't tear apart its mind as easily. Or reliably, for that matter."

Ethan sat up. "How long would you need to watch for?"

"Five or ten minutes for a dumb brute like that if you can work him over," he said.

"Well, that should be easy enough," Ethan said. "We'll just sneak up on it and watch him for a few."

Maii shook his head. "No, I'll need you to talk to it so I can get a good idea of how its mind works. Besides, as the sergeant pointed out back there, he'll smell us coming."

"That's a long time to chat up an ettin," Ethan replied.

"Then I suggest you don't get drawn into a fight," Maii said with a grin. "Or if you do, you avoid getting hit. I can't bring the dead back to life."

Four hours or so into their search, a voice—strained, gravely, and failing miserably at sounding feminine—cut through the air.

"Somebody saves me, pleases! He's so bad!"

Ethan, Zoey, and Maii stopped dead in their tracks and threw perplexed looks at each other.

"Tell me that's not our ettin," Ethan said.

Maii wrinkled his nose and shuddered as he took in a good whiff of air. "That voice is coming from the same direction as that stench I've been tracking the last twenty minutes."

"Oh, saves me! Help! Help!" came the cry. "He's so big!"

Before the trio could confer with each other again, a second voice, close to the first in distance and tone, added, "He's strong, too."

"Yes! He's strong! And handsomeses."

"So handsomeses! I can't take it!"

"Well, if he is this noisy and stupid, maybe we have a good shot at this," Ethan said. "Maybe we could convince the guards to tow some cannons over."

Zoey shook her head. "He knows we're here, and I'm sure he'd smell anyone else who tried to creep up on him. Besides, if we don't chat him up now, I'd wager he'll skip whatever stupid thing he's got cooked up and jump us on the road."

"Only if there were some of my goodest humans to come rescue me from this clever ettin!" came another cry. It, as before, was joined by yet another. "And looks at all the lovelies loots to be had for saving me! Oh, saves me please!"

"We better get moving," Zoey said. "He sounds anxious."

Ethan nodded, and the group pressed on for a few minutes before they reached a small clearing in the woods. In the center of the clearing was an old stump about four feet high. On it sat a pumpkin with a crudely painted face on its front and a handful of straw stuck on top. Wrapped around its "torso" were a few pieces of old rope that had been used to tie mismatched clothes to the stump. Directly in front of it was a pit, poorly concealed with a dozen thin branches and some leaves thrown on for good measure.

"Oh, good sir knight man! Will you be my truester loves and rescue me? We could marry the morrows if you's likes."

Ethan followed the sound of the voice and spied a good-sized boulder about twenty yards from the damsel. Good-sized, however, was all relative, because Ethan could easily see the giant huddling behind it. It had its two balding heads ducked low, and judging by the creature's short, erratic movements in its rag-covered body, it looked like it was trying to hold back from bursting into laughter.

"Alrighty, then," Ethan said, smirking at the scene before him. "This is going to be easy."

Zoey shook her head and nudged him forward. "Be careful. Stupid can still be strong."

"Will do," he said. "And Maii, think you can drive him crazy enough to fall into that pit?"

"I can do much better than that," he said, giving a devilish grin. "You stay alive and keep him talking, and I'll take care of our friend."

Ethan nodded before stepping free of the tree line. Immediately, the ettin grew quiet—for a few seconds, that is. Ethan had barely made three strides before the creature was giggling to itself like a couple of grade school kids about to bring down the teacher's wrath for not paying attention.

"He's going to falls right in!" one head whispered.

"I bets he gets all squishy splitty on them spikes," replied the other.

Ethan stopped, deciding that his spot was as good a place as any to entertain the giant. Well, at the very least, he would be the one being entertained. The ettin, he guessed, might not be, especially when Maii did whatever it was he planned on doing. "Whatever has happened to you, my fair damsel?" Ethan called out, hand over his heart, and milking his performance for as much over-the-top drama as he could.

Out of the corner of his eye, Ethan saw the ettin hunker down even more before raising a hand to one of its heads and issuing its reply. "This big, mean ogre took me aways, he did!"

"Ettin!" the other chimed in, trying unsuccessfully to match the first's voice.

"I meant ettin!"

"That's terrible!" Ethan said. "What does he look like so I can watch out for him?"

"Big!"

"Very big!"

"And strong."

"So strong."

Ethan shook his head out of pity for the giant. This was too easy. "He sounds enormous. I bet he had lots of muscles."

"Oooo! So many muscles!" the two said together, voices quivering. Then one hand bopped one of the heads, and only one voice sounded next. "Come untie me, and I'll gives you's kissy as rewards."

"Yers so handsomeses."

Ethan chuckled, but had the presence of mind to recompose himself quickly before the giant brute took notice. "Why did he tie you up, my fair maiden?"

"'Cuz he's mean!"

"I mean, shouldn't he have eaten you?"

"Oh! Yes, he did. I means, he says he wills! Keeping us fresh for later."

"Me! Not us!"

"Yes, yes. I meant me! Now hurry and unties us!"

The tone in the giant's voice hinted at impatience, and so Ethan decided to give in a little to his damsel's demands. "Of course, my sweet, fair maiden!"

Ethan glanced at the ettin. The two-headed giant was now peeking over the boulder like a giant Kilroy. His eyes were filled with excitement, and it was probably all the not-so-little ettin could do not to jump over the boulder and charge.

When he was only a half step from the edge of the poorly concealed pit, Ethan stopped. "You won't trick me, foul witch!"

"Huh? I's no witch!"

"Not one bit. I's a sweet maidens, I is."

"That's what you'd like me to think," Ethan said, crossing his arms. He then decided to draw on one of his favorite movies to confuse the creature further. "You are clearly made of wood, and everyone knows that's what witches are made of."

"Are not. Are they?"

"They are," Ethan said with a nod. "Why do you think they burn at the stake?"

"I don't know why they burns, but we're nots a smelly witch."

"Don't think so, at least. Hey, what if we made one?"

The last bit was probably meant to be whispered, but the nervous edge in the ettin's voice at this point was a good indicator that the thing probably wasn't worried about Ethan—or at least, wasn't thinking about him.

Ethan remained quiet as the two heads argued more, tone and tempo rising.

"You's made a witch, you did!"

"You's the one that said to use that stump! This is your fault!"

"Well, you's the one that painted its face and got the witch's hair!"

"Then I's going to be the one to smash her ugly head in!"

"No!" Ethan called out, trying to infuse his voice with terror in an effort to stall for more time. "Please don't turn me into a frog!"

The ettin leaped from behind the boulder, coming down ten yards ahead of it with a mighty crash. In one hand, it carried a club the size of a horse while all four eyes of the monster carried the look of crazed madness.

Ethan scrambled away as the brute closed the distance, but to Ethan's surprise, the giant didn't go after him. Instead, it swung its club in a high overhead arc, smashing it down on their decoy's head. Pumpkin flew in every direction like it was the final sacrifice at a Gallagher event. The witch's body cracked under the blow and then split when hit a second and third time. But even then, the two-headed giant did not relent. It let loose a string of obscenities as it pounded its creation over and over, all the while screeching about how she would never have a chance to turn him into a frog.

"That's a good and dead proper witch right there," one head said.

"Course, nows we's all out of distressing damsel," replied the other. "What we do now?"

At this point, Ethan realized he was standing a little too close for comfort, something that seemed all the more troubling when the ettin turned and gave Ethan toothy grins with both heads.

Barnaby attacks!

Ethan jumped at Narrator's intrusion into his head, and then again as the ettin took a swing at Ethan like his head was the ball, and it was the bottom of the ninth with bases loaded. Ethan prayed as hard as he could as he dodged.

The club whiffed by, failing to connect with Ethan's skull by less than an inch.

Luck point used!
Barnaby missed!

"Hang on a sec. Luck?" Ethan said, rolling to his feet. "I can use my luck?"

"You can also use your feet and get out of there!" Zoey called out. She was several dozen yards away at the tree line, cutlass in one hand, pistol in the other. "Run!"

Ethan did not. He needed an ettin head, and knowing he could tap into his immense luck reserves changed things. A lot. After all, a good crit, either in speech or combat, might be all it would take to bring this monster down so he could get into Weynock and be back to finding his dog.

"Barnaby, is it?" he said, pulling the pistol Zoey had lent him from his waistband and trying to buy some time. "Why don't we talk this over?"

The ettin grunted, eying the weapon. During the brief lull in combat, Ethan tried to find the perfect place to fire a shot, which wasn't nearly as easy as it sounded. What was the anatomy of an ettin anyway? Did they have one heart or two? And where were those hearts, exactly? On either side of his chest or both in the middle? Or could he shoot one in the head and have the whole thing drop? Or would the other one still be able to control half the body and hop around on one leg while batting Ethan till the sun went down?

"You ought to be more grateful, you know," Ethan said. "I did save you from that witch."

Barnaby howled and charged.

Ethan reflexively pulled the trigger to his gun. The weapon kicked like a mule, belching smoke and fire, before flying out of his grasp. The shot struck Barnaby in the right shoulder.

Ettin hit!
Ettin barely wounded!
Critical failure!
Weapon dropped!

Narrator seemed to take great pleasure in pointing out that last point, which ended up bothering Ethan more than the pissed-off, barely wounded giant who was about to turn him into paste.

"Hey! I'm not the one with the dice, damn it!" Ethan said. "Give me some better rolls!"

The loud rapport of a black-powder pistol cracked through the air. Barnaby twisted sideways, looking over his shoulder as if a bee had stung him a moment ago. A few dozen yards away, Zoey dropped her first pistol, raised another, and fired. This shot caught Barnaby in his left throat. The giant stumbled backward, clutching the wound. Though it was momentarily distracted, Ethan could tell neither shot had done any serious damage.

"Ethan, run!" Zoey yelled.

Ethan balked as he realized he was at a decisive point in the battle. While the ettin was focused on Zoey, he knew he could either opt for a sneak attack or run away. The latter would no doubt yield him many a song by local bards for gallantly chickening out, while the former could end the battle right then and there.

Opting to be the hero, Ethan sprinted forward and leaped through the air with his cutlass ready, intent on severing both of the ettin's heads with a single blow. As he flew at his target, he prayed that he'd spend every last bit of luck in this final exchange to finish things once and for all.

His plan, as far as he was concerned, was perfect, even if he didn't precisely understand how the mechanics of everything worked in game.

A split second before he could land his blow, Barnaby spun around and promptly knocked Ethan into a low orbit with a single well-placed strike of his club.

CHAPTER XIV
SMACKED

IN THE DARK world that had to be the limbo that separated life from death, Ethan could still hear Barnaby arguing with himself. The ettin's voice sounded distant as if it were at the far end of a long, empty tunnel.

"Oooh! Looks. I killed the squishy in one hit."

"You dirty goblin gagger. That's a filthy lie."

"That's his bloody goo all over the ground, ain't it? I bet that's half his brains, it is, and squishies can't live without their brains. Even I knows that."

"No, you stupid sod, I mean, I'm the ones who killed the squishy. Not you. That was my swing."

"My club."

"My aim."

"Bah! Fine. We both killed him. Where the other squishy go?"

"She buggered off, I thinks."

There was a snort of disgust. "Figures. Let's find some horses. I need a snack that's still wrigglin' when I's puts it in me mouth. He's no good all dead like that."

"Oh, I like horses. Fills me right up, they do. Remember to pull off the shoes this time. Nearly broke me tooth on that last one."

The ettin left, voicing its pleasure on good horse steaks as it did; all the while, Ethan wondered how long it would take for him to finally die. Surely not that long, given that his brain had been forcibly evicted from its home in his skull.

As he waited, he decided death wasn't nearly as scary as he had thought it would be. Then again, he had met Death already, and he wasn't all that scary, either. Hopefully, whatever awaited him in the next life would treat him well. He also hoped his dog would be there waiting for him, but felt his throat tighten and his eyes mist as he feared he'd never see Anne again.

After waiting a bit and realizing Death was taking his sweet time in collecting him, Ethan tried counting to pass the time while in limbo. He got to twenty before he decided he should probably count something other than numbers. Sheep? That was for sleep. What animal was a reliable choice to summon the Reaper? Something that saw or dealt with a lot of dead things? Rats? Vultures? Funeral directors?

Ethan settled on the latter but spruced up the counting with the other two as well. He pictured tall, pale men in black suits with vulture emblems on their jackets while jumping over rats. Ethan got to the count of twelve before he heard Maii's voice clear as the bright blue sea.

"You know, if we'd let him die, we could've gotten some boots out of all this."

Zoey sighed. "We're not letting him die."

"But the boots. They could be ours."

"They're not even nice boots," she said.

"Nice enough to trade for some mead."

"Sure about that?"

"At least a mug's worth," Maii replied after a pause. "Well, half a mug. We could split it. A swallow each. Wouldn't that be enjoyable? You'd have to clean the blood off of them, of course. Or maybe lick them clean. Do you lick blood as much as you suck it?"

Zoey huffed. "You just want to eat him, don't you?"

"The thought had crossed my mind," the jackal replied. "I do need to grow, you know, and I don't think he'll let me dine on you."

"I won't let you dine on me, either."

"All the more reason I could eat him in your stead," Maii replied. "Then you could have the ring. I'll even let you have a bite first."

"Tempting, but no. I'll pass."

Maii grunted with displeasure. "I don't see why you got to eat him, and I don't."

"I nibbled," Zoey corrected.

"I could nibble, too, you know."

"True, but we both know you won't stop."

"A technicality at best."

At this point, Ethan realized he had enough wits that he could probably wake up if he tried, which he did. Groggy and unsure of what sort of predicament he'd find himself in, Ethan slowly opened his eyes.

Zoey and Maii stood nearby. The jackal sat near his feet while Zoey stood a little closer. Golden rays of sunlight came down from above, striking her head and shoulders just right to give her a heavenly look, which was more than enough for Ethan to forget the conversation he'd been privy to moments ago. "Are you an angel?"

"Me? An angel? Ha!" she said with a snort. "Fallen, maybe. If Saint Pete wrote down even a tenth of the crap I did in college, I'd be lucky to get a referral to hell. Now come on. We've got to go before he comes back and decides you look enough like a horse that you might taste like one."

Ethan's brow dropped, and he blinked a few times to get the rest of his surroundings to come into focus. Heaven did not surround him. The forest that he had been traveling did. His cutlass lay off to the side by a couple dozen yards, and farther away, he thought he could spy his pistol, too. Stiffly, he sat up and rubbed the back of his head before cringing as pain laced through his ribs. "Oh, for the love of all," he moaned. "That hurts."

"I can't believe you're not dead," she said. "How much damage did you take?"

Ethan shrugged and then immediately wished he hadn't. "I didn't catch that part."

"Check your combat log," she said.

"I have one of those?"

"Yes. It's on the back of your character sheet."

"Why didn't you tell me before?"

"Because when you got it, you hadn't seen any combat, so it was blank. Did you want me to have you stare at a blank piece of paper? Because I could if that would make you feel better."

"No, I guess not," he said. Ethan rummaged around in his pockets until he found his character sheet. Slowly, he unfolded it. The front had changed in two places. The first line he saw was near the bottom, and it read:

Health: Gravely Wounded

And the second that caught his eye sat near the top. It was one of his stats, his luck stat to be specific.

Luck: Depleted.

"What the hell?" he asked, staring at the sheet.

Zoey leaned over. "That explains why you didn't run when I told you to."

"What does?"

"You tried to sneak in an uber crit, didn't you?"

"Well, yeah," he said. "It was a good plan, you know? Charge in with Glamborleg before he realized what was going on. Not sure what went wrong, though."

"Stats matter, you know. You didn't take into account that the ettin had a higher initiative than you," she explained. "He got to swing first, and when he connected, all that luck you threw into the exchange saved your life instead of ending his. I told you he wouldn't go down easy."

"Oh. Huh," Ethan said. "I guess I should've taken all of that into account. How was I supposed to know he got to swing first?"

"You could've started by realizing he was moving before you, or I don't know, read the manual as I suggested because backstabbing is not currently part of your repertoire of abilities," Zoey said. "I've still got it if you want to check it out."

"No one has time for that," he said with a wave of his hand. When she shot him an angry look, he amended his statement. "Okay, if we have time, I will. But there are more pressing matters we need to direct our attention to."

"Like what?"

"Like finishing off that ettin so we can get our crowns," he said. "Then I'll need a good tavern, bad rum, and plenty of wenches."

At first, Zoey gave him a sour look. Said look, however, quickly morphed into a mischievous one.

"What?" he asked.

"I would love to see you tangle with these quote-unquote wenches."

"As would I," he replied. He then turned to Maii. "I thought you were going to help."

Maii coolly licked his front paw and used it to clean his muzzle. "I did make you look a lot more dead than you were, which you still haven't thanked me for," he said. "And I can still help finish the brute off, provided you keep him entertained long enough to find out what he's terrified of."

"Okay, I can do that," Ethan said as he stiffly pushed himself to his feet.

"You might want to drink one of your health potions before we go," Zoey said, motioning to his pack. "They're the red vials you picked up in your shack."

"Right," Ethan said, grabbing one and downing it all. Relief washed over him in a matter of seconds, and after a minute or so, he felt as if most of his strength had returned. "Now, come on and let's catch up before my sense returns and I decide taking him on again is a really, really bad idea."

Ten minutes later, Ethan's sense hadn't returned, mostly because he didn't have much of it to begin with—a fact he was quickly coming to terms with. If his actions as of late hadn't reinforced the idea, along the way, he took another look at his character sheet, specifically, his stats.

"This has to be some sort of typo," he said. "This can't be right."

"How's that?"

"My intelligence is lower," he said, double-checking that yes, indeed, that was what he was staring at. He tried flipping the sheet over a few times, thinking that maybe it was a trick of the light. It wasn't. The number fifteen that had once been next to the letters INT had been replaced by an eight.

"It's been nearly halved," he went on. "Is this a temporary thing from getting knocked silly?"

"Any debuffs listed? They'll be beneath your primary stats."

Ethan checked. "It says 'humbled 1m.'"

"Humbled?" Zoey repeated, perking. "Quick, look at the rest. See what else changed."

"Why?"

"Just do it before it wears off!"

Maii trotted next to her and plopped down on his haunches. "This could be good," he whispered.

She waved an annoyed hand at his face. "Shh."

During that brief exchange, Ethan pored over his character sheet, trying to see what, if anything, had changed since last he'd seen it. It wasn't an easy task, and he realized he was having a hard time recalling exactly what it had said before. But when he reached the section on traits, his eyes stopped scanning the parchment. His brow dropped, and he twisted his mouth to the side as he took in what he saw. "It says I'm rash."

"And there it is," Zoey said with a heavy sigh. "Damn."

"I'm not rash, though, am I?" Ethan asked, more to himself than anyone else. As he went on, his voice grew more and more downcast. "I mean, I guess I did screw up with the guard. And I probably could've planned our encounter better with the ettin, all things considered, but rash? I'm not that stupid, am I?"

Zoey wore a pained look on her face, and she bit down on her lower lip before answering. "When you were with Madam Nataliya, you didn't pick anything that bolstered your wits, did you?"

"No. I mean, I'm sure I did," Ethan said as his mind furiously tried to recall the specifics. After a few beats, his memories started to solidify, and he had his answer. "I don't remember the questions, exactly, but I do know she said I was very clever—which, we've definitely seen as being true."

Zoey cursed softly. "And there goes the humbled. Guess he's back to thinking he's a genius."

Ethan glanced at his character sheet, and it was all that he remembered and more. "I probably read that wrong," he said. "It probably said bumbled, not humbled, on account of my brains being clobbered. Besides, with this cursive handwriting, it would be easy to mistake an 'h' for a 'b.'"

Maii grinned as he nudged Zoey once more. "You're going to regret not letting me eat him when you had the chance."

"Hey, you, be nice," Ethan said, showing off the ring he wore. "No one is eating anyone in the group. Don't make me use my ring on you."

Maii's head dropped as he gave a reluctant reply. "As you wish."

"Since we're not completely headlong into danger yet, do you think you could maybe read a touch of the manual?" Zoey asked. "Or at least realize that your continued insistence on this is making me annoyed. And when I'm annoyed, I like to eat to my heart's content. Savvy? I'm tired of being polite about this."

"Uh, yeah," he said. "I'm savvy. But what if the ettin gets away?"

"What if you think you can do something you can't, only this time, you don't have any more luck to spend?" she countered. "Just read the damn thing."

"I think right now my time would be better spent trying to come up with a plan. Just give me a few, I'll think of something great. You'll see."

Zoey snorted. "Yeah. I bet. That stunning eight INT is going to come in handy for that."

"Fine," Ethan said, caving to her demand. "I'll make a quick flip through of the important stuff. Okay?"

Zoey breathed a massive sigh of relief. "Finally," she said before unslinging and digging through her pack. After a couple of moments, she produced a small leather book that had no lettering on its cover whatsoever, but it did have a set of three interlocking rings with a pair of crossed swords behind them embossed on the cover.

Ethan took the manual and started flipping and reading at the same time. "Let's see, yadda...yadda...lore...yadda yadda, character creation. Talents...bestiary. Oh, that might be handy—"

"You think?" Zoey said with a snort.

Ethan ignored the remark and flipped to the appropriate section and then scanned down the list until he reached the ettin section. There wasn't much, maybe a couple of paragraphs along with a picture of the brute they'd encountered. Though he wanted to toss the manual back to Zoey, especially since the more he read, the more it made his head hurt, he didn't. He'd made a promise. He was going to read. "'The Oregons of ettins—'"

"Origins," Zoey corrected.

"That means where they come from," added Maii with a devilish grin.

"I know what Oregonians—origins—means," Ethan said, cursing to himself as his brain misfired yet again. God, he had to do something about this low INT of his. It was getting harder and harder to pretend that it wasn't affecting everything he did.

"Keep going," Zoey prompted.

"Right. Well, it says, before I was so rudely interrupted, 'the origins of ettins are unknown, but these large brutes have an aff-in-it-tee—there, see? I got that one on my own—have an affinity for violence but can carry around interesting items from time to time, should one manage to bring it down.'"

Ethan looked up from the book, unimpressed by it all. "There. Happy now? I read your manual, but I don't see how any of that helps right now."

Zoey nodded reluctantly. "Yes, you read it. Now read some more."

"Well, there are some stats," Ethan said, looking back at the text. He didn't read these aloud, and most of them didn't interest him as they seemed obvious. Ettins seemed like they had enough strength they could chuck a clipper if they wanted and high enough vitality they could shrug off a six-pound cannon shot. Well, maybe that last bit was stretching it, but it didn't matter. Ethan hadn't brought one along, regardless.

Then there was the bit about them being highly skilled with smashing and clubbing and throwing things, which meant he'd probably not be able to aim and shoot a cannon before it was too late, anyway. That said, there was one little bitty stat he noted and liked. "An ettin's INT typically scores at a whopping six," he said.

Maii snickered. "Finally, someone you can marginally outwit."

Ethan shrugged. "Maybe. But I've always said I'd rather be lucky than good."

"Can't rely on it forever," Zoey said. "Trust me. I've seen that strategy go three sheets to the wind, fast."

Ethan nodded with a bright smile. He'd been toying with an idea for a few seconds, and now he was certain it would be nothing but spectacular, so he was ready to share it with the group. "All we have to do is get the ettin to fess up to what he's scared of, right?"

"According to him, yes," Zoey said, gesturing toward Maii with one hand.

"What if I can make him scared, does that count?"

"I can work with that," he replied, initiating another tongue bath with a forepaw. "But he has to be honestly frightened."

"I'll stop you right now," Zoey said. "There's no way in the nine hells of the deep you are going to intimidate this guy."

Ethan shook his head and grinned like a little kid who'd discovered the secret behind stealing someone's nose. "I know but hear me out on this: All I have to do is get inside his head."

"You think you can do that?"

"With my eight INT versus his six? You bet," he said.

"Mind filling us in?"

"Well, it's a work in progress," he admitted. "But I figured if I was dumber, what would I believe?"

"And?"

"And with the right coaxing, I bet I can make him think he's surrounded by witches," he said.

"How's that?"

"Well, he was starting to buy into that Monty Python bit earlier," he said. He then made a sweeping gesture of the woods they were in. "You know, witches. Wood. Wood, forest. That kind of thing."

Maii tilted his head. "Who and the what thing?"

Zoey, on the other hand, clearly knew the reference. She rolled her eyes and gave an exasperating sigh. "This is the stupidest plan I've ever heard. It's never going to believe the forest is a bunch of witches in disguise."

"Or is it so stupid, it will work?" Ethan said, raising an eyebrow. "Things don't work that way. Ever."

"Only because you're too smart to give it a try," Ethan countered. He then tapped the side of his head. "Look, Maii, all you need to do is be ready with some illusions to help sell it all. I promise, to beat this guy, we've got to think dumb. And apparently, I've got that down."

Maii chuckled. "No argument there." He then turned to Zoey and flashed his teeth at her. "When this doesn't work, I get his ribs."

Ethan opened his mouth to scold the jackal when a heavy crash of foliage interrupted the rest of whatever was left in the conversation. Ethan spun to see Barnaby plow through the brush with a club held high and a stupid, happy look on both of his faces.

Chapter XV
Round Two

O
H, THANK THE seven seas you're here!" Ethan cried out, running toward the ettin as fast as his legs would carry him. "You've got to save us from all the witches! We'll do anything you want! Anything!"

Ethan's pleas, though overdramatic for anyone with an ounce of brain, were enough to halt Barnaby in his tracks. The two-headed giant twisted both of his faces into huge balls of confusion while keeping his club raised.

"Wot you's on 'bout?" one head demanded. "We's knockered that ugly ole witch already."

"Dun thumped it right proppa," the other added as he smacked his club a few times into a meaty palm.

"And now we's going to thump you a second time. Serves you scrawny right, not dying when you should."

Ethan backpedaled, hands up defensively. "They're everywhere! Look around you! They said you weren't smart enough to see them, but I know that's not true. I know you can see each one and thump them all right proppa."

"We's smart," the head on the left said with a growl. "Who's says we wasn't?"

"Smart enuff we thumped that witch we made before she turned all tricksy on us."

Ethan nodded enthusiastically, grateful that they hadn't forgotten the details of their previous encounter. "Remember when I said everyone knows witches were made of wood?"

"Yeah, wot of it?"

"I was wrong. They're not made of wood." Ethan paused so he held both heads' undivided attention and then spoke slowly and softly, hunching his shoulders and inching toward the giant as if he was about to pass on the most coveted secret ever to grace the lands. "The woods are made of witches."

Barnaby straightened. All four of his eyes darted left and right, and he laughed nervously. "No. That's not right, is it?"

"It is! You think I'd run up to an ettin that just smashed me in the head if not?" Ethan said. He then dropped to his knees and clasped his hands in front of his face. "Please, please, please, bash them all!"

At first, Barnaby seemed excited, eager even, at the news. However, when Ethan caught Maii out of the corner of his eye, whispering, the expression on the ettin's faces changed from enthusiasm to trepidation.

"Did you's see that?" the head on the right asked. "Dat tree right 'ere is lookin' at us funny. "Little bugger might be right."

"Then we thump that tree till it stops staring at us and then—" The left head stopped midsentence. "Hang a second. Runty's trying to be tricksy with us!"

The right head growled and furrowed his brow. "I's not like being trixied with. Dat deserves an extra thump'n."

Ethan's eyes went large, and he started backpedaling as he realized that yes, even an ettin wasn't as stupid as his idea was. "No, no," he said, now in a near full retreat. "I'm not trying to trick anyone. I'm—"

Barnaby attacks!
Barnaby missed!

"Crap!" Ethan yelled as he came out of the roll that had saved his life. As he pushed himself up, he realized just how close to death he'd come, and just how cozy with death he was about to be. And in that brief instant, he had a new idea. One that seemed a little smarter than his last and could work, but it did rely on Maii casting a spell or two at the right time, as well as one hell of a coin trick. Or fungi trick as the case may be.

"Okay! Okay!" Ethan said, holding up his hands. "I was trying to trick you. But the witch made me after she brought me back to life. She doesn't want you to have her powers. But if you spare me, I swear I'll tell you how to get them. Then you can conjure up all the horses you want to eat."

Barnaby stopped a few paces away, club raised, and tilted both his heads. "Talk, runty. Or I's gonna make you even deader again."

"The glowing mushrooms," Ethan said with a hushed voice. "They eat them, and that's how they gain their power. That's all I know."

"There's ain't no glowy mushrooms here," the ettin replied, grunting. "We'd have seen them a long time ago."

"They're rare! I swear!" Ethan said. His eyes darted left and right, scouring the forest, and when they found a small patch of death caps, they lit up. "There's five right there! Look!"

The ettin turned to where Ethan pointed, and right as he did, sure enough, five mushrooms inside a clump of ten started to glow while tiny, harmless flames of white and red danced across their caps.

"Those mushrooms all glowy for you's?" the left head asked the right.

"They sure is," the right replied. "But I still says somefin's not right. Those them death ones. Kill you right proppa, they will."

"No, not the magic ones," Ethan said. When Barnaby narrowed all four of his eyes and let slip a growl, Ethan edged toward the mushrooms, knowing it was all or nothing at this point. "I'll prove it. Okay? I'll eat one, and then I'll glow with some of their power, and you'll see."

"Ha! I's like to see a little humie eats himself to death."

Ethan nodded and hurried over to the death caps. Carefully, and making sure the ettin could plainly see, he picked a small one lit with magical fire, pinching it off from the base of the stalk. "You can only eat the cap because the rest is poisonous," he said, taking the top off and tossing the rest. Then in one smooth motion, he popped the cap in his mouth, chewed, and swallowed.

At least, that's what he hoped the ettin thought he did. As he kept the cap palmed in his left hand, he extended his right, palm up, and stared at it with such intensity, the ettin was drawn into the show as well. "Watch," Ethan whispered, eyes still focused on his hand. "I didn't eat that much, but we should see the magic start to flow."

A moment passed, then two. Then three and four.

"I's not seeing nuffin' flow," Barnaby said with equal amounts of skepticism and annoyance.

"Any second now," Ethan said, keeping his voice steady. "You'll see."

Thankfully, a heartbeat later, flames, tiny and painless, engulfed his fingers and raced over his hand before running up his arm. Ethan smiled broadly, and as the ettin gasped in astonishment, he took the opportunity to discreetly pocket the death cap he had in hand.

"Out of the way, runty!" Barnaby yelled, nearly trampling Ethan as he stormed the pile of mushrooms. To the ettin's credit, he avoided picking the non-glowing fungi. To his detriment, he picked—and ate—the other ones, which, as it turned out, were just as deadly. With three already swallowed whole, Barnaby was about to eat the fourth when his face went rigid, his skin turned scarlet, and his legs gave out.

The two-headed giant crashed to the ground in a heap.

Ethan exhaled sharply and wiped some sweat that had formed on his brow. "Holy crap, that worked," he said. Pride filled his chest, and his face beamed. "What do you guys think of my ideas now?"

"Not bad," Zoey said, sounding genuinely impressed. "Not bad at all."

"Sorry, Maii, if I ruined your dibs on my ribs," Ethan said, looking over at the jackal.

To Ethan's surprise, Maii not only didn't seem disappointed, but he, too, looked at Ethan with hints of respect. "Do that a few more times, and you'll start making a name for yourself," he said. "A name I might allow myself to be associated with."

"Thanks," Ethan replied. He then looked back to Barnaby, and while the giant was still on the ground, he hadn't entirely stopped breathing yet. "Uh, shouldn't he be dead?"

Zoey's face twisted in revulsion. "I don't even want to think how much he's suffering right now. Go finish him off."

"A vampire with a heart?" Maii scoffed. "Now, I've seen it all."

"If you think my heart isn't dark enough, I could always dine on yours," Zoey said, dropping her hand on to the butt of her pistol. When Maii stayed quiet, she prompted Ethan once more. "Go. Make it quick."

Ethan pressed his lips together, not liking what he was going to have to do. For some reason, poisoning a giant that was about to smash his head in was a lot higher on his morality scale than executing one who was gravely wounded, foe or not. Should he show the giant compassion by ending his suffering? Or was it justice that Barnaby should die by his own stupidity, even if that end was a painful one? Or was there something spiritual at stake here, something about all life being sacred, and now that the giant wasn't a threat, he should have a chance at life? Should Ethan maybe try and find a way to neutralize the death caps? Zoey had those potions, after all. Maybe the giant would see the error of his ways and join them?

He didn't mean to balk and weigh those choices for any considerable length of time, but apparently, he did.

"What's wrong?" Zoey asked.

"I feel like this is a big decision, is all," Ethan said. "Like, really big."

"Big like...?"

"Like one of those things that'll affect the future, big," Ethan admitted. He wasn't sure how he knew that, only that he did.

"Oh," she replied. "I'd suggest reading the manual, but you might not have enough time, to be honest. No decision, in the end, is still a decision."

"Can you give me the short version?"

Zoey nodded. "From time to time, you'll hit a crossroads. Your actions may permanently alter stats—virtues and vices, especially. Not to mention, open and close doors with people you encounter later."

"Then what should I do?"

Zoey shrugged, which was every bit as unhelpful as her reply. "Do what you think is right. Or hell, do whatever it is the person you want to be would do. It's your choice. Not mine."

Ethan grunted. And after a few seconds more of internal conflict, he made his decision. "Can I borrow your pistol? I think I should use two."

Zoey nodded and handed the weapon over.

As Ethan walked over to the giant, everything became automatic, and he felt as if he were watching the scene unfold as an onlooker, not a participant.

A pace away, he addressed the giant. "Sorry, Barnaby," he said. "This will be over in just a moment."

He then watched himself take aim on the first head, fire, and then do the same to the second. Each shot, made from three feet away, struck Barnaby dead on.

Barnaby killed!
+1 Compassion gained.
You feel a lot more experienced.
You feel like some skills could improve after some rest.

"I guess that's that," Ethan said, surprised at how little he felt about it all. As he handed Zoey back her weapon, he asked the only question that came to mind. "Now what?"

Zoey smiled. "Now, my budding swashbuckler, we collect our reward, celebrate you no longer being a total noob, and get that gem."

"I like the sound of that," Ethan said with a nod. "I like the sound of that a lot."

Chapter XVI
Thirty-One & A Bone

ETHAN FILLPED THE shilling.

It sailed upward, light from the busy tavern glinting off its coppery surface and hypnotizing everyone around the table. As it came back down, Ethan swiped it out of the air and slammed it onto the oak table.

"Alright, lads," he said, giving the four men around him a bright smile that had been bolstered by plenty of ale. "Let's play for more than pennies. What do you say?"

Looks of concern and amazement circled the table. Two of the four grumbled before adding their own shillings to the pot. One did so eagerly, a portly man with no hair and a pair of flintlock pistols jammed in the red sash across his waist. The fourth man, a wiry, greasy-haired fellow who apparently was an apprentice leather-worker and was already down ten pennies—a sizeable amount of money—simply shook his head and left, muttering that the game was rigged.

"I guess things were a little too rich for his blood," Ethan remarked with a shrug. "What do you think, ladies?"

Both of the barmaids who flanked him on either side giggled. The pair, who anyone in their right mind would swear were sisters (and be dead wrong), had instantly taken a liking to Ethan when he tossed the barkeep/tavern owner a couple of shillings to ensure three things: first, he'd have as much food and drink as he wanted; second, his "pet" jackal would receive the same treatment along with a private table he could dine at in peace; and third, the two tavern maids he handpicked would serve him exclusively for the night.

During the transaction, the barkeep snatched the money so quickly, Ethan wondered if he shouldn't have included breakfast in the deal. In the end, however, he didn't care all that much. He could easily afford breakfast and then some. Hell, maybe he'd be buying these two lovely freckled redheads who sat beside him breakfast, too. As it turned out, ten crowns—his share of the bounty—was a lot of money.

Not enough to buy his own ship, sadly, but still, it was *a lot* of money.

Ethan sort of had that idea when he got the reward from the Sergeant at Arms, and both Zoey and Maii looked as if they were staring at a dragon's horde. He also sort of felt like it might be a sizeable amount of coin when Zoey took him straight to a clothing store for new apparel, and the tailor said he'd have it all adjusted to Ethan's measurements by morning *AND* Ethan still had a purse full of nine crowns and change.

Then, of course, when he only paid a couple of crowns to replace his bargain-bin cutlass with weapons that actually looked like they could kill something, he knew he'd done quite well. Weapons, despite what computer games had tried to tell him up until now, were costly things and took a long time to craft.

"I think playing for pennies is far too common for the likes of you," said Katherine, the maid on his left.

She, like her counterpart, Alice, wore a black skirt, padded petticoat, white corset, and the clearest and cleanest of fair skin along with curly red locks. Prior to their temporary employment, Ethan had insisted the two take a little time off—compensated, of course—to bathe and refresh themselves after a full day's worth of work.

Alice chuckled and put a delicate hand against her mouth. "Oh, Master Ethan. You don't want to be seen as such, do you?"

"Ladies, ladies," Ethan said, leaning back and throwing an arm around each. "You'll find I'm anything but ordinary."

Roger, the big guy who'd thrown in his shilling without complaint, cleared his throat and shot Ethan a perturbed look. "Are you finished?" he asked. "Because I thought we were here to play Thirty-One and a Bone?"

"Master Roger," Ethan said, loving how saying that title really put him in the moment. "I am more than willing to continue taking your money if you are obliged to provide it to me."

Alice giggled again at the remark, as did Katherine, and both girls snuck their arms around his and cozied up to him. The fact that they were more than willing to press their ample chests against his body was not lost on him, nor the reasons for doing so. Though the very primal male side of Ethan loved the attention from the pair of beautiful girls, he knew deep down they were after his coin.

Some things never changed.

But did he care?

No. Because for once in his life, it felt damn good not to be an afterthought at best. They even got his name right.

"We'll see about that," Roger said, narrowing his eyes. "Are you going to deal?"

Ethan nodded and picked up the deck of cards. With the smoothness of a Vegas dealer thanks to one of his recently invested perks, *Natural Gambler* (which gave a slight bonus to his already solid *Gambling* skill), Ethan tossed cards around the table until each player, himself included, had been dealt three face down.

The object of Thirty-One and a Bone, as Ethan had quickly learned, was almost identical to Blackjack, except for a few notable changes. First, one had to reach thirty-one instead of twenty-one without going over. Second, other players didn't know what you had until the reveal at the end, provided you didn't bust. And third, once, and only once a hand, you could pay double the initial wager to buy a different card than the one you were dealt.

Thus far, Ethan had been doing well. Thank his skills and hefty luck score for that.

Edmund, the first player dealt, took two cards and ended up with a bust, even after he paid another shilling, which was enough to send him away from the table, cursing up a storm. Henry, the next player, ended up taking three extra cards, and at the end, he sat rubbing the stubble on his narrow chin, which told Ethan the old man probably had either twenty-six or twenty-seven in total. Nothing spectacular, but too close to thirty-one to risk going over.

Then came Roger, who didn't take a single extra card. Since he didn't automatically go for the pot, Ethan realized he didn't have thirty-one. As such, he most likely had thirty, possible twenty-nine or twenty-eight. The way the rotund gambler sat back with an air of satisfaction, however, made Ethan think he was sitting on thirty.

Ethan glanced at what he had. A jack. A king. A five. Not a winning hand at all.

"I'll take a hit," he declared before dealing himself a card.

A four popped up, which gave him twenty-nine in total. Strong, especially since the dealer won a tie. But if Roger had thirty, it wouldn't be enough. That said, chances of him going over were pretty high.

Ethan drummed his fingers on the table, unsure what to do.

"What do you think, love?" Ethan said, turning to Alice before toying with her hair. "Should I take another card and put him out of his misery?"

"Oooh," the woman said as her hand found her cleavage. "You'd have to be pretty brave to do that."

Katherine leaned over so her lips were a hair away from his ear. "I think a real man wouldn't care either way," she whispered.

Ethan sucked in a breath and grinned. What did he care about the pot, anyway, when it was all said and done? Not that much, especially since he'd already won much more over the last hour. As such, Ethan thought about letting things fall as they may. Even if the guy won, his lackadaisical attitude at the loss would no doubt get under Roger's skin. That could be a valid long-term strategy to empty the man's purse over the course of the rest of the night.

That said, however, Ethan wanted more. He wanted to take everything this guy had and then some. Even though Roger looked nothing like Melissa's date from the fair, he reminded Ethan of him to such a degree that Ethan was deadest on making sure he lost. It wasn't as if he didn't have the skill now to make that happen, Ethan told himself. Or at least, a decent shot at making it happen.

A little under one in four, Ethan noted, after counting the cards that had been dealt. Those were his best odds of snagging either a five or six, assuming one had already been dealt elsewhere.

That, however, didn't factor in his luck stat. How that would work out for him, he didn't know, game-wise, but he sure as hell felt lucky. And his winnings thus far testified as such.

"Go big or go home, right?" Ethan asked. "I'll take another."

A queen made an appearance, which immediately put Ethan over. However, he didn't flinch whatsoever. Instead, he raised an eyebrow, grinned, and then casually set a couple more shillings in the pot before dealing himself one final card.

Six of spades.

The girls let out a collective gasp. Alice even fanned herself as her chest and neck turned scarlet.

"I believe that's thirty-one, gentlemen," Ethan said, revealing his facedown cards for all to see.

Henry laughed and downed what was left of his full mug of ale. Roger, on the other hand, scowled, and when Ethan reached for the pot, he had a pistol pointed in Ethan's face.

"You're a liar and a cheat," Roger growled. "No one's that lucky. No one."

Ethan, not moving a muscle, but feeling his heart pound relentlessly in his chest, caught a glimpse of Zoey moving toward the table and decided to play things cool. "I don't think you want to do this," he said.

"I think I very much want to, Master Ethan," Roger answered, narrowing his eyes. "Unless, that is, you want to admit to your trickery and forfeit your earnings."

The loud, distinct click of a flintlock pistol immediately drew Roger's attention. To his left, Zoey had her own weapon pointed at his temple. "I haven't killed someone all day," she said. "But you know what they say."

"What do they say?" Ethan prompted.

"The day's not over yet," she said.

To Ethan's surprise, Roger didn't immediately back down. The man slowly wiped his greasy left hand across his dirty cotton shirt before leaning forward. "You're no man," he said. "And your girl here won't always be around to protect you."

Zoey chuckled and stashed her pistol back into her waistband after carefully decocking it. "I think there's something you ought to know," she said, bringing her face so close to the side of his that her wide-brimmed hat grazed his ear. "So pay attention, because I'm only going to say this once."

"And what's that?"

"He doesn't need me to protect him, you see, because this man who you've so unwisely pointed a pistol at," Zoey said, sliding behind Ethan and slinking her arms over his shoulders, "is the same man who collected the twenty-crown bounty on the ettin today."

The pistol in Roger's hand wavered. "No, he's not," he said, sounding unsure of himself.

"You can go ask the guards yourself if you don't believe me," Zoey said. "But that might be hard if he opts to take your head first."

The man balked but didn't lower his weapon. Ethan knew he had to do something to see this through. More importantly, as a plan came to him in a matter of moments, he felt as if Zoey was reading his every thought on the matter, for she squeezed his shoulder reassuringly ever so slightly.

"I'd like to keep this cordial," Ethan said before slowly pushing the remaining deck of cards toward the man. "If you think I'm cheating, by all means, count the cards in front of us all."

Roger nodded slowly. For a brief second, his weathered eyes darted to the cards, and then it all happened.

Ethan drew his pistol, and as it cleared his belt, Zoey struck Roger on the inside of the wrist, knocking his weapon to the side. But her blinding speed didn't stop there. Before Ethan could blink, she'd slid to the side and wrenched the gun out of the fat man's grasp.

"As I was saying," Ethan said, coming out of his shock quickly enough to play it all off. "I'd like to keep this cordial, but at this point, that's going to depend on what you do next."

Roger's eyebrows shot up almost as fast as his hands did. "My mistake," he stuttered. "I meant nothing of it all. Just took the fun a little too far. My apologies."

"You have a strange concept of fun," Ethan said. "But apology accepted."

"Then I'll take my leave," Roger said, backing away. He looked at Zoey expectantly, and when she didn't say or do anything, he cleared his throat. "May I have that back?"

"This?" Zoey said, tilting her head to the side and looking at the pistol. "I don't know. I kind of like it."

"Then I think it's yours to keep, love," Ethan said. He'd tossed in the pet name completely impromptu, but he figured since he was fully invested in this mini-roleplay of a seasoned gambler and veteran bounty hunter, he might as well have a little fun with it.

Zoey didn't seem to mind. Especially when she was getting a new weapon out of it. "My deepest thanks," she said. She then pressed her lips together and waved the man off. "You might want to leave while you're still able. You can always buy a new pistol. New head? I doubt that very much."

Roger obeyed and not even reluctantly at that. He scampered off and left the tavern completely without word, much to an approving uproar of the tavern's patrons and goading of the barkeep.

"Did you actually kill that ettin?" Katherine asked as she and Alice came back to the table.

"I did," Ethan said, chest bulging with pride. Though he loved boasting of the deed, he couldn't in good conscience not include Zoey and Maii. "I can't say I did it on my own," he said, nodding to each of them. "They're both worth their weight in gold."

Alice set her elbows on the table and rested her chin on her hands. "I bet it was exciting," she said with a longing voice. "Here's good, proper work, don't misunderstand, but it's a dull life for the most part."

"That card game didn't seem dull," Ethan said, chuckling.

"I can't remember the last time something like that's happened," Katherine said.

Zoey dropped into Henry's old seat. Her eyes narrowed before she tilted her head as if considering something she hadn't thought of. Ethan was about to ask what was on her mind when she snapped her fingers and drew the girls' attention.

"You two," she said. "Our jackal looks hungry. Be so kind and feed him something delicious, would you? I'd like to talk to Ethan for a few moments in private."

The girls didn't leave right away and instead turned to Ethan for direction, which was understandable since he was the one paying to have them on call.

Ethan simply nodded. "That's fine," he said. "I'll see you two soon."

Chapter XVII
Perks

ZOEY WAITED A few seconds for the barmaids to be well out of earshot before speaking. "Before we talk about anything," she said, looking at him with newfound respect. "I want you to know, I'm impressed by how you handled that guy."

Ethan's ego swelled to the size of a large galleon. "Thanks," he said. "I guess taking down a two-headed giant will do that for you."

"I also want you to know that was potentially the stupidest way to handle him," she said. Despite her unexpected remark, her tone stayed light.

That said, confusion ran rampant through Ethan's brain. "Didn't you just say you were impressed?"

"I did. And I am," she replied before taking a swig from her mug. "I'm impressed that you didn't freeze up, cower, or run for the hills. But after that first fight with Barnaby, I would've thought you'd have learned your lesson about trying to beat someone when it came to reflexes. So, I'm curious why you decided to make that move."

"Because I had him distracted," Ethan said, frowning. He then pointed to the deck that sat off to the side. "He was looking at that, remember?"

"I do, which is what let me grab his pistol before you got shot in the face," she said.

"I know," Ethan said, not missing a beat. "I was counting on it. In fact, I thought we were on the same page."

Zoey smiled brighter than the sun. "Certainly seems that way, and that's what I was hoping for. I'm glad we're turning into a great team."

"Me too."

"It also means you're thinking things through, which, no offense, is awesome given your negative rash trait. There's hope yet you might be rid of it."

Ethan nodded. "Always a plus."

Zoey's eyes flashed to the side. He wasn't sure what had caught her eye, but before he could turn to see, she spoke, voice dropping a little. "Listen up," she said. "I want you to keep looking at me, keep smiling, and whatever you do, don't let it go to your head when I kiss you."

"When you—"

Zoey cut him off when she leaned across the table, grabbed him by the collar, and pulled him forward so she could press her lips into his. When they finally parted, she caressed the side of his face before easing back into her seat, gazing at him as if they were star-crossed lovers. "Perfect."

Stunned, confused, but not complaining, Ethan grinned. "Glad I could help?" he replied.

"Me too," she said. "I'll explain in a second, but for now, act natural."

Ethan wasn't sure how to do that, seeing how being kissed by Zoey was anything but. He did, however, end up smacking his lips and perking. "You taste like cherries."

"Like that?" she said, tilting her head. "Bought some lip balm."

Ethan decided to push his luck and step out of his comfort zone. It might not be natural for him, but he wanted it to be. He leaned forward as confidently as he could. "I think you should kiss me again, you know, to make sure that balm is good."

"Oh, Ethan," Zoey said, with an overly exaggerated pained, but playful look. "Pets don't get to make requests."

Ethan chuckled and waved a dismissive hand toward her. "Ha. Ha. Very funny. I'm not your pet."

Zoey arched an eyebrow.

"You're not serious, right?" Ethan asked with a nervous edge. "There's no way I'm a pet."

"I did buy a leash," she said, glancing at the leather pouch that hung off her belt.

Ethan huffed and folded his arms over his chest. "I'm not letting you put me on a leash."

"What if I ask nicely?"

"No."

"What if I ask really, *really* nicely?" she asked, putting a magical tone to her words.

Goosebumps raised across his skin, and Ethan felt himself sink into a warm bliss where he hung off every little thing she said and did. Charmed, he knew, but with that same thought came another: he didn't care.

"Relax, Ethan," she said, letting go of the spell she had over him. "Or, I guess you already were. I've had my fun. We do need to talk seriously. I wasn't lying about that."

"Right, seriously," Ethan repeated, shaking his head to try and rid himself of the bubbly feeling that still lingered. "What's on your mind?"

"A few things," she said. Her right pinky flicked to the side, but only for a brief second that Ethan almost missed. As she continued, she kept her gaze elsewhere. "When you get a chance, look at the man in the corner."

"Okay," Ethan said. The clattering of a dropped plate followed a moment later, giving him the perfect excuse to jump and spin around. In the corner Zoey had referenced sat a thin, dirty man dressed in a dark, frayed longcoat with yellow trim who had a lit pipe sticking out of his mouth. He toyed with a bowl of soup that had been placed in front of him, but he wasn't looking at it. His seedy eyes seemed forever focused on Zoey.

"He's watching you?" Ethan asked, casually turning back around. "Why would some ugly Spanish guy do that?"

"Since he arrived," Zoey said, pretending to inspect the pistol she'd taken from Roger. "Well, myself and the barmaids. That's why I kissed you. I wanted to see what he'd do, and why do you think he's Spanish?"

Ethan gestured to his clothes. "The colors of his uniform," he said. "Makes him out to be a guy in the Spanish Navy."

Zoey blew out a puff of air that quickly told Ethan he was wildly wrong. "First, those aren't the colors of the Spanish Navy," she said. "Second, there is no Spanish Navy around here."

Ethan furrowed his brow. "How do you know? Their armada sailed the Caribbean a lot."

"Because there is no Caribbean here. Or Spain for that matter," Zoey said.

"Oh, right," Ethan said sheepishly. "Is he part of any navy?"

"I don't know," she said. "All I do know is that he's making me uneasy."

"You'll be fine. You could probably kill him ten times over before he knew what had happened," Ethan said, trying to make her feel better.

"Maybe," Zoey said, much to his surprise.

"Maybe?"

"I might be a little more seasoned than many," she said, carefully picking her words now that a trio of sailors took the table next to them. "But I'm not immortal, and I don't have godlike powers. I've also learned to trust my gut."

Ethan drummed his fingers on the table as he thought about this new development. "What do you want to do? Leave? I was under the impression we couldn't find passage to the island until the morning."

"I don't want to do anything," she said. "Maybe's he's just someone with the social skills of a kraken. Maybe he's trying to find a whore to bed. I have no idea. All I'm saying is, keep an eye on him. Hell, for all we know, he's an opportunist, and since we both have a hefty sack of coin now, he might be looking to relieve us of that weight."

"Will do."

"Good," she said. "Two more things. First, have you decided where you want to spend your last perk point yet?"

Ethan shook his head as he pulled out his character sheet. "Not yet," he said, spinning it around to face her. "This is where I'm at now. What do you think?"

"I knew about *Natural Gambler*," she said. "That'll come in handy."

"Maii said I ought to win an extra four and a half percent of my games with it. I tried to do the math, but it made my head hurt."

"Sounds about right," she said before chuckling. "On both counts."

Ethan shrugged. He still didn't like it, but he'd come a long way in accepting the fact that his mind was a few sheets short of full sails. Well, maybe a sheet, he told himself. "I also grabbed *Navigator*, not so much for the not needing a compass or sexting anymore, but because the next rank I'll increase ship speed by ten percent if I also pick *Master Rigging* down the line."

"That's sextant, not sexting," Zoey said. "Big difference. You can't get the next rank of *Navigator* for a few levels, you know, and two more levels until *Master Rigging* on top of that."

"I know," Ethan said. "I read a little more of the manual, and ultimately, I need to win that race, which is why I picked it."

"You read more?" Zoey said. "On your own?"

"Yes, thank you."

"You're full of surprises tonight, Ethan," Zoey said. "Keep thinking ahead, though."

"I'm trying, but honestly, I really do have a headache from it all."

Zoey smiled and tapped the side of her head. "That's your gray matter trying to grow from a whopping eight INT to a nine. Push through it, and hopefully, you'll get a chance to raise it soon. Unfortunately, aside from a few extremely rare items, getting an opportunity to raise primary stats is a little random."

"I'll keep that in mind."

"Good. That said, what are you looking at for your last pick?"

Ethan shrugged and sighed. "No idea."

"You can always sleep on it," she said, scooting the character sheet back toward him. "I don't like telling people how to play, but if I were you, I'd think about picking up a combat perk or two soon. *Deadeye. Resilient. Ambidextrous.* Or even *Finesse* might be a good choice for you—your normal hits will do less damage, but your crits can be devastating. That's a good perk for anyone as lucky as you."

"Yeah, I was eying that one," Ethan said. "I also saw one that looked promising: *Nine Lives.*"

Zoey's brow dropped, and her lips pursed as if his words left a sour taste in her mouth. "Don't take that," she said. "It's garbage."

"But it lets you survive something fatal no matter what."

"Yeah, once," she said. "And only once—like you never get to use it ever again. And it leaves you unconscious and near death, which doesn't do you any good if you're being chewed on, drowning, caught in a fire, or about to be hit again. Which means you may technically live another second or two."

"I'll still end up dying," Ethan said. "Got it. Maybe I'll take *Finesse*, then."

"Or *Resilient* if you're worried about biting the big one," she said. "Being healthier is always a good thing, especially where we're going."

"True."

"I might like that, too."

"How's that?"

Zoey flashed a wry grin. "I could suck a little more out of you."

"You know, that should turn me on more than it does," Ethan said, keeping it light.

"Are you saying you don't like it?" she asked, cocking her head to the side.

"I think the only reason I do is because you're the queen of charm," Ethan replied.

"Every relationship is give-and-take," she said. "Could be worse. I could go straight to the biting."

"I think I'd like that even less."

"Probably. But back to the subject. As I suggested before, sleep on it all," she said. "No need to pick that last perk right this instant. Once you mark it on your sheet, that's that. No rerolling here."

The conversation paused when Katherine came over and slid a plate bearing a juicy turkey leg and boiled carrots in front of each of them. "Didn't mean to interrupt," she said. "Thought you might be hungry."

"I'm famished," Ethan said, snatching up a drumstick. He quickly took a chunk off with his mouth and savored the taste as he slowly chewed. "This is fantastic," he said.

As he ate, Katherine gently placed a full bottle of wine in front of Zoey. "Compliments of the house," she said.

Zoey eyed the bottle suspiciously. "Because?"

"Because Master Ethan here has spent a lot of money," the barmaid answered. "And we'd like him to come back."

Zoey snatched the bottle and laughed. "Sounds about right." Before she put it to her lips, she looked over at Ethan. "You don't want any of this, do you?"

Ethan shook his head and replied with a half a mouthful of turkey. "No, but you should try this turkey. It's fantastic."

"Thank you, but I'll pass," Zoey said, taking a drink from the bottle.

"Are you sure?"

"Very."

"Not hungry?"

Zoey politely shooed Katherine away before answering. As she did, she kept her eyes fixated on the young woman's back. "Oh, I'm hungry," she said, wiping the bottom of her lip with a finger. "But not for turkey."

Ethan sighed. "Please tell me you're not about to do what I think you're about to do. They seem nice."

"They do, don't they?" Zoey said, her attention still focused on the girl and doubly so when Alice joined her near the kitchen door, and the pair started chatting. "Which brings me to the last thing I'd like to talk about."

"What would that be?" Ethan asked.

"Alice or Katherine?"

"Come again?"

"Who do you like better? Alice or Katherine?" Zoey answered, finally turning around. She held Ethan's gaze for a moment before flicking the tip of her tongue over her lips and showing off a bit of fang that hadn't been there before. "If you're trying to score an evening with one, which it seems like you are, I don't want to ruin your chances when I need a little snack."

"We haven't even been here a whole day, or evening for that matter, and you're already plotting the demise of our gracious hosts," Ethan said after finishing another bite of turkey. "Doesn't that seem a little evil to you?"

"I'm not killing anyone, Ethan," she said. "A girl's got to eat, too, you know. You don't want to see me cranky. I promise. Besides, you're the one all squeamish about me dining on you."

"Yeah, but still. A little self-control would be nice."

"My little self-control, as you described it, is what keeps my dinner guests alive."

Ethan tutted. "Dinner guests? That's what you're calling us now."

"There's dinner, and I consider you my guest. So, yes," she replied, shrugging.

"I still find all of this morally ambiguous at best."

"Life here *is* morally ambiguous at best," she said, helping herself to more wine. "Besides, don't act like you wouldn't do the same if you were in my boots."

Ethan shook his head. "I wouldn't."

"No, you would," she countered. "I promise. There are no vegetarians when it comes to my kind."

"Then you can strike me right off the list of ever becoming one of you," he said, pointing his fork at her. "I don't want anything to do with it, ever."

Zoey frowned as if she took the remark personally. "It's not that bad, Ethan. You might like it."

"I wouldn't."

"Maybe you should at least try," she said. Zoey leaned across the table and took his hands in hers, all the while, captivating him once more with her smile. "I could change you tonight."

Ethan pulled away, furrowing his brow as he did. "I said no, and I meant it. I don't want to be that. Ever. It's not right."

"Fine," Zoey said with a groan. "You really are a stick in the mud sometimes."

The topic died right then and there, and they made small talk for the next quarter-hour or so. In that time, Zoey polished off the entire bottle of wine and now sat—no, slowly swayed—in her chair, with her eyes half open and a happy grin on her face.

"That," she said, pointing an accusing finger at the bottle while narrowing her eyes, "is one devilishly strong little guy."

"Are you drunk?" Ethan asked with a snort of disbelief.

Zoey's eyes looked up and over as she bit her lower lip and stuck a finger in the air as if she was testing the wind. After holding that for a few seconds, she plopped both of her palms onto the wooden table and leaned forward so far, she nearly fell. "I believe, Master Ethan," she said with a slow tempo, "that I am."

"I can't believe you're drunk off one bottle," he said. "I figured you'd be the type to need an entire barrel of rum to even get tipsy."

Zoey made a pillow out of her arms and rested her head on them on the table. She then adjusted her wide-brimmed hat to cover her eyes. "I'm not tipsy," she said. "I'm sleepy."

"Maybe we should find our room."

Zoey didn't answer.

"Zoey?" Ethan asked. "You okay?"

When she still didn't reply, he reached over and gently shook her by the shoulder. With all the grace of a rag doll, Zoey slid to the side and flopped to the floor, not stirring in the least, even when she struck her head against a table leg.

Chapter XVIII
White Knight

"Zoey!"

Ethan flew to her side. Panicked, he knelt and pressed two fingers into the side of her neck. He didn't feel a thing. But would she even have a pulse on account of her bloodsucking ways? She should, right? Or not?

"Come on, Zoey, wake up," he said, shifting his fingers on her neck. He pressed harder this time, and after another moment of total dread, he found a pulse: strong and steady.

Zoey's eyes fluttered open. "Did you say something?" she asked, slurring her words in an alcoholic stupor.

"Oh, thank god, you're alive," Ethan sighed.

"My dear, sweet Master Ethan," she said. "I am most certainly not alive. You know this already."

"Whatever."

Zoey lolled her head to each side and shooed at him with her hand. "Whatever, whatever."

Ethan slid one arm behind her back and the other under her knees and picked her up. Once standing tall, he glanced over to the barkeep who was watching with keen interest and worry. "I think we'll take that room now," he said.

The grizzled old man motioned to the stairs with the cleaning rag he had. "Up there, first door on the left is yours," he said. "Is your lady friend okay?"

"I think that wine snuck up on her," Ethan explained. "Nothing a good night's rest won't solve."

"Glad to hear it," he replied. "I've some wallar root in the cellar. Bitterest thing you'll ever take a bite out of, but it'll ward off any headache that might take to her. Give a shout if she wants some once you set her down."

"Thanks, and I will."

Ethan then made his way to the second floor, and carefully at that, since he was starting to feel the effects of his ale as well. Along the way, Zoey giggled at something she found funny, but she didn't share whatever it was that tickled her so.

He found their room with ease and even managed to turn the handle and bump open the door without dropping her. Zoey, meanwhile, reached up and tried to grab the side of his face, but with her coordination impaired, it came across as an awkward slap.

"Sorry," she giggled. "That was...that was...supposed...to be gentler..."

"That's okay," Ethan said, still feeling the sting in his cheek. "I doubt you'll remember any of this anyway."

"Remember what?" She narrowed her eyes, which was quite an accomplishment given they were barely open to slits already and pointed a finger at him. "Are you trying to charm me? I'll have you know, you rapscallion, I am immune to such things."

"No, you're the only one working charms around here."

"That's right. And don't...you...forget it...mister noob."

"Well, this noob still has to get you in bed," he said, turning his attention to the room.

Unfortunately, darkness shrouded everything, save for where the pale moonlight poured in from a pair of large windows opposite the door. From what Ethan could tell, it would probably only take a few paces at most to walk from one end of the room to the other, and he had no idea what sort of furniture happened to share the space with him, except for the oak bed which thankfully he could see half of.

"Alright, here you go," Ethan said, crossing the room without incident and easing her on to the mattress.

Zoey rolled on her side and tucked her legs against her chest. With her eyes closed, she smiled and whispered something Ethan didn't pick up.

"What was that?" he asked, leaning over.

"Nothing, my little white knight," she said, cracking a grin.

Ethan felt his heart warm. He dropped in a nearby chair, and for the next couple of moments, he sat there, watching her, not sure what to do, but having a thousand things he wished he could say.

Zoey peeped an eye half open. "What?"

"Nothing, I—" Ethan caught himself. He didn't want to slip back into old ways. "I was thinking that maybe when this was all over, we could go see a movie or something."

By the time he'd finished, Zoey had already closed her eye and had gone to sleep. Ethan sighed heavily and then smirked at himself for asking such a thing. The girl lived across the country, which made a casual meetup a little tricky, to say the least.

Unsure what else to do, Ethan thought about jumping into bed on the other side and simply getting some much-needed rest. However, his brain wasn't ready to switch off yet, especially when he realized he didn't know where Maii had gone.

Playing mind games with some hapless townsman, no doubt. Or maybe he'd found a warm place by the fire downstairs to curl up by. The innkeeper had offered the spot to them for Maii after Ethan and Zoey had flashed their crowns.

Ethan was about to run down and check when a light rapping sounded at his door. He glanced at Zoey to see if she'd stirred, which she hadn't, and when the knock came again, he hurried over.

"I'm coming. I'm coming," he said as loudly as he dared since he didn't want to wake Zoey.

When he got to the door and opened it a tad, he saw Alice and Katherine huddled close to one another, grinning like mischievous schoolgirls. Katherine held a small, lit lantern, while Alice kept a massive bottle of port close to her chest, as if she'd borrowed it from its owner without him knowing.

"Can Master Ethan come out and play?" Alicia asked.

Ethan's heart jumped. He wasn't sure what to make of two ladies suddenly appearing at his door, interested in him, no less. His mind screamed over and over that they simply made him out as a mark, wanting another crown or two from his purse, but his groin quickly told his mind to shut up.

Besides, Zoey was the only one he'd met so far who could literally charm anyone, and even then, she seemed to have difficulty with him. Ethan decided he must be special, and it wouldn't hurt to at least *see* what the two wanted.

Was that going to be a bad decision if he went with them? Maybe. But he figured with his ginormous Luck stat, he was much more likely to regret things if he didn't.

Alice cleared her throat. "So, can he?"

Ethan straightened, shook his head, and laughed at himself. "Sorry," he said. "It's late, and I wasn't expecting anyone." He glanced over his shoulder and saw that Zoey remained in bed, unmoving, save for the rise and fall of her chest. In that moment, doubt washed over him. Could he leave her?

Should he leave her?

As if reading his thoughts, Alice grabbed his hand and pulled. "Come. She'll be fine."

Ethan held his place for a moment, still looking at his sleeping friend, and hated the idea that she might wake wanting to know where he was—or worse, needing him for something. Though he'd never said it, he felt indebted to the vampire for the help she'd provided thus far, and he wanted to repay that kindness.

Besides, she *did* expect him to watch over her, being the white knight and all. White knights didn't simply up and leave their post and abandon their charge. "I'm not sure I ought to," he finally said, voice full of regret. "I should stay with her."

Alice let go of him and put her hands on her hips. "I thought you liked us."

Katherine nudged her friend with her hip. "I told you they were together," she said. "That kiss she planted wasn't an act."

"No. I mean, but even so," Alice stammered. She caught herself before saying something Ethan didn't follow and looked at her friend and arched her eyebrows. "We're employed?"

Katherine sighed. "Right." She then turned to Ethan who looked at them both inquisitively. "Your wife will be fine, Master Ethan, but we would be remiss in our duties as hostesses to not insist on entertaining you the rest of the evening."

"Duties?" Ethan said, scratching his head. "Oh, right. I paid you."

Katherine nodded. "Come. Surely you can spare an hour or two of your time."

Ethan smiled, and he wanted to, but again, his gaze drifted back to Zoey. It wasn't just that he felt indebted to her. He just didn't want to go. Then a thought struck him, one that he hadn't considered before that moment. He had no desire to be around anyone else but her, and even if he had employed the two girls to lavish him with attention earlier, in the end, he only wanted the attention of one woman: Zoey.

"No, I—"

"Master Ethan," Alice cut in. "We're not looking to make you an adulterer. But we're not ones not to earn our keep, either. Now come. We'll only be a few rooms away. If she needs you, I promise, you can promptly attend her needs."

Ethan balked some more, but in the end, he realized Zoey was as passed out as they came, and given that he wasn't tired in the least, he figured he might as well do something to pass the time. "Okay, dear Katherine, I suppose I could kill an hour or two."

"Lovely," she replied, taking his hand and pulling him out the door. "I guarantee we'll keep you well entertained."

Ethan nodded and swept the hall with his hand. "Then lead the way."

The girls did, taking him down the corridor, which hooked right at the end, and after a short stint, they stopped at the end where a set of narrow, steep stairs led up into the attic.

"What's up there?" Ethan asked as Alice started up.

"Our room," she said. She paused after a few steps and twisted enough so she could look at him over her shoulder. "We're proper ladies, so you know, even if we do keep the tavern," she said. "Don't get any ideas."

"I wouldn't," Ethan said. Though his tone was even and unassuming, a worry settled in his heart. The last time he'd spent a night with a woman in this world saw him turned into a midnight snack. Were they creatures of the dark, too, luring men to their deaths? Hopefully not. Surely, not. Zoey would've sensed it right away, wouldn't she? And certainly employing such girls would be bad for business, he reasoned.

"Ethan?"

Ethan jumped off the train to his runaway thoughts and snapped back into the moment.

Katherine, a few steps up, waved for him to follow. "You're not getting any improper thoughts, are you?"

"No," he said.

"Good," she said before she hurried up the stairs.

Ethan followed and entered the attic. The area wasn't terribly wide, but it was long, with slanted wood walls on both sides, while the far wall was made from rough stone. An oil lamp hung from one of the crossbeams, giving the area ample illumination. At the opposite end sat a pair of low-lying beds with brass frames, each having their own foot chests nearby. A circular table took up a sizeable portion of the middle. On it sat a few metal plates and a simple vase with a handful of lilies that could use a little water.

"Come and sit," Alice said, motioning to one of the stools at the table as she set her lantern down.

Ethan did, cringing reflexively as the floorboards creaked underfoot.

"Everything around here does that," Katherine said. "Don't worry about it."

"Gotcha," Ethan replied, dropping onto one of the stools. He sat there for a few moments as the two girls kicked off their shoes before joining him at the table.

"Want a drink?" Alice asked, offering him the bottle.

Ethan took it and brought the bottle to his lips. The port tasted rich against his tongue with strong notes of plum. He savored it for as long as he could before passing the bottle back to Alice. "What did you two lovely ladies have in mind when you said you didn't want to waste the night?"

"We thought that a strong, adventurous man who takes on ettins would have all sorts of fun things to do," Alice said after a brief glance to Katherine.

"Sounds as if you two have been talking," Ethan said.

"We're best friends. What else would we do?" Katherine replied, taking the bottle from Alice and helping herself to the port.

"I don't know," Ethan said. "But I'd love to find out."

Katherine raised her eyebrow. "Would you, now?"

Alice giggled and brushed her red hair back over her ears. "How about a game of Bold & Meek?"

"With only three of us?" Katherine asked.

"Sure, why not?"

"Not sure it'll last long enough."

"Then we'll play again, silly," Alice said, laughing. "And again and again and again if need be."

"Would either of you ladies mind tell me what I'm about to get myself into?" Ethan asked.

Katherine took a drink from the bottle and passed it to Alice before explaining. "We each take turns issuing one another challenges. So, if it's my turn, I might press you to eat a cricket or smack a bull on its ass. If you do it, you get ten points. If you don't, I have to do the same. If I do, I get fifteen points. If I don't, I lose ten. First person to a hundred wins the match."

"If I'm hearing this correctly, the idea is to dare someone to do something you think they won't do, but you are willing to do?" Ethan asked, thinking it sounded simple enough but wanting to be sure he'd followed along correctly—eight INT and all.

"You've got it," she said, eagerness in both her eyes and voice. "Shall we, then?"

"We shall."

"What say we play for pennies?" Alice added.

And there it was, he thought. They wanted coin, probably lots of it. He sized the pair up for a few seconds, quickly realizing that this was far from their first time at the game. In fact, if he had to bet on it, he'd wager the two frequently worked rich men in such a way, no doubt tag-teaming a mark, which would be easy if they were both in on the take.

That said, he had crowns to spare and decided to cap his losses at a few shillings. That, he figured, was perfectly reasonable as an entertainment expense, especially since he'd done well at cards earlier.

"Okay. Pennies it is, but I'd hate to take all your money," Ethan said as he dug through his coin pouch and set a penny on the table. "But if I must, I must. Who goes first?"

Both girls did the same, and Katherine was the one who answered. "You can if you like," she said.

"Okay," Ethan said. He looked around the room, trying to think of something both fun and mildly embarrassing to kick things off with and bring the ice—*break* the ice, he quickly corrected.

Stupid eight points of INT. "Alice, are you bold enough to sing a song as loudly as you can with your bare ass out the window?"

Katherine, who'd been taking a drink at the time, laughed so hard she ended up spewing half of what she had across the table. "Master Ethan," she said, wiping her mouth. "You get right to it, don't you?"

Ethan gave her a wry grin and shrugged. "I have my moments." He then turned to Alice. "Well, my good Alice. Are you bold? Or are you meek?"

Alice narrowed her green eyes, though her glare was one of the most flirtatious he'd ever seen. Her words, however, weren't directed at him, but at her best friend. "Tell me, Katherine," she said. "Should I play to take his money or to watch him make an ass out of himself?"

"You do what you like, dear," she replied. "But if I were you, I'd love to see what happens when his rump is exposed for all of the night's vagrants to see."

"As would I," she said. The grin that spread across her face would've been the envy of any devil, and she nodded to the window. "I'm afraid, Master Ethan, I'm far too meek for such a challenge. Are you bold enough, I wonder?"

Ethan frowned. He hadn't expected her to turn it down, and at first, he didn't think it would be a big deal for him to moon the world. However, that was before they seemed especially keen on him doing such a thing, not to mention painting an uncertain picture as to what those in the street might do. He sucked in a breath and held it for a few counts, unsure which course to take. However, it didn't take him long to make up his mind.

Old Ethan would've passed, coming up with some lame excuse not to. That was the Ethan too scared to ask the girl who lived across the hall on a date—or hell, talk to her for more than a few seconds at best or tell her his name was Ethan, not Evan. New Ethan, the ettin-slaying Ethan, wasn't about to let some barmaid call him out like that.

"Hail to the king, baby," he said with his best Ash Williams impersonation he could muster. "It's on."

Ethan strutted over to the window, pulled it open, and spun around to see both Katherine and Alice watching with no small amounts of giggles and whispers being shared between them. Without a sliver of hesitation, Ethan unbuckled his belt and let his trousers fall before backing up to the window and letting his ass kiss the warm, salty air. He ended up shifting slightly to get a little more comfortable but quickly stopped when he realized he really didn't want to inadvertently end up with a splinter or two in his butt cheeks.

"Now sing," Katherine said flatly.

Ethan cleared his throat and belted out the lyrics to the only appropriate song he could think of for this place, "Yo Ho!" from the Pirates of the Caribbean ride. He actually knew every line, having ridden it at least a hundred times one summer when his family went to Disney, and he was ten. That said, he only got through half of the second stanza when someone yelled from the streets below.

"Sirens almighty! Shut it bilge sucker!"

Following the sharp rebuke came an even sharper sting against his right ass cheek. Ethan yelped and jumped forward. Still, with his trousers around his ankles, he twisted to present the wounded buttocks to the light so he could inspect the damage. The skin wasn't broken, but there was a hefty welt.

"I guess that's fifteen points to Master Ethan," Alice said with another giggle.

"Does that mean I can pull my pants up?" Ethan asked, trying to play it cool but probably failing miserably.

"If you like," Katherine said. "Either way, I believe it's Alice's turn."

"Oh, it is?" she said with an unexpected squeal of delight. Her eyes darted between Ethan and Katherine, and she tapped her nails rapidly on the table as she made cute little mulling noises. Finally, her gaze fell on Katherine. "You know, love," she said while toying with a simple pendant—a toying, Ethan knew, no doubt, was designed to draw attention to her ample breasts. "I do believe I owe you from the last time we played."

Katherine cocked her head. "Are you sure you want to take this game to the next level?"

"What did you say before? 'Play for keeps,' I believe," Alice said.

Ethan had no idea what they were referencing, but his imagination ran wild with all the things he hoped it could be. Those hopes seemed to come to practical fruition when Alice faced him and issued her challenge.

"Master Ethan," she said. "Are you bold enough to be blindfolded without your pants for the next ten minutes?"

Ethan grinned, not because he had somehow lost his mind to a wave of horniness (which was tempting, admittedly), but because her challenge confirmed his suspicions: they were sharks looking for a meal. Sex may have been hinted at, but it wasn't on the menu. It was a ploy, nothing more.

That said, he felt confident with both his newly picked *Natural Gambler* perk and innate high luck, he could come out on top—or at the very least, make an enjoyable loss out of it all.

"I believe, Miss Alice," Ethan said, pretending to think about it longer than he did to keep them guessing, "I will take you up on the challenge. So yes, I am quite bold enough for that, my dear. Quite bold indeed."

Alice motioned for him to sit, which he did. Once settled in the chair, she flashed him a smile that would launch a thousand ships, and he gave her one in return. Alice took a long silk scarf that had been draped across one of the footlockers and tied it around his eyes. She did so in a slow but graceful manner, one that told Ethan that this was only the tip of the iceberg for her when it came to such skills and again reaffirmed in his mind what they thought of him: a mark.

But did he care? Not in the least. He reminded himself of the amount of money he was willing to lose should things spiral out of control and went along with it. Soft hands gently took his wrists and eased them downward. The lightness to it all and the enjoyment in his heart, however, disappeared in a flash when a thick rope cinched around his wrists and pinned them to the chair.

Ethan pulled against the bindings. "What the hell are—"

A delicate finger pressed against his lips, firm but not malicious, and Katherine's voice whispered in his ear. "It's my turn," she said. "Are you bold enough to stay like this for the rest of the game?"

"If I'm not, then I get to tie you up, is that right?" Ethan said, considering the options.

"You get to challenge the same," she said. "But seeing how you're blindfolded, I doubt you'll enjoy it as much as I will."

Her soft hands caressed the side of his face, and though in his heart, Ethan knew she was working him over for the long haul, he couldn't help but relish her touch over the next few seconds.

But only for a few seconds.

Something didn't feel right, and it wasn't his mind reminding him that the two barmaids wanted coin. What was it? Danger? No, that wasn't it, he decided. These two were as harmless as they came, skill at playing to a man's lust aside.

He furrowed his brow, wracking his meager eight INT, wishing to God Almighty he had invested a little more in smarts during his time with Madam Nataliya. He was about to give up when it wasn't his brains that popped the answer, but his heart.

Zoey.

Ethan held his breath.

Was that it?

If it was, why? She'd made it perfectly clear what his role was with her—his only role. She wanted him as nothing more than a personal blood doll. Well, helping to get a gem aside, but mostly being a doll, right?

What else could it be? Worry?

The creases in Ethan's brow deepened as he tossed that in his mind. What did a vampire have to worry about? Nothing, as far as he could tell, at least not there. But then he realized she'd been left alone, drunk as a skunk. Helpless. Vulnerable.

Maybe that was it. It had to be.

Ethan frowned. No, not worry. Or rather, not only worry.

He did worry about her. But a longing had settled in his heart, one that only just then had made itself known, and he realized he'd have liked the night a thousand times more if she'd been a part of it.

He wanted more with her.

A lot more.

Moreover, he didn't want it with anyone else.

Ethan slipped one hand free of the rope and used it to tear the blindfold from his face. The two barmaids looked at him with confusion. "I'm sorry, ladies," he said. "It's been a lovely evening, honest, but I have to go."

Alice frowned. "But…"

"No, I do," Ethan said. "Another time, perhaps? My penny is yours."

Katherine sighed heavily, apparently realizing things had come to an abrupt end. To his surprise, a sweet, longing smile spread across her face. "Returning to your wife?"

"Yes. I mean, no," he said. "Returning, yes. But she's not my wife."

"She should be," Katherine replied. "In the morning, I'll tell her that myself. I can count on zero fingers the number of men who've left us as you're about to."

"I don't doubt that one bit," Ethan said, tipping his head toward them both.

"Do us a favor, at least?" asked Alice.

"Of course."

"Don't tell your friend," she said. "I want him to think he got his money's worth."

Ethan tilted his head, unsure if he'd heard correctly. "Money's worth?"

"Your friend gave us half a crown each," she explained, though it wasn't much of one.

"But only to entertain you," Katherine quickly added. "Properly, I should add. We're not whores."

Lines of worry formed across Ethan's brow. "Friend?" he asked. "What friend? You mean Maii?"

"Is that the fellow's name in the black coat?" Alice replied. "He looked like a Christopher to me."

"I thought he was more of a Charles," said Katherine.

"Charles? He looks nothing like a Charles."

"As if he looks like a Christopher."

"Ladies," Ethan barked, a little more forcefully than he intended. "Are you saying the guy with the coat gave you money?"

"Yes," Alice said. "Have the bats made a home in your noggin? I could've sworn to the patron saint mother I said that not even a moment ago."

Ethan's eyes lost focus, and he ended up staring at a seam in the floorboards as he tried to figure out what was going on. It only took him a second. His heart stopped, and one single word barely escaped his lips.

"Zoey."

Chapter XIX
The Chase

THE BED WAS empty.

Ethan stood at the foot with lantern in hand, and he stared at the spot where he'd left Zoey. He stayed there for only a moment before sweeping the room with the light and racing out.

"Zoey? Maii?" he called.

Muffled curses and threats of death for screeching at this ungodly hour answered him from multiple rooms, but he didn't care. He ran to the end of the hall, calling for them both before bolting downstairs and into the tavern.

Shadows draped the large room, with the only sources of light being the moon filtering in through a few of the windows and the warm glow cast by dying coals in the fireplace. In front of said fireplace slept the cook, a burly man whose hairs on his head numbered exactly nine. He was propped up in a large wooden chair, snoring loudly as his massive belly rose and fell. Maii lay curled up at his side.

"Maii!" Ethan shouted, running over to him. He nailed his shin on a stool in the process, nearly falling flat on his face, but stayed upright by catching himself on the table. "Maii, wake up!"

The jackal shot into the air, and his head snapped back and forth as he took in his surroundings.

"Maii, where's Zoey?"

Maii tilted his head but didn't answer.

"Damn it to hell, Maii," he said. "She's not in the room anymore. Just tell me."

"Ethan? I don't think he can talk," Alice said from behind, concern in her voice.

Ethan spun around to see the two girls standing on the first step to the second floor, huddled together. "He...I know," he said, realizing it was probably in both his and Maii's best interest not to draw attention to the fact that Maii wasn't an ordinary thing. "I treat him like anyone else," he said. "I get a little carried away sometimes."

Ethan then sucked in a breath and blew it out slowly. "Okay, do either of you know if that guy got a room?" he asked.

"Your friend?" Katherine asked. "No, I don't think so."

"He's not my friend, but I'm pretty sure he has my friend."

"But why?" asked Alice.

"I don't know!" Ethan said, throwing his hands up in the air out of frustration. "He was watching Zoey all night, and he obviously paid you two to distract me. Now she's gone, and he's not here. What else could it be?"

Alice, face full of fear, covered her nose and mouth with her hands.

Katherine put an arm around her shoulders and spoke softly. "We didn't know. Honest."

"Ugh," Ethan said. "You two, check the rooms. I'll check the kitchen and basement."

"You want us to go into the guest rooms?" Alice asked.

Ethan narrowed his eyes and drew his pistol. "If you don't, I will," he said. "I'm not going to stop looking for her until I know she's safe."

Alice nodded, but before anyone could move, Katherine shook her head. "She's not here," she said, pointing to the door. "The bar on the door is off."

Ethan spun and brought the lantern up to see. Sure enough, the thick beam that was used to secure the tavern at night had been placed to the side. Furthermore, the door itself was open a crack.

"Crap," Ethan muttered.

Before he knew it, he stood in the dirty streets with a light rain drizzling on his head and Maii a few paces away sniffing the air.

"God, I hope you're a good tracker," Ethan said.

If there ever was the perfect embodiment of are-you-freaking-kidding-me, it wouldn't have been found anywhere but with the look Maii shot him.

"Right, nose and all," Ethan said with a huff. "Can we stop the dramatic looks now?"

The jackal nodded and bobbed his head down the street to their left before breaking into a light trot. Ethan quickly followed, his shoes thumping hard against the cobblestone. As he ran, the rain fell harder, and an ocean wind swept through the town, bringing with it the smell of salt and...and what was that? Ethan wrinkled his nose and ended up gagging. Something rotten.

A glance to Maii showed he wasn't imagining the horrific odor, for the jackal had his eyes tightly shut and was shaking his head in a vain effort to be rid of the smell. "By a witch's cold tit, that's the most putrid thing I've ever been witness to," Maii said with a low growl.

"What is it?"

"Dead whale, I think," Maii replied. "Myriden only likes eating their hearts and ends up leaving the rest. Usually, whatever's left gets eaten by scavengers and sharks, but sometimes they wash up nearby and stink up the place."

"Ugh," Ethan said, trying to shake the image of a bloated, decaying whale corpse from his mind. "Does that mean it's near the docks?"

"Probably," Maii said. "Or washed up on one of the barrier islands nearby."

"But you can still track Zoey, though, right?"

"Yes," Maii replied. "She went this way, or rather, rode this way with a couple of horses. Probably in a wagon."

"Rode?"

Maii sniffed the air again and wrinkled his nose. "If I have to do this much more, I'm going to stick my snout in dung to be rid of this smell," he said. "She's with the man who was watching her back at the tavern."

"Damn it," Ethan muttered, shaking his head. "I was afraid of that. All the more reason to find her quickly."

"What do you plan on doing once we find her?"

"Assuming he's taken her?"

Maii nodded.

"Kill him."

"That's cold," Maii said with a surprisingly approving tone. "Not going to even offer a chance for parley? Or an arrest and proper trial?"

"He kidnapped Zoey," Ethan growled. "He'll be lucky that's all I do to him."

"Why, Master Ethan," the jackal said. "I do believe I'm getting to like this side of you. May I be so bold to ask what brought it on?"

Ethan paused at the unexpected question. He wasn't sure how to answer it at first, but it didn't take much honesty with himself to find the answer. "I'm her white knight. I've never been that before."

"Her what?"

Ethan shook his head. "It's nothing. It's just a stupid thing to be where I come from," he said. He then snickered at himself. "Hell, half the time it's a bad thing to be called that."

"I see," Maii said, even though Ethan was sure he didn't.

"Look, it all comes down to this," Ethan said. "She trusted me to keep her safe, and no girl has ever actually asked that of me. Not seriously, anyway, and definitely not in a life-or-death situation, so that's exactly what I'm going to do. I'm going to make sure she's safe, which includes killing the dude who ever thought he could get away with taking her in the first place."

Maii flashed a devilish grin. "Afterward, can I eat him?"

"Absolutely," Ethan said, feeling his body temperature rise. "And if he's broken even one strand of hair on the top of her head, I want you to do it slowly, while he's still alive."

"Now, *that* is the kind of thing I like to hear my master say," Maii said.

The jackal went back to his tracking, and Ethan closely followed. They passed through the narrow streets of Weynock with greater speed than before. Ethan wasn't sure if that was due to Maii being sure of the trail now or if he was trying to act quickly before it was washed away thanks to the rain. Either way, the faster pace gave Ethan hope they'd reach her before any one of a thousand nightmare scenarios unfolded that were plaguing his mind.

Who the hell kidnapped a vampire, anyway? Did he know who she was? Or was he simply some sick creep looking to drag a woman off to have his way with her? Ethan had no idea, but in the end, he didn't care either. He was completely serious when he answered Maii. The only thing he planned on doing was putting a bullet straight through the man's heart.

Five minutes or so came and went, and Ethan was now thoroughly drenched thanks to the rain that had become a torrential downpour. His clothes chafed his skin, and water streamed into his eyes, causing him to wipe them clear time and again. Lightning streaked through the sky at regular intervals with thunderous claps that were so loud they'd easily silence any cannon. With them, at least, they brought flashes of light that helped illuminate the way.

"I'm coming, Zoey," he muttered. "Hang in there."

The two rounded a bend in the road and quickly found themselves at the guardhouse that led to the town's docks. Huddled inside the stone walls, taking refuge from the storm, were three guards, seated around a small table with mugs and playing cards in hand.

They almost didn't notice him.

Almost.

Ethan was a couple of steps away from slipping by when the guard closest to the door happened to look over and jump to his feet. The man, a boy of seventeen years at best, really, came running out, sword in hand.

"You there!" he said. "Halt!"

Ethan did, reluctantly. He didn't have time for this, but he also knew he had to handle this encounter perfectly, and perfectly definitely didn't include entertaining the idea of running. "Is something the matter?"

"It's past curfew!" the guard said. "What business do you have at this hour?"

Ethan balked at first, unsure of what to say or do. Thankfully, he quickly realized if he didn't respond at all, he'd get to know the stockades faster than a mutinous crew would get to know the hangman's rope. So he did the only thing that came to him. He went on the offense. "You dare question me?" he shot back, hoping he could throw whatever luck he had regenerated since his fight with Barnaby into whatever fast-talk skills the world had, assuming it had any.

The guard faltered but ultimately didn't back down. "Who are you?" he asked. "And I best be seeing some sort of papers to identify you with."

The two guards in the guardhouse took to their feet. They didn't approach, but one did call out. "Anything the matter?"

"That's what I'm determining," the guard in front of Ethan replied, glancing over his shoulder. "Now, you best be answering me, *sir.*"

Ethan had no idea who was important, let alone what he could say to impersonate them. But he did realize one thing: money was a universal language. With one hand, he held up a finger, bidding the guard wait, and with the other, he reached into his coin purse and pulled out a crown. "I was never here," he said. "Understand?"

The guard's eyes went wide at the offer, but the young man quickly recomposed himself. "It's a high crime to bribe a guard," he said, voice low and eyes filled with greed. "I could take you in right now. Then I'd have your whole purse."

Ethan swallowed reflexively and tried his best to keep calm. He couldn't back down now from the bribe, and he knew he'd have a hard time beating this guard in a fight, given his own inexperience. He definitely wouldn't best three of them. Ethan did the only smart thing he could think of that tapped into his gambling skills. Or maybe a dumb thing. He doubled down.

"You could," Ethan replied. "But if I'm willing to toss a crown at you, think about how much I could toss to others to bury you, even if you did try and stick me in prison."

The guard shifted his stance uneasily, no doubt trying to decide whether or not Ethan was bluffing.

"Look, lad," Ethan said, hoping he could get away with such language, despite the fact that he wasn't much older. "A man came through here on a horse with a woman. No one is going to stop me from getting to her. Now, you can stand in my way and face the consequences, or you can tell me where he was headed, and if it checks out, I'll even pay you a second crown for making my job easier."

That got the guard's attention. The young man straightened and glanced over his shoulder to his comrades, who were casually watching. Apparently, the rain was enough of a deterrent to keep them inside for now. "How do I know you're not a wanted man or up to no good?"

"If I were, do you think I'd stroll right by?" Ethan replied.

"No."

"Exactly," Ethan said. "Now, be smart. Take the crown and tell me what I want to know."

You feel a little bit more deceitful.

Startled at Narrator's voice, Ethan jerked back. Thankfully, the guard was already glancing over his shoulder to see what the others were doing before turning around and snatching the coin from Ethan's hand and pocketing it.

"Jacob Linden passed by not even ten minutes ago," he said. "Had a lady with him. Said she was sleepy, but I know what a drunk looks like. I take it he's the one you're after?"

Ethan nodded. It took all his self-control not to show his building anger, but he managed. "He is."

"He's got a small cutter tied up at the end of the third pier," he said, motioning out to the docks. "You'll find him there."

Ethan tipped his head at the young man. "You have all my utmost gratitude, good sir," he said. "I'll be back with your crown shortly."

With that, Ethan took off toward the docks, Maii at his side. At first, he simply broke into a light trot, but once he was a dozen yards away from the guardhouse, and the man who'd stopped him had returned to his post, he broke into a full sprint and didn't stop running as fast as he could until he'd reached that third pier and had traveled nearly to its end.

Tied to the pier maybe twenty yards away, a fifty-foot single-mast ship with a handful of small deck guns rocked in choppy waters. All of its sails were furled, but thanks to the lanterns carried by its crew—a total of three, by Ethan's count—and the illumination by the still-constant flashes of lightning, Ethan could see that preparations for launch were being made despite the stormy weather.

"Harrison!" one called to the other. "Go round up the crew!"

"Aye! On my way!"

With that, the three on the ship became two as one of the men hopped off and hurried by Ethan without giving him a second glance.

"I don't think we have a lot of time," Ethan said.

"I'd say you're quite right about that," Maii replied. "Do you have a plan?"

Ethan drew his sword and nodded toward the ship. "Board the ship. Kill the bad guys. Save the girl before a dozen more show up."

"I like it," Maii replied, grinning with enthusiasm.

Ethan, not expecting the energy in the response, straightened. "You do? Thanks."

"Brave. Straightforward. Completely stupid," the jackal said, bobbing his head with each point. "Possibly more stupid than you trying to bribe the guard back there."

"I *did* bribe the guard back there."

"True, but you were incredibly lucky the other two didn't notice and demand in on the bribery action."

"Maybe you missed it, but I'm a lucky kind of guy," Ethan said, puffing his chest.

"If you say, Master Eight INT," Maii said, grinning. "I just hope they toss your body on the docks and not overboard into the water. I don't like my snacks marinated in brine."

Ethan narrowed his eyes and pointed a finger at the jackal. "Don't call me that."

"Little too close to home?" he asked. "Look, you might get the drop on one, and I emphasize the word might. But you're hardly the swashbuckler, now, are you? These men are seasoned, and there could be more below deck we don't know about."

"Maybe, but in a few minutes, we're going to have a lot more to worry about," Ethan said.

"Then I suggest you think of a better plan, quickly."

Ethan grumbled to himself, and then some more when he realized that Maii was right. He was being rash and stupid, both of which had nearly gotten him killed with Barnaby. That said, as hard as he tried to come up with an idea that could work, all that he succeeded in doing was giving himself a headache. He was about to ask for any suggestions when he saw one of the men disappear below deck, leaving the other alone near the bow of the ship.

"Now's our chance," Ethan said. "Can you distract that one long enough for me to sneak up on him?"

"And how would you like me to do that?"

"I don't know," Ethan said. "Just be you. Mess with his head."

"As you wish," Maii replied before darting off.

Ethan waited a few seconds for the jackal to get ahead before following. He tried to be as quiet and sneaky as he could in his approach of the ship, and he felt that the storm did a fantastic job in keeping him hidden.

Right as he got to the ship and stepped aboard, Maii darted in front of the man's view at the very bow and sat. At first, Ethan wasn't sure what the jackal's plan was, but it soon became apparent. Tiny blue flames erupted across his fur, softly illuminating him in light and giving him a magical appearance.

The man still on deck, with a wood belaying pin in hand, stared blankly at the jackal, unmoving as the rain pelted his face, and Maii swayed gently with the natural rocking of the boat.

Realizing he didn't have long, Ethan moved toward him as fast as he dared. A couple paces away, the man spun around unexpectedly. At that moment, Ethan realized what had given him away: his lantern. Oddly enough, or perhaps luckily enough, that same light was what let Ethan react first as the man spent a moment shielding his weathered eyes with one hand.

Free attack!

Narrator's voice barely registered in Ethan's mind as he struck the man across the face with the hilt of his cutlass.

Mercenary lightly wounded!

Mercenary stunned!

The man staggered backward, and Ethan seized the moment. He leaped forward and smashed the sailor once more across the cheek with a right cross that sent him spinning, and then struck again, hitting him square in the back of the head.

Mercenary seriously wounded!
Mercenary unconscious!

Ethan stood over the now fallen sailor, heart pounding in his chest, and inspected his handiwork. The man lay unmoving as blood poured from his head and was quickly washed away by the rain.

"Finish him," Maii said, hopping over to Ethan's side. "I'll eat later."

Ethan shook his head. "No. He's just some hired hand, and he's done anyway."

Maii grunted. "Going soft on me?"

"Not partaking in murder sprees is hardly going soft," Ethan explained.

Maii gave a look of indifference. "If you say so," he replied. "I suppose if this compassion of yours gets you killed, it's no fur off my back."

"No one is getting killed."

"That's my point."

"You know what I mean," Ethan said with a grunt. "Now, come on. Let's go get Zoey."

CHAPTER XX
THE SECRET

ETHAN TOOK THE stairs below deck, pistol and lantern leading the way. He passed through a small cargo hold as well as the crew quarters, which thankfully only held a half dozen or so empty hammocks. At the other end, he reached the captain's cabin, a cramped space with a single bed built into one side and a small table on the other, that was surprisingly devoid of anyone, as well. At the far side of the room, however, stood an iron-barred door that led to a tight three-foot-by-three-foot brig where a figure lay chained and curled inside.

"Zoey," Ethan hissed as loud as he dared. He bolted over to the door and yanked on the handle as hard as he could, but it refused to open. "Zoey, wake up!"

The figure on the ground stirred, and Ethan dropped to his knees to get a better look. Zoey, indeed, lay inside with her hands bound behind her and her ankles locked tightly together. Her clothes had been torn in multiple places, and when she looked up when he called her name a third time, her face stole Ethan's breath away.

A massive bruise marred her left cheek, and her lower lip had been split off to one side. Blood caked her chin and neck, and she looked more scared and helpless than a day-old fawn cast to the lions.

"Oh my god, Zoey," Ethan whispered. "I'm getting you out of there right now."

"Thank you," she mouthed.

Ethan tried the door again, even though he didn't think it would open, and then spent the next minute turning the cabin inside out, looking for the key. "Where is it?" Ethan asked once he realized he was on borrowed time. "The key, I mean."

Zoey's head fell, and she shook her head. "With the captain, I'm sure."

"Damn it," Ethan said. He then hurried back to the door and tried inspecting the lock. "Can I pick it? I mean, I don't know how, but maybe you can walk me through it?"

Wood creaked behind him, and Ethan whipped around to find Jacob a foot inside the door with a pipe stuck in his mouth and surprise splashed on his face.

"Let her go right this instant," Ethan said, leveling his weapon at the man's head.

Jacob cautiously raised his hands into the air, but he didn't seem nearly as afraid of having a gun in his face as Ethan would've liked. "I can't do that," he said, and when Ethan's finger twitched on the trigger, the man quickly held up a finger. "Hear me out before you shoot: if I let her go, we both die."

"No, if you let her go, you won't die."

The man took a puff from his pipe before using it to motion to Zoey. "Do you know what she is?"

"I do," Ethan said evenly. "My friend."

"She's a lot more than that," the man said with a short laugh. He then gave a curious look before sighing heavily. "You *do* know what she is, don't you?"

"Ethan," Zoey said. "Don't listen to him."

Jacob laughed once more, but this time twice as hard. "She's charmed you, hasn't she? And going by those marks on your neck, I'd wager she's dined on you a little as well."

"I don't care what you think," Ethan said. "I said let her go."

"And I told you I can't," Jacob replied evenly. "I'm not looking to get shot, but I'm not lying either. If she goes free, we both die."

"She won't kill me," Ethan said.

"She's not the one I'm afraid of," Jacob replied evenly. "It's Lord Belmont. He wants her, and he'll kill everyone in his way to have her—and that especially includes bounty hunters who let his prize go once she's been captured."

Ethan's brow dropped, and he retreated a half step as he tried to make sense of this unexpected news. "Lord Belmont wants her?"

"Aye, he does," Jacob replied.

"Why?"

"Ethan, please," Zoey begged. "Don't listen to him. He's trying to kill me."

Ethan snapped his eyes up in time to see Jacob step forward. Operating on pure instinct, Ethan pulled the trigger to his pistol, but when the hammer fell, only a distinct click hung in the air.

Jacob blinked and then grinned broadly. "Only a fool tries to fire wet powder," he said, drawing his sword. "I guess I greatly overestimated you."

Out of pure instinct, Ethan slung the lantern at Jacob's head. It sailed through the air and was easily dodged, but when it struck the floor and its glass shattered, the impromptu missile served as a decent enough distraction. By the time Jacob had ensured no flames had taken to his cabin, Ethan had his cutlass up and ready.

"I'm going to tie you to the yardarm and flay you alive for that," Jacob growled as he took a half step back and adopted a dueling stance.

"This is your last chance to walk out alive," Ethan countered, hoping he could bluff his way out of this. "Leave me the key, and I'll leave you with your life."

"Bravo," Jacob said with a hearty laugh. "You're not a coward. I'll grant you that. But I'll see you under hatches before the next clap of thunder."

Ethan had no idea what that last part meant, but it sounded bad. He didn't have time to think about it, either, as Jacob drove forward with a straight thrust aimed squarely at Ethan's heart.

You parried Jacob's attack.

"Ugh! Get out of my head," Ethan groaned, hating Narrator's intrusion. Thankfully, Narrator seemed to do just that. Either that or the fact that he was fighting for his life allowed Ethan to ignore him completely for the next few moments, which was just fine with Ethan because Jacob's next two attacks came harder and faster than before.

Ethan barely parried the first thrust, steel clanging loudly against steel. But when the next attack came, he didn't fare as well. Though he managed to trap Jacob's blade against his own and the hilt of his cutlass, the two ended up being nearly face-to-face. As such, Jacob was close enough to jab Ethan in the side with his free hand, sending him stumbling back.

They parted, and Ethan swung wildly, feeling his guard drop. Jacob ducked the haphazard blow and issued a low cut of his own. Unlike Ethan's attack, this one sliced across the outside of Ethan's left thigh.

"Damn," Ethan growled, stumbling backward yet again. He didn't get far as he was now pressed up against the door to the brig.

"Soiled your kicksees, have you?" Jacob mocked, dipping the tip of his blade toward Ethan's bloodstained breeches. He was about to say something else when he dropped his sword and staggered forward, Maii latched firmly to the back of his neck.

Ethan, operating on pure instinct, sliced open the man's belly with a single cut before stabbing him once more in the gut.

Jacob critically hit!
Jacob gravely wounded!

Jacob lurched sideways, and Maii released his grip. The man, with clenched eyes and jaw, fell against the wall, hand pressed against his gut and blood seeping through his fingers. The strength in his legs gave out, and he quickly slumped to the floor.

"Should've known you weren't alone," the man said with a pained, shaky voice.

"I told you to let her go," Ethan said, keeping the point of his cutlass aimed at his adversary's throat.

Jacob coughed, blood frothing out of his mouth as he did. "Tell me, what did she promise you?" he asked. "Bountiful treasure? Life eternal? Her everlasting love?"

"Too bad for you, you'll never know."

Jacob chuckled, which turned into a violent cough that took hold of him for several seconds. "For your sake, I hope it's not a ruby amulet," he said, resting his head against the wall. He closed his eyes, grimacing, before coughing again. When he was finished, his eyes met Ethan's. "Blood and 'ounds," Jacob said, grinning. "She did, didn't she? She promised you Lord Belmont's ruby, and you were fool enough to believe her."

"What are you talking about?"

Zoey lunged forward, snapping hard against her chains. "Ethan, don't listen to him," she said. "He's trying to trick you."

Jacob shook his head weakly, looking like he was a single breath away from death. Yet somehow, he still managed to summon enough strength to gesture to his broken body. "Look at me," he said. "What tricks could I possibly play? No, Master Ethan, if anything, the truth is far sweeter revenge on the two of you at this point."

Ethan, unsure of what was going on, stepped sideways, so he could see both the fallen bounty hunter and Zoey at the same time. "Talk."

"She's only after that gem to destroy it," he said. "There's no selling and splitting the fortune, which I assume is what she promised you. It's what she's promised everyone else she's tried to get help from."

"No, that's insane," Ethan said.

"What's insane is thinking she'd keep it," Jacob said. "That ruby is what grants Lord Belmont his power, his immortality. She wants to destroy it."

"I don't care about that, Ethan," Zoey said, tugging again. "Please, listen to me. He's going to try and turn you against me. Yes, the gem holds Belmont's life force, but I don't care. We can still sell it for a ton of coin. Let someone else worry about trying to figure out how to shatter the damn thing if they want."

The fallen bounty hunter turned to face Zoey, and he managed a snort. "Shatter? Is that the story you're going with?"

"It's the truth," she shot back, narrowing her eyes.

"Tell me, Master Ethan, you've seen her run around with dragon's breath, have you not? A powder that, when lit, melts steel faster than a torrent of lava? What do you think that's for? Cutting locks and chain?"

Ethan, hating the fact that there was an air of truth to the man's words, inadvertently dropped the tip of his sword. "You're saying she's going to melt the gem?"

Jacob nodded.

"Why?"

"I wouldn't!" Zoey yelled. "God, Ethan, don't let him get in your head like that. Why the hell would I risk my life to destroy something worth so much? I need funds as much as you do, if not more so! I've got people I'm playing for, too."

"Yeah," Ethan said as he turned her words over several times in his head. "But you don't talk about them much, do you?"

"Because I've messed up, okay?" she said, eyes watering. She tried clearing them, but the chains kept her hands from her face, and all she could do was shake her head and try and sniff the snot away. "It's worse than what I said earlier, and I didn't want to say much about it because I didn't want you to think I didn't know what I was doing—or that I was a failure. I already think that about myself enough."

Ethan felt his heart break for the vampire, and all he wanted to do was sweep her up in his arms and hold her tight. "I'd never think that about you."

"How touching," Jacob said with a slow clap. "I'll tell you why she wants that gem, and it has nothing to do with getting money."

Ethan spun back around and glared. "What is it, then? She's doing it for shits and giggles?"

"Ethan, kill him!" Zoey begged. "Please, for my sake."

Ethan shook his head. "No. I want him to die knowing his lies had no effect on me."

"That's the spirit, Master Ethan," Jacob said as a devilish grin spread across his face. "The reason she's so keen on destroying that gem is because it binds all the curses Lord Belmont has ever cast."

"Ethan!"

Ethan held a hand up to Zoey, bidding her quiet. "What curses?"

"Hundreds by now," the bounty hunter replied. "As for your lady, here, she's been cursed by him as well, and she'll never break free of it until that gem is destroyed—and the fastest and easiest way to do it is to melt the gem with dragon's breath."

"No," Ethan replied softly, but even as the words passed his lips, doubt overtook him.

"Tell me, when was the last time she's done something that would make her a queen of the undead?" he asked, suddenly gaining a bit of strength to his voice. "Blood sucking aside, has she charmed the masses? Shrugged off a hundred shots? Moved faster than a tempest or disappeared into mist?"

"No, but she must have."

"Is that a fact?" he asked, not missing a beat. "Then, take a moment and tell me when."

"I can't recall."

"Exactly," he said. "That curse has stolen it all from her. She may be a vampire, but it's in hunger only. Her powers are all but gone."

Ethan was at a loss of words. All he could do was watch the man as he settled back down with a smile across his face. He didn't want to believe a word of any of it, but at the same time, he knew the man was telling the truth. Why the hell would Zoey be carrying that volatile mixture otherwise? And in the end, the man had nothing to gain by lying, but Zoey certainly had everything to lose if that were the truth.

Ethan stood there, feeling all emotion and attachment to his surroundings drain away. He felt his eyes glaze over, and he didn't know what to think or do. A deep sense of emptiness filled his soul, and he wasn't sure whether or not he felt more angry, sad, or foolish for ever trusting her. The only thing he knew from all of this was that even in another world, one where he should've been able to reinvent himself as anything or anyone, he was still just an afterthought when it came to the fairer sex at best and something to be taken advantage of at worst.

"Ethan? Ethan, listen to me, damn it," Zoey begged. "He's lying through his rotten teeth."

"No use now, love," Jacob said with a bloody, cough-filled laugh. "He knows who's telling the truth."

"Shut up!"

"Or what? You'll yell at me some more?"

Ethan snapped out of his daze. With one clean thrust, he drove his sword through Jacob's heart. The man stiffened for a moment before slumping forward and falling over when Ethan withdrew the blade.

"Thank god," Zoey said, sighing. "I thought he'd never stop. Now get me out of here before his crew gets back."

Ethan's eyes met hers. He tried to give off a flat affect, but a wellspring of agony ripped through his gut. Instead of letting it break him down, he channeled it into righteous indignation. "Piss off."

He then turned and headed the door.

"Please don't go," she said. "I can explain."

Ethan stopped, a foot away from the threshold. He half glanced over his shoulder. "Tell me the truth: were you planning on destroying that gem?"

"Yes, but—"

"Then no buts," he said, cutting her off. "I'm done with you."

With that, he left.

Chapter XXI
Dying

I'M DYING, ETHAN," Zoey called out, her voice pleading. "I can't do this without you."

Ethan halted right outside the cabin, one hand holding the door. He could hear the storm thunder above, its fury matching the storm of emotions he had raging inside.

After a few beats, he turned around and stepped back in the cabin. He had no intention of listening to anything she said, but at the same time, he wanted to give her both proverbial barrels.

"You think I'm going to believe anything you say?" he said. "You've lied to me from the start."

"I know," she said weakly. "I know, and honestly, I wouldn't believe me either if I were in your shoes. But I'm not lying. I don't have a lot of time left anymore—less than you do."

"How's that?"

"That gem, the curse it holds over me, keeps me from healing at all," she said. "The only reason it didn't kill me is because I'm a vampire."

"Why?"

"Because it affects the living more than the dead," she said. "Either that or I heal as fast as it kills. Either way, it hasn't killed me yet."

"Anything else I should know before I walk away?"

"If I die here, I die for real, too," she said.

"I thought you said you didn't know what happens if we die here."

"I don't, not for you, at least," she said. "I lied about the chess match but not the duel. Death had me beat, and as I bled out, I got him to agree to a double or nothing by throwing my soul into the pot. He was gracious enough to let me heal and said whenever I was ready, he'd welcome the rematch."

Ethan balled a fist at his side and started cracking his knuckles as he turned her claim over in his head a few times. "Is that why you never wanted to fight?"

Zoey nodded. "It is. I can't risk being hurt at all. Death by a thousand paper cuts is still a death."

Though her story elicited sympathy from Ethan, in the end, he still couldn't get over the fact that she'd been using him for her own gain, stabbing him in the back as she toyed with his emotions. All he'd wanted to do when coming here was to save his dog, Anne, and Zoey had practically cost him that already given how much time of his she'd wasted. "You shouldn't have lied to me," he said.

Zoey surged forward, the chains around her snapping tight with the distinct clink of metal on metal. "I know," she said. "But no one around here would help me, a vampire at the mercy of anything and everything. Please understand, I was going to help you get your ship once I was whole again. I wasn't trying to screw you out of that. I'm not that evil of a person."

"Then why didn't you say all of this from the start?"

"Because I've been scared out of my mind since it all began," she said. "I might be good at hiding things, but that doesn't mean I wasn't terrified. Do you have any idea what it's like to know that even the smallest bruise could wind up being your last?"

Ethan shook his head. "No, I don't."

"Well, it makes you second-guess everything," she said. "What if you didn't believe me? What if you took advantage of me? What if you ran? It's not like I'd have much chance of finding someone else. So, when I saw you, I decided to go for it, because the only thing I knew for sure was that I needed someone fresh, and nice, and—"

Zoey cut herself off, but Ethan filled in the rest with a solemn voice. "Didn't know any better, right?" he asked. "You needed someone stupid and gullible enough to trust you, who'd fall for you. Who'd also..."

His voice trailed, and he didn't have the heart or energy to finish the sentence.

Zoey fell back on her haunches and sighed. "Who'd also what?" she asked. "You might as well say it."

Ethan swallowed hard and forced the words out despite the immense heartache they brought. "Who'd die for you," he said. "That's who you wanted. Someone so enamored with you, that even with or without your charms, they'd follow you to the ends of the world and back, right? Because let's face it, I'm kind of pathetic that way seeing how I'm hardly the ladies' man back home. I was an easy mark."

Zoey opened her mouth as if to argue, but she instead collapsed in a heap and sobbed. "Yes," she said. "You're right."

"Then you can piss right off and die in that jail for all I care," he said, starting to walk away again. "There's nothing you can say or do to make me ever trust you again. I'm tired of being used."

He didn't get even a pace away before Zoey called out one last time. "Their names are Gail and Zach. Just so you know."

Ethan froze and looked over his shoulder. "What?"

"That's the names of the kids I'm playing for," she said. "Gail and Zach Peterson. They're both in ICU at Mount Sinai hospital in

Great Falls, Montana, in a coma, fighting for their lives after a car accident."

Ethan snorted. "Let me guess, drunk driver?"

"No," she said. "Someone blew a tire on the highway. Spun out, hit their car, which ended up wrapping around a tree."

"How do you know all of this?"

"I'm their nurse," she said.

"Which means what?"

"Which means if I die, so do they since Death will win by default," she said. "Look, you can hate me all you want. Spit in my face if that's what it takes. I certainly deserve it. But help me for their sake, if no other reason."

Ethan balked for a moment, but ultimately shook his head and sighed with disgust. "No, you're lying," he said, refusing to be toyed with any longer. "As I said, I'll never trust you again. Ever."

"Ethan, I'm not lying."

"Yeah, sure you aren't. I'm done with you."

"Fine," she said, her voice suddenly growing sharp and cold. "You don't have to believe me. But once you're out of here and back in the real world, go look their parents up. They'll be easy to find, especially if you check the newspapers. And when you find out they died about the same time as their nurse did, I'm sure you'll be able to sleep well for the rest of your life knowing you couldn't be bothered to try and save a couple of kids."

"Damn," Ethan muttered. He wanted to keep walking, wanted to leave her to rot. Hell, he almost had the inkling to bring her to Lord Belmont himself and collect whatever bounty the lich had put on her head. But he couldn't. The ring of truth in her words was so loud in his ears, he knew she wasn't lying. "Damn. Damn. Damn. Damn. Shit!"

Ethan slowly turned around and made his way back to Jacob, cursing both himself and the situation a thousand times over in the process. He didn't look Zoey in the eyes, though he knew she was watching his every step.

"Ethan?" she said. "I—"

"Just shut up," he snapped as he searched the bounty hunter's body and took the iron key from one of his pockets. "I don't want to hear your voice right now. Maybe ever."

Zoey nodded and slumped. To her credit, she didn't speak. She simply put her hands together in front of her face and cried softly.

Ethan went to the brig, put the key into the lock, and gave it a turn. It took a little more effort than he'd expected, but it opened with a sharp metallic clank. He then opened the door and unlocked the shackles on her ankles and wrists.

For what felt like an eternity, neither one said or did anything.

"You should've been straight with me," he eventually said, standing to the side. His gaze rose from the floor, where it was often aimed when he was doing his best thinking, and his eyes met Zoey's. They were large, fearful, and watery. And in all the time he'd known her, she'd never looked so small. "I would've helped you, regardless."

"I—I know," she said, clearly unsure if she should say anything. "I've been here so long, Ethan, and I've become jaded and untrusting of others. I'm not saying that makes any of what I did okay, but that's the truth of it. Everyone here is only out for themselves. I forgot what decency was like, and I'm sorry. I'm so, so sorry."

The world seemed to pause, and everything took on a surreal nature. He felt like he had back when Barnaby was dying, and he'd had a choice to make. Whatever actions he took at this very moment could not be undone, he knew, and somehow, he also knew they'd forever affect both himself and his future in this world.

"I should make you pay for what you did," he finally said, tapping into his desire for justice. When Zoey shrank, only to find herself pressed against the back wall of the brig, he quickly shook his head. "I should, but I'm not. I forgive you, on the promise that you never lie to me ever again, because I swear, Zoey, I won't give you another chance."

"On my life, Ethan, I won't ever lie to you again," she said. "Never, ever, ever."

Ethan forced a smile and extended his hand. "Good. Now come on and get out of there. We've got a gem to destroy."

Zoey bolted out of the brig and threw her arms around him, right as Narrator did what he did best:

+1 Compassion gained.

Out of pure reflex, Ethan rolled his eyes and muttered, "Damn, that's annoying."

"What?" Zoey said, pulling back.

She didn't get far. Ethan quickly put his arms around the small of her back and kept her close. "Not you," he said. "Narrator."

"Oh," she said, sounding relieved.

His hands slid to her hips and tightened, and she sucked in a sharp breath in response. "I meant it," he said. "Don't ever lie to me ever again."

"I won't," she said, shaking her head. "I promised you that already, and I meant every word."

"Okay," Ethan said, taking a deep breath to calm himself. "I just needed to hear that again, is all."

"Ahem," Maii interrupted. "The crew?"

Ethan straightened and pulled away. "Right," he said, laughing. "We've got to get out of here before they return. Any chance the two of us can sail this ship?"

"Absolutely," Zoey said with a nod. "But we'll need to move fast. Can you do that with the leg?"

"With all the adrenaline pumping through me, you bet," Ethan said. "Anyway, I don't think I have much of a choice, do I?"

With that, the three of them raced through the ship and flew up the stairs leading to the deck. Along the way, Zoey snatched a small hatchet from the crew quarters. Having a weapon in hand put a smile on her face, but that smile quickly faded once they'd gone topside.

Having taken only a few steps across the deck, Ethan froze and pointed a finger at the docks. "Oh, damn," he said. "The crew's here."

Chapter XXII
An Old Friend

"OH, CRAP," Zoey muttered. The group of men Ethan had pointed out was still fifty or so yards away on the docks, stumbling drunkenly along, the light from their lanterns making them easy to spot. "Ethan! Center mast! I need the mainsail unfurled!"

"How do I do that?"

"It's a Bermuda rig with a single headsail!" she barked. "Use the halyard and cunningham to get us underway! I'll cut the mooring lines!"

Ethan bolted across the deck to where she pointed, nearly slipping twice as he half-ran around, half-jumped over the backs of the cannons. His hands worked the lines around the cleats, freeing the mainsail from its wrap. He had no idea how he knew what line, pulley, or wench did what, but it all came to him as naturally as breathing, and so he chalked it up to his character's skill and simply ran with it.

He was about to drop the main sheet when he caught sight of movement out of the corner of his eye. Ethan turned a split second before he caught a belaying pin with his face. Thankfully, Ethan had fast enough reflexes to raise his left arm, which promptly took the brunt of the attack.

"Holy god balls on a stick, that hurts," Ethan cried out, jumping back.

The man came at him again, swinging wildly and screaming like a madman. Ethan ducked under the blow and drove forward, hitting the guy in the chest with his shoulder. Ethan kept running until he rammed the soldier into one of the deck guns, his back making a satisfying crunch.

The mercenary had the wind knocked out of him, and he let go of the belaying pin. As the man slumped down, gasping for breath, Ethan punched him with a right cross before grabbing the fallen pin and issuing a wicked backhand with it that shattered the man's cheek and sent him to the land of unconscious beings for a second time. Ethan was about to finish the guy off when Zoey came running over, screaming.

"No, Ethan! Don't kill him! We need him alive!"

Ethan stopped, arm raised. "Alive for what?"

"For Myriden!"

"Who?"

"The baby kraken who ate your ship when you first got here," she said, pointing to the water. "He's somewhere out there, nearby, and if we don't donate a fresh meal to him, he might come after the ship. Now finish dropping that sail!"

Ethan did as he was told, and within seconds, the main sheet fell from its wrap and caught the wind. The ship immediately tilted and lurched forward. Zoey perched at the helm, muscled the wheel, and peeled them away from the docks. They'd only gone a few yards before the approaching crew took notice. Shouts of confusion quickly followed, and a few of the more sober members ran down the docks, but by the time they'd reached the space where the gangplank had been, the ship was far enough away that all they could do was watch Ethan and Zoey disappear into the night.

"You look like hell," Zoey said once Ethan joined her at the wheel.

"Thanks, but I just hope it's not broken," he replied, inspecting his arm as best he could in the rain. He tried flexing his fingers a few times, which he was able to do, but not without considerable pain. "It still hurts. A lot."

"Once we're clear of Myriden, I'll take a look," she said. "We'll probably need to stitch the leg up, too. I can't believe you're still walking on it."

At the mention of his leg, Ethan looked down and immediately wished he hadn't. Nearly every square inch on the left side of his breeches was shades of crimson and dark red, and he was certain a half-carved turkey from Thanksgiving had less tissue damage than he did.

"Damn it to hell, that can't be good," he said, suddenly feeling weak.

Zoey laughed. "You'll live. Don't worry. I'm sure it looks worse than it is."

"I hope so."

"Honestly, you wouldn't be walking if it weren't. What's your character sheet say?"

Ethan took it out and spent a few seconds trying to read it in the dark. "Moderately wounded," he said. He then stuffed it away. "That sounds bad."

"It's worse than a few bruises," she said. "You'll suffer some minor penalties to most of your rolls, but at least you're not serious, or worse, critical."

"Or dead," Ethan tacked on.

"Exactly," she said, beaming. Her smile faded as her eyes lifted and focused on something far ahead in the dark. "Speaking of dead, I think I can see that dead whale."

Ethan turned and strained his eyes, trying to see what she was referencing. Even with the moonlight glimmering on the water, it wasn't enough for him to see much of anything. "You can?"

"Jacob was wrong about me," she said before pointing to her eyes. "That curse didn't take everything but the hunger. I still have my night vision and a few tricks left."

"Oh, that's handy," Ethan replied.

"Very."

The conversation died, and the ship cut through the waters at a good clip. Ten or fifteen minutes later, the storm had blown by, and Weynock was a distant speck of light. Ethan had checked on the mercenary a few times during that, and other than moaning incoherently from time to time, he hadn't shown any signs of waking up. Eventually, Ethan made his way back to Zoey, who was still at the helm, eyes constantly scanning the water around them.

"Maybe Myriden's decided to leave us alone," Ethan said.

"Maybe."

The flutter in her voice told Ethan she didn't believe that at all, which in turn put Ethan on edge. After all, the last time he'd tangled with the baby kraken, his ship had gone down, and he'd barely made it to shore alive.

"Should I load the cannons?" Ethan asked.

Zoey took her eyes off the water long enough to look at Ethan and shake her head. "Those aren't big enough to scare him off," she said. "Most they'd do is make him angry."

"Really?"

"Really."

Zoey looked like she was about to say something else when her face drew back in a grimace, and Ethan couldn't help but mimic the gesture. "What?"

"Pretty sure I just saw a giant tentacle," she said, turning the ship about twenty degrees starboard. "Get over to our friend and be ready to chum the water."

Ethan shook his head and frowned, trying not to envision chopping up the sailor into fresh chunks of meat. "Can we not use the word chum?"

"Use whatever word you want," she said. "But we're going to need him dumped overboard in about two min—"

Her words cut short when the boat rolled sideways, sending both of them sprawling across the deck. The ship then pitched forward, and the wood groaned as its bottom scraped across something large and unyielding.

"What the hell was that?" Ethan asked, scrambling to his feet.

Zoey didn't have time to answer, but she didn't need to either. A large tentacle shot out of the water and crashed onto the deck. Suckers, each the size of a fist with a pair of bony hooks set inside, lined one side, and the moment the appendage struck the wood, it began feeling around, looking for a victim.

The tentacle swept the deck. Zoey darted behind one of the deck guns, and Ethan dove over the attack, but not nearly as skillfully as he'd have liked. His boot grazed the top of the monster's appendage, and instantly the tentacle changed course.

"Holy crap, that thing is fast!" Ethan yelled, diving to the side. Like Zoey, he ended up taking cover behind one of the cannons right before Myriden would have gotten his hooks into him.

An instant later, a second and a third tentacle shot out of the water on each side, sending a fine salty spray in all directions. These, too, joined the blind search for a meal. And although they futilely battered the deck, with each strike that came up empty, the next one rained down harder and faster. It didn't take long for Ethan to realize that if Myriden wasn't fed soon, he'd send the ship to the bottom of the ocean in pieces.

Right after a tentacle smacked the cannon he hid behind, Ethan dared a glance over it to see where the mercenary was. The sailor had rolled up against the railing, unconscious still, but not likely to be found, especially since Myriden was currently searching the back half of the ship.

"Zoey!" Ethan shouted. "Can you reach the mercenary?"

The vampire peeked around her hiding spot, and for a brief moment, it looked like she had an opening. Zoey raced forward, trying to take advantage of a gap in Myriden's search, but when the baby kraken added a fourth tentacle to the mix, it was only a small miracle that kept her free of Myriden's gasp.

"I can't," she said. She then glanced around the deck. "Where's Maii?"

"Probably down below," Ethan said. "Or abandoned ship."

A fifth tentacle came up, but instead of using it to try and find a meal, Myriden wrapped it around the mast.

"Ethan! He's going to wreck the boat!"

Ethan, desperate, looked around for something he could use, hoping maybe he'd stumble upon a randomly dropped vorpal sword or a legendary pistol especially attuned to slaying sea monsters. Sadly, all he had at his disposal other than the pistol in his belt and the cutlass at his side was the wooden belaying pin he'd used to clobber the sailor.

None of those seemed useful, and at most, he figured they'd only manage to get Myriden's attention for a half second before he was eaten.

Rigging lines snapped, and the headsail, which had been furled, unrolled. As it caught the wind, the boat listed hard, sending a barrel careening across the deck and into Myriden's tentacle. The moment it hit, the baby kraken snatched it up before tossing it away.

"Why couldn't that have rolled next to the chum?" Ethan moaned. As soon as the words left his mouth, he got an idea. He stood up, ducked a tentacle, and threw the belaying pin as best he could, aiming at a tentacle that happened to be near the mercenary. The wooden pin flipped through the air, and bounced off the top of the appendage.

Myriden hit!

Myriden grazed!

Myriden went into a flurry of activity, smacking everything this way and that, trying to find the offending person who'd touched him. While the kraken flailed near the fallen sailor, Ethan worried Myriden still wouldn't find him. So he threw the next two things he had: his pistol and then his sword.

The pistol missed Myriden by a foot or two and ended up flying overboard, much to Ethan's dismay. The cutlass, however, not only hit Myriden, but it did so right next to the mercenary.

Myriden hit!
Myriden grazed!

Again, the baby kraken went into a frenzy, but this time, he found the unconscious sailor. Like a hungry python enjoying a fresh meal, Myriden struck the mercenary with lightning speed, wrapped him up, and yanked him overboard. Narrator narrated accordingly, all the while, Ethan relishing his words for the first time since he'd arrived in this world.

Mercenary hit!
Mercenary grabbed!
Mercenary is killed!

The rest of Myriden's appendages lazily withdrew, and the ship righted itself. After a few tense seconds of neither Ethan nor Zoey daring to move, Narrator tacked on one last tidbit of info.

Myriden is satiated!

"Dare I ask if we're clear now?" Ethan said after exhaling a tense breath he'd been holding for a while.

"Yeah," Zoey said, blowing out a puff of air as well. "We're good. Now let's get that leg of yours looked at before you catch an infection, and we have to amputate."

Chapter XXIII
Stitches

THE MYSTERY OF Maii's absence during Myriden's attack was solved in a matter of minutes once Zoey engaged the autopilot—a rope tying the ship's wheel in place.

They found the jackal inside the captain's cabin, rolled on his back, snoring loudly. His belly, swollen, gently rose and fell with his breathing, and his tongue hung lazily out the side of his mouth. The fur on his face was stained in hues of reds and browns, and the only signs that Jacob had ever existed were some tattered clothes and some boots—one of which had a bone sticking out of it.

"I didn't need to see that boot," Ethan said, turning away.

Zoey took a completely different approach to her reaction. Her eyes were wide, and she looked at the jackal, thoroughly impressed. "Damn," she said after a long, slow whistle. "He's one hell of an eater."

"Tell me about it," Ethan said. "Can we fix my leg now?"

"I mean, like, really, he's one hell of an eater," she said. "I bet he'd put a school of piranhas to shame."

"Mm-hm. Now, come on, let's go," Ethan said, tugging her arm.

Zoey shrugged him off. "Does he look bigger to you?"

"His belly does."

"I'm serious," she said. "I think he's bigger."

Ethan looked at Maii. He did seem as if he'd gained weight, and not just because of his bloated stomach. The jackal looked broader in the chest and might have even gained a few inches in height at the shoulder. But no, that couldn't be right. Nothing grew that fast, did it? Certainly not a jackal. "Probably a trick of the lights," Ethan said, liking that explanation.

Zoey twisted her mouth and grumbled to herself for a few seconds, which did a fantastic job of making Ethan feel uneasy.

"What?" he asked.

"I don't think he's a just a jackal."

"Yeah, I figured that part out already," Ethan replied. "He talks, and he can cast illusions, remember?"

"Correction, then: I don't think he's just a talking, spell-casting jackal."

"What is he, then?"

Zoey exhaled sharply, and then her lips went tight into a thin line before replying. "I don't know, but someone went to a lot of trouble making a ring that controls him."

"Which is a good thing for us, right?"

"Maybe."

"Maybe?"

"Fire is good if you can control it," Zoey said. "If you can't..."

Ethan grimaced. "Right. Any idea on how to discover what our little friend is, then?"

Zoey shrugged. "No, but I suggest finding out sooner rather than later."

Ethan agreed, and the two left Maii to his full belly and dreams of, well, whatever it was magical-creatures-who-were-pretending-to-be-jackals dreamed of. They soon procured some bandages from the ship's stores, as well as needle, thread, and a dark bottle of rum.

Ethan was keen on using the last of those three, but given the size of the first, and the coarseness of the second, he was leaning toward a thorough scrubbing with saltwater and a nice wrap as opposed to Zoey playing trauma surgeon, even if they had the rum, which he'd no doubt be drinking all of.

"Hold still," she said, once she had him sitting on the stairs with his leg extended.

"Easy for you to say," he said. "You're not the one about to be jabbed with that thing."

"Hush," she said, kneeling down and leaning in for a better view. "I'll get you plowed before I stick you. Don't worry."

"I'd worry less if we had some healing potions. Don't suppose you still have any?"

"Yes, but they're back at the inn, along with everything else I had," she replied. "You wouldn't want to waste one now anyway."

"I think I very much would."

"It's going to take a couple of days to sail to the fortress," she said. "You'll have regained your strength by then."

Ethan snatched up the bottle and took two swigs as big as he could muster. To his surprise, though strong, it had a fantastic taste of roasted sugar, and within seconds he could feel the alcohol beginning to warm his belly. "Alright," he said. "Give me a few more minutes and a few more drinks, and I'll be ready."

"Glad to hear it," she said. "In the meantime, let me see what I'm working with."

Her hands gingerly peeled back the split fabric to his breeches. She was about to prod the wound with her forefinger, when she stopped an inch away. Her head dropped unexpectedly, and her shoulders slumped.

"I haven't said it yet, but I need to," she said, her voice nearly a whisper. "Thanks for saving me back there."

"You're welcome," Ethan said with a coldness that surprised even him. Now that things had calmed and they were no longer fighting for their lives, thoughts of what she'd done and what she had been planning on doing resurfaced, and with them, came renewed feelings of resentment. "I'm still mad at you, FYI."

"You sure you want to say that to a girl who has a needle in hand?" she asked, obviously trying to keep things light.

"I'm serious."

Zoey grew quiet, and her half smile faded as her head dipped. "I know," she finally said. "And as I said before, I understand if you never forgive me. If I were in your shoes, I probably wouldn't."

"I don't know about forever," Ethan said. "But at least for the next few minutes. Or hour. I haven't decided yet."

Zoey stood and placed a shaky hand on his shoulder before using her thumb to massage it gently. She focused on the act, which seemed to be more an outlet for nervous energy and lingering fear than anything. After a few moments, her hand snaked up his neck to the back of his head where her fingers began to play with his hair.

"I could make it up to you," she said hesitantly.

Ethan's lips curled upward, but he ended up shaking his head with a long sigh. "No," he said. "I don't want you to have sex with me out of feelings of guilt. I don't think you want to do that either."

"No, but I know how guys are," she softly said. "Both here and back home."

"I am still bleeding," he said. "Kind of a mood killer."

"Maybe for you," she said, flashing her fangs in a moment of levity.

"Yeah, well, I don't have those," he said.

"I could give them to you, if you like," she offered. "I don't like turning people. It's a big deal—life-changing, literally. But for you, if you wanted, I would. You'd heal overnight if you did. Even faster if we had someone you could dine on. But even without a midnight snack, you could avoid the needle and thread."

Ethan drew back and made a face as if he'd just walked into a morgue that had lost its AC for a week. "Eh, no, thanks," he said. "I'll take the stitches."

Zoey furrowed her brow. "Really? Why? Most people jump at the chance. It's not like being turned into a zombie."

"I know, but did you ever see that movie *From Dusk till Dawn*, or was that after you got here?"

"No, I saw it. Why?"

"Remember the part when that guy makes the speech about how if there are vampires, then they have had to come from hell, and if there's a hell, there has to be a heaven?"

"No, but let's pretend I do."

Ethan snorted and threw up his hands. "How can you not remember that? That was, like, one of the best parts."

"I don't know. I just don't."

"I guess it doesn't matter," Ethan said. "Point being, if there are unholy monsters, there have to be holy kickass clerics, priests, paladins, and whatever else who love launching crusades against the undead. And I'd rather not be blasted by any of them the moment I cross their path. And that doesn't even count all the vampire hunters I'm sure are running around here, too."

"Oh, you mean like Blade?"

"Exactly."

Zoey cracked a grin and nodded. "They're annoying. I'll grant you that."

"Just annoying?"

"Deadly if they realize who you are," she said. "But I've got rules I follow that I could teach you. Stick to them, and you'll stay alive. The same goes for steering clear of the clergy."

"I'll still pass. Besides, I don't like the idea of having to suck the blood out of others on a regular basis."

"Okay, I understand," she said. "But if you change your mind, let me know."

She returned to dealing with Ethan's leg. With one hand, she kept the fabric peeled back, and with the other, she started cleaning with one of the bandages. At first, she dabbed at it, but when that wasn't going as well as she would've liked, she pulled back and straightened.

"I'm going to get some freshwater," she said. "Lose the pants in the meantime."

"Say again?"

"Lose the pants," she said. When Ethan balked, she tacked on. "I'm a nurse. There's no reason to be bashful. I promise you've got nothing down there I haven't seen before. Now strip."

Ethan stood, unbuckled his breeches, and let them fall before sitting back down. "Fine. Happy?"

"Quite," she replied. "Be right back."

Zoey left and returned in a couple of moments with a small bucket of water. Using said water, she cleaned the wound with every bit of skill and care he would've expected from a nurse working the ICU. At least, right up until the moment that she squeezed his leg and fresh blood oozed out, coating her finger, which she promptly stuck in her mouth.

Her lips pursed as she closed her eyes and sucked. Her cheeks blushed, and the redness in them quickly spread to her neck and the top of her chest. For a few seconds, she seemed lost in a world that Ethan had only had a glimpse of the night before, but then her eyes popped open, and she quickly popped her finger out of her mouth.

"Sorry," she said with a nervous chuckle. "I'm a little hungry."

"I figured."

Zoey cleared her throat and went back to work. It wasn't long before she'd tended to the wound to her satisfaction. While she had made Ethan wince a couple of times while prodding, not to mention scream bloody murder when she disinfected the wound with the rum, he'd also managed to down about a third of the bottle by the time she was finished. As such, when she held up the threaded needle and asked if he was ready, he managed a drunken smile.

"Do your worst," he said, words starting to slur. "Actually, check that. Do your best. And nothing but the best. And all that stuff."

"I will," she said. "But try not to move, okay? That'll only make it hurt more."

Ethan nodded and sucked in a breath, trying to prepare himself for what surely was going to hurt like hell. It didn't. But only by a degree or two. A split second after Zoey pushed the needle through his skin, Ethan slammed his hand into the step next to him and let loose a string of curses that somehow ended with "horny-piss-ass-flying-crap monster."

"That was one I hadn't heard before," Zoey said, grinning. "And I've heard a lot through the years."

Ethan sucked in a sharp breath and forced himself to relax. "Yeah, but how many of those people had a nurse use a worn-out needle the size of a battleship on them?"

"Uh, none," she admitted. "But you did well on that. Honest. I'm really impressed you didn't pull away."

"Thanks."

"Only fifteen more to go."

"Damn it to hell," Ethan muttered. He then held up a finger before she stuck him again and took the opportunity to help himself to more rum.

Another four stitches came and went, and the number of creative obscenities that flew from Ethan's mouth would've made even the most hardened drill instructor take notes. Stitches six and seven felt as if someone was grabbing his wound with hot pliers and twisting, but after Zoey gave him a ten-minute break, at which point he drank even more, all the rum he'd imbibed since the start finally kicked in at full strength.

You're drunk.

Narrator didn't actually say that. Or at least, if he had, Ethan couldn't remember. He'd made up that bit on his own as he felt as if it was something Narrator was dying to tell him. He was quite the guy, Ethan figured, that Narrator fellow. Always hanging around, making sure he didn't miss something important. Too bad he never had him back in the real world. He could be handy from time to time, even if it was a little creepy that he followed him *everywhere*.

And how did that work, Ethan wondered.

Zoey stuck him again, interrupting his train of thought, which was just as well, because after the dull prick against his leg, Ethan couldn't remember what he was thinking about. Probably something to do with the incredible angle he had when it came to admiring Zoey's chest.

"See something you like?" Zoey said, catching his eye as she looked up.

"You...hic...you might...hic...say that."

Zoey gently reached up and took the bottle. Ethan tried to protest, but when he nearly lost his balance, and the room went spinning, he decided it was probably for the best.

"I did say that," she said, putting the bottle to the side. "The question is, would you say that?"

"Say what?"

Zoey laughed, hitting light, sweet notes that struck a chord in Ethan, ones that made him happy to be around her. "Never mind."

Immediately, Ethan shook his head. That wasn't right. He was mad at her about something. Or was she mad at him? He furrowed his brow, trying to figure it out, which served as the perfect distraction while Zoey said something or other and finished sewing him up.

"There you go. Good as new," she said, tapping him on the knee. "Or will be in a few days. No heavy lifting, and absolutely no swimming until I say. Doctor's orders."

Zoey stood and turned to leave. In the half second before she left, Ethan grabbed her by the hand. "Wait."

"What?"

Ethan rose, and feeling as if the moment had turned into a now-or-never sort of deal, he tried to kiss her.

Zoey, ten times nimbler than he was thanks to his inebriation, easily slipped from his grasp and hopped out of the way. "No."

Ethan dropped his brow, confused, and still feeling like it was a good idea. After all, they'd almost hooked up, and not that long ago, if his blur of a memory proved to be correct.

"Why not? You...hic...were going to...before...I think."

"Not exactly," she explained. "You're really drunk. Like really, *really* drunk."

"And?"

"And you turned me down sober."

"I did? Why?" Ethan scratched his head, which ended up spinning the world. "Oh, that was a bad idea."

"You did," she said with a sigh. "And thank you for that."

"I still think we—"

Zoey put a finger on his lips to quiet his protest. "Trust me," she said as she backed a couple of paces. "You'll thank me in the morning. I promise. Or maybe not, all things considered."

Ethan stumbled to the side when the ship rocked unexpectantly, and he had to take a few seconds after catching himself on a post to make sure his footing was solid enough to keep him from kissing the floor anytime soon. Even after he'd done that, it was still iffy. Everything around him seemed fuzzy and moved far more than it should have. All of that was more than enough to overload his alcohol-saturated brain so that when he finally remembered Zoey was standing nearby, he hadn't a clue what was going on. "Um, what were we talking about?"

"You climbing into one of the hammocks for the crew," she said, gently pulling him forward by the wrist.

A couple of minutes later, she helped him into one of the hanging beds. Blissful, drunken sleep quickly followed.

Chapter XXIV
Land-Ho!

ETHAN WOKE, GROGGY, sore, and thoroughly hungover. After he massaged his temples, he managed to roll out of the hammock without smashing into the floor, at which point he noticed a clear bottle filled with water nearby, which he promptly drank.

Still feeling like crap, Ethan flopped himself back in the hammock and passed out again. When he woke for the second time, aside from a dull ache in his left leg and head, he felt halfway decent. Except, he noted, he had to pee. Bad.

"Christ," he said, rolling out of the bunk. He raced up the stairs and out on the main deck where a steady salty breeze greeted him. In a flash, he bolted over to the portside rail, and once he was done with his much-needed bio break, he buttoned up his pants and took a look around.

The first thing he noticed was the sun on the horizon, its warm rays putting a golden glow over the waters. The sails, at full, flapped hard against a stiff breeze, and he could hear the waves skipping off the ship's bow as it glided effortlessly across the open waters.

Behind him, much to his surprise, he found Maii manning the helm with Zoey nowhere to be found.

"Sleep well?" the jackal asked, tilting his head to the side for a better view.

"Well enough," Ethan said. "Thought I'd have slept at least past dawn, though."

Maii laughed and nodded toward horizon. "That, Ethan, is a setting sun," he said. "Not a rising one."

"Oh, well, that would explain why I'm famished," Ethan said, noting his rumbling stomach. "What's to eat around here?"

"Tack. Hard tack. And even harder tack."

"That's it?"

"I think Zoey said something about finding some salted meat as well, but honestly, I wasn't paying much attention at the time."

"Why's that?"

"Too busy keeping my distance."

Ethan, not liking the tone in his voice, glanced around the deck once more. "Come again?"

"She's hungry, too, Ethan."

"Well, yeah. I figured that."

"And she's a vampire," he added, slowly.

"Oh, right."

Despite the jackal's warning, Ethan continued his search for Zoey, partly out of curiosity about where she was but mostly out of concern. True, he still hurt over her backstab, and yes, she probably still deserved his ire and scorn, but that didn't mean he didn't want to make sure she wasn't suffering some hellish torment.

Eventually, he found her in the bowels of the ship, slowly rocking in a dark corner. She sat with her back turned to him, arms drawn across her chest, mumbling incoherently. Her skin had turned a pasty white, and even across the room they were in, he could see the sweat beading on her back.

"Zoey?" he said softly, unsure what to say or do.

The vampire perked before groaning and shaking her head. "Go," she ordered. "I'm fine."

"You look like crap."

"I don't care what I look like!" she snapped. "Go!"

Part of him wanted to leave, to tell her to piss off because he was only trying to be nice, but in the end, he couldn't. Whether it was a general sense of pity or the extra compassion he'd gained earlier, he wasn't sure. All he knew was that he couldn't leave her.

"I know you're hungry," he said, slowly approaching. "I can only imagine."

Zoey clutched her sides and whimpered before glancing over her shoulder with her eyes narrowed. "You will never understand," she hissed. "Ever. Now, if you value your life, leave. I'll find something to eat when we get to the island."

Ethan shook his head. He came up behind her once she turned back around and placed a hand on her shoulder. Zoey shook her head, and for a half second, he thought she might pull away, or attack even, but in the end, she did neither. In fact, what she did surprised him to no end. She trembled.

"I can't hold out around you," she said, her voice choking.

"You don't have to," Ethan said. Before he could think himself out of it, he embraced her fully. He wrapped one arm around her midsection and pulled her against himself, and with the other, he presented his wrist to her mouth. "It's yours."

Zoey touched it with shaky fingertips. "I can't," she said.

"You can."

"No, I mean, I might not stop," she said. "I might kill you. You lost a lot of blood already."

Ethan brushed her hair and tensed at was about to come. "I know," he whispered. "But I can't see you like this, not when I can do something about it."

For a second, Ethan thought the vampire was going to argue more, but instead, she lunged forward and sank her fangs into his flesh. Lightning pain shot through his arm as his wrist felt as if it had caught fire. The pain, however, quickly gave way to a heavenly sensation, and whatever struggles he'd put up out of reflex gave way to quiet relaxation and submission.

For the next several moments, Ethan felt her mouth hungrily suck on his flesh. A tingling sensation spread through his limb, relaxing his body and putting a smile on his face. The tips of his fingers grew cold and numb. His hand followed suit a few seconds later.

Zoey's grip on his arm tightened. In the back of his mind, he realized her strength returned with each beat of his heart more and more, but he also realized the longer she fed, the more it seemed as if she had no intention of releasing him.

Ethan's legs weakened, and his knees buckled. He faltered, and Zoey suddenly relinquished her hold on his wrist. The vampire spun around and grabbed him under the arms and helped to steady him on his feet.

"Are you okay?" she asked, worried.

Though a little lightheaded, Ethan nodded and spent the next few seconds breathing deep. "I'm okay," he said. "Any chance you've had enough?"

Zoey wiped her mouth. "Yeah. Thanks."

The two stood awkwardly together. Ethan hadn't a clue what was running through her mind, but a whirlwind of conflicting feelings ran through his.

"Zoey?" he said, realizing there was still something he longed to do.

"Yeah?"

Ethan reached up and gently framed her face with his hands. She didn't pull away, and before he lost his nerves, he pressed his lips onto hers.

Pressure built between the two. Her hands found his sides, nails slightly digging in. After a few beats, or maybe a thousand (Ethan couldn't tell as the world melted away), they slowly parted.

"I'm not drunk anymore," he said, smiling and holding her gaze. When she kept quiet, he reached up and toyed with her hair. "And I'm probably about to confess the most obvious thing in the world, but I've wanted to kiss you for a long, long time."

A smile slowly spread across the vampire's face. "When did you decide that? Before or after I kissed you at the inn?"

"Before. Long, long before."

"I'm glad you did," she said.

Ethan felt his soul dance high above the heavens. "Does this mean we're a couple?"

"Not after one kiss," she said playfully.

"You did kiss me at the inn," Ethan pointed out, not missing a beat. "So, that's twice now."

"Then I guess you'd better see if the third time's the charm," she said. "Think you can muster the courage to make it happen?"

Two days came and went, the majority of which was spent keeping the ship on course—something that took a lot more time and effort than Ethan had originally realized. The rest of the hours were spent recuperating his strength and replenishing lost fluids with what stores the ship had. Eating was simple, as several barrels below contained salted meats and cheeses that weren't half bad. A few other barrels held freshwater, which Ethan had to drink from a lot as Zoey drank from him nearly as much.

Nights were spent sharing the bed in the captain's cabin, which ended up being a lot less frisky than Ethan had thought it would be, on account of Maii insisting on having a spot inside the room, too. And with the jackal there, watching and commenting on their new relationship, what time he had with Zoey was PG at best.

Still, she did snuggle up to him each night and rested her head on his chest. She inevitably would nod off first, and Ethan would simply hold her with a bright smile, thinking he had to be the luckiest guy alive.

On the third day, about an hour after golden rays broke the horizon, Gibbon Isle crested the horizon, and an hour after that, Ethan and Zoey rounded its southern peninsula in search of a place to lay anchor.

When they came around, Ethan let loose a long, slow whistle as he took in the enormous, sheer cliffs off the port side.

"Damn, those are big," he said. "How long will it take to sail around them? They seem to go on forever."

"About nine miles in either direction," Zoey said.

"And how much farther do we have to go?"

"About five hundred yards."

"Five hundred yards?" he repeated, certain he'd heard wrong. "We're not stopping here, are we?"

"We are," she replied before pointing up ahead while easing the ship's wheel to the starboard side several degrees. "There's a small inlet up ahead. We'll lay anchor there and make our ascent."

"Right, our ascent," Ethan said, eyes scouring the area. He picked out the inlet without trouble—a small recess that was maybe fifty yards deep and maybe three times that in breadth—but that's all he could see, cliffs aside. "I take it there's a secret staircase in there?"

"Nope."

"Wooden elevator cleverly painted to match the rocks?"

Zoey snickered. "Wouldn't that be nice."

"Nest of griffons you've tamed who are eager to whisk us away?"

The vampire sighed and looked at him with pity. "Do I need to shatter your dreams any further?"

"Well, I hope you've got a better idea than the one I think you're about to suggest," he said crossing his arms. "Because in case you've forgotten, I didn't spec mountain goat. There's no way I'm climbing that."

"Yes, I know, and yes, you are."

Ethan grumbled, mostly to himself, and before he knew it, they'd laid anchor, and somehow, Zoey had convinced him to start climbing. The first few feet weren't too bad, he decided. There were, as she'd promised, quite a number of handholds, and the rope they'd brought from the ship did indeed offer a bit of extra security that he felt good about, especially since they used it to not only tie themselves together but to anchor themselves to a number of pre-anchored grips. That said, they hadn't even scaled fifty feet before Ethan was having serious reservations about it all.

"You know," he said, hoisting himself up to the next mini-ledge where he could take a break. "We could still climb back down, hop in the boat with Maii, and find a better shore to come in on. One that's not so filled with cliffs."

"Anywhere else will undoubtedly be under watch," Zoey said, looking down at him.

"Yeah, well, if there's a lich at the top of these cliffs, I'm not going to be happy with you. I don't care how much of a cute couple we've become."

"Cute?" she repeated as if she was mulling over the concept for the first time.

"Not the word for this world?" asked Ethan. "How about dangerous? Or pirate-y?"

Zoey laughed. "Pirate-y? That could work. Then when you forget our anniversary, I'll make you walk the plank."

"Gee, thanks."

"You're the one forgetting important dates, not me."

Talk quieted for a moment as Zoey turned her attention on the next part of the climb. Once she had it conquered, and Ethan had as well, he decided that he really needed to keep the conversation going, lest he might think about not only what he was doing, but how insanely high he was going to be.

"So, what do you like to do for fun?" he asked, grabbing the next handhold and pulling himself up.

"What do you mean?"

"You know, like fun, like back in the real world. I should probably know some real stuff about you now, right?"

"Oh," she said. "Read, I guess."

"That's it?"

"Well, no," she admitted. "Sometimes I'll go see a movie with friends, or maybe binge stream some movies and stuff myself with chocolate. What do you do?"

"The last thing I tried to do was go to a fair," he said. "But that, obviously, didn't end up the way I thought it would. I guess I figured a hot little nurse would do more."

Zoey laughed. "What makes you think I'm a hot little nurse? I could be a sweaty three-hundred-pound dude with one leg and a beard full of lice for all you know."

Ethan froze, and his stomach made it known it was one wrong answer away from puking. "You're not, right?"

Zoey held his gaze for a moment before laughing again. "No," she said. "I'm just messing with you."

Ethan sighed. "Oh, thank god."

"But to be honest, I wish I did more," she said.

"Why don't you?"

"Because working ICU takes its toll, you know?" she said. "Half the time when I get home, all I want to do is nothing at all."

"Yeah, I can't even imagine," Ethan said, knowing he could never relate. He tried a more universal topic. "What's the last movie you saw?"

"Tremors."

"Holy balls," Ethan said. "Tell me not in the theater."

"No. Streamed it. Why?"

"'Cuz it's super old."

"I know, but it's funny as hell," Zoey said. "I love every bit of it."

"Ever see the sequels?"

"No. I didn't even know there were any."

"Like four or five," Ethan replied. "Worth checking out if you liked the first, but I wouldn't call any of them groundbreaking."

For the next half hour, once they moved on from Zoey's last seen film, the two went over their top-ten list, then worst ten, and finally moved onto their should've-been-a-sequel-but-wasn't list. Zoey was about to tell Ethan what her number one on that list was when they finally reached the top of the cliff.

Ethan, eager to hear what she had to say (yet annoyed she hadn't spoken to him at all once she'd reached the top), quickly pulled himself up and over the cliff. When he pushed himself to his feet, thoroughly exhausted—but utterly proud of himself for finishing the climb—his heart stopped.

Zoey knelt a few feet away, her hands clasped behind her head. Surrounding her in a semi-circle were three dozen skeletal warriors dressed in ragged clothes, armed with sword and musket, and next to the vampire stood a man dressed in a long blue coat with golden embroidery, white trousers and undercoat, and a black bicorne hat.

Only he wasn't a man. Whatever the thing was that filled the uniform was decayed, ancient, and powerful. He looked at Ethan with glowing eyes, filled with amusement, and an emaciated face that was probably a few thousand years older than that of an Egyptian mummy.

"Ah, Ethan," the creature said before giving a sweeping bow. "Allow me to introduce myself. Lord Belmont, at your service."

Stunned, all Ethan could do was shake his head and try to make sense of things. "You know me?"

The lich chuckled. "No," he said. "But you'd be surprised what I can draw out of someone in a matter of seconds."

Ethan glanced at Zoey, who, in turn, glanced at him. "I'm sorry," she mouthed.

Ethan shook his head. "Don't be."

"Exactly, my dear man," Lord Belmond said, smiling broadly. "There's nothing to apologize for. Now, why don't you lay down your arms so we can have a more civilized discussion."

Chapter XXV
Interrogation

I BELIEVE I told you to kneel."

Lord Belmont, who sat on an obsidian throne inside the great hall of his citadel, flicked a bony finger, and the skeletal guard behind Ethan struck him with the shaft of his spear right behind the knee.

Ethan's leg instantly gave out, and down he went. Though he managed to catch himself with his hand before his face rammed the stone blocks of the throne room, that was a consolation prize at best. He had no delusions he was getting out of this alive, and as such, he figured he might as well die well. Or at least, not as a blubbering coward.

"Where's Zoey?" Ethan growled. "She'd better be alright."

The lich chuckled. "Or what?"

"Or I'll make sure that when I tear you apart, it's painful and slow," Ethan said. It was a total bluff, of course, one that Lord Belmont no doubt understood as well, but as cliché as it all was, it still sounded good. Besides, he did have a half-baked idea that might see at least Zoey out of this mess. She, after all, still had kids to save. And as much as Ethan loved his dog, Anne, the lives of children mattered more.

The lich drew back his thin lips to reveal a rotting mouth with more than one wooden tooth. "I must say, Master Ethan, I admire your tenacity even in the face of certain death. Pray tell, if you would be so kind as to entertain me, why do you insist on angering me for her sake?"

"Because I'm not going to let anyone hurt my friends."

The lich cocked his head. "She's a friend, is she, now? I wonder, then, do you know what she is?"

"If you mean, do I know she's a vampire, then yes. I've even had the experience of being around her when she's hungry."

"In other words, she's charmed you, and you're her blood doll."

Ethan shook his head. "Only in the beginning. Not anymore."

"And why is that?"

"You ask a lot of questions."

"Such things happen during pleasant conversations, do they not?" he replied, seemingly taking no offense to Ethan's remark.

Ethan tutted as he rolled his eyes. "I'd hardly call this a pleasant conversation seeing how you're about to kill me."

"All in the name of progress, Master Ethan," the lich said. "It's much better than the alternative."

"I think I'd rather live."

"I didn't mean that," Lord Belmont replied. "I meant, at least this way, your life will be full of purpose, which is indeed better than a life devoid of meaning. Those lives are wasted opportunities and the leeches of resources."

"Whatever. Just tell me where Zoey is."

"Why?"

"Why does it matter?"

"It doesn't, which is why I'm inclined not to say a word. However, I am curious to see your reaction," he replied. "She's locked away, under guard, whilst I have the ritual room prepared."

"For?"

"To have her soul taken, of course," Lord Belmont said before gesturing to his skeletal guards. "These fine lads, as you can see, are the results of how I usually mete out justice. Why throw them in jail only to rot—or worse, execute—when their labors can be put to good use? Your friend Zoey, however, presents me with the rare opportunity of safely taking her powers and adding them to mine. Thus, to simply change her into what amounts as cannon fodder would be a terrible waste."

Ethan lunged forward, intent on ripping the lich's head off. He'd barely gotten a foot before one of the guards drove the butt of his spear into Ethan's stomach. As he doubled over, another guard cracked him across the head, while a third put the point of a sword against the side of his neck.

The lich cocked his head before tipping his hat. "Full marks for concern for your fellows, Master Ethan," he said. "But your anger is misplaced. If anything, it should be directed at your friend for getting you involved in such ill pursuits."

"She hasn't done anything to you," Ethan said. "And neither have I."

The lich held up a finger. "On the contrary, Master Ethan. She's tried to rob me once already, and now has attempted the same thing a second time, not to mention, she—and you, I might add—has, up until recently, tried to kill me as well. That's also not counting the murder of Jacob and the stealing of his ship. Let's be honest, now, my good sir, you are as much of a scoundrel as any other."

"I did what I had to."

"That's what they all say, Master Ethan," Lord Belmont said as he settled back into his throne. "That's what they all say. No, correction, some of those I take instead beg for mercy. And I'll have you know that I grant them what mercy they've granted others— which is usually none."

Ethan dropped his brow and glared. "And you think that gives you the right to make people your slaves?"

"They're not innocent people, Master Ethan," the lich casually replied as he toyed with some of the beads on his staff. "They're the worst people. The morally repugnant. The hopeless. The absolute dregs of society who will do nothing but tear it down if given a chance—which is exactly the kind of person your vampire is."

"No. You're wrong."

"I can appreciate your point of view, Master Ethan," the lich said, leaning forward. "If I were you, I might say the same. She is a pretty thing, isn't she? I think any gentleman would be hard-pressed not to defend her honor until his dying breath. That said, you know in your heart that such a vile creature cannot be permitted to live. Ridding the world of her is nothing more than killing a rabid dog."

"You're one to talk," Ethan spat.

"Yes, my ghastly appearance," Lord Belmont said, gesturing toward himself with a smile. "An unfortunate side effect for taking on immortality. But you of all people should know that outside appearances have little to do with the heart inside. Whereas I look to save the world, she looks to end it."

"All she wants to do is save a couple of kids. She's not the one trying to make the world burn. As far as I can tell, that's what you're out to do."

The lich took to his feet and laughed. "You think you know this world or the people in it?" he asked. "I've been here for centuries, and truth be told, it was a fine place long ago. A place where men and women cared for their fellow neighbors, where the trade of goods and ideas flourished, where wars were waged on chess-boards and it would've been thought unconscionable to let the sun set on an unsettled disagreement. Look where this place is now. No one gives even as much as a passing glance to the poor and wretched, and robbers, cutthroats, and pirates brazenly take what they want in broad daylight while people—good people—are forced to cower in their homes and pay what little they have to corrupt guards and governments."

"You think you can change that? Or even better, you expect me to believe you're going to be the savior of the world?" Ethan scoffed.

The lich idly tapped his staff on the ground a few times while inspecting the skull attached at the top. "I have no reason to lie, Master Ethan," he said. "I have no ego to bolster, especially regarding the likes of you. But yes, I intend to restore this world to its former glory, and to do that, I must conquer it first before I can reinstate justice and order."

"You've got a long way to go."

"Indeed, I do," Lord Belmont said. "Hence the need to take the wicked and have them serve a righteous cause."

"Zoey's not wicked. Killing her only proves you're the evil one."

Lord Belmont sighed heavily and grinned as if he were being lectured by a toddler. "My dear friend, even if her heart hasn't rotted away as of this moment, it will soon enough," he said. "Vampires are ultimately unwanted by society, and eventually succumb to their thirst for blood, making them desperate to satiate their undying appetite. Not everyone is willing to give them what they want like you do, Master Ethan. And when the cattle refuse to be slaughtered, they are so anyway, usually with much more horrific results."

Ethan pressed his lips together. "Zoey's not like that. What if she got her hunger under control? She deserves a chance."

Lord Belmont chuckled and began slowly pacing around Ethan. "Give a vampire a chance?" he asked as if the notion were the most alien thing he'd ever heard. "I wonder, Master Ethan, would you be so eager to give her a chance at the risk of your life?"

"I already have."

"Agreeing to be her blood doll is hardly a risk worth noting. I'd have been more impressed if you'd refused yet kept her in your company." Lord Belmont then smirked and tapped Ethan on his head with his staff. "But you disagree, don't you?"

Ethan flipped him his middle finger.

Lord Belmont shrugged and, leaning on his staff, drew his face close to Ethan's. "Since we still have time to enjoy one another's company, what do you say we test this hypothesis of yours?"

"That I'd risk my life to give Zoey a chance?"

Lord Belmont nodded.

"What did you have in mind?"

"I assume you are a man who enjoys a round of cards," the lich said, pulling out the deck Ethan had been using at the tavern, cards that he'd forgotten he'd stuffed in his pocket when he took Zoey back upstairs. "I thought perhaps you'd care to play a game."

A tiny wellspring of hope bubbled in Ethan's soul. "I would if we're playing for Zoey's life."

"And what of yours?"

"I'll gamble with mine if that's what it takes to make it happen."

"I'd expect no less," he said. The lich then riffled through the cards before pulling out two clubs and a heart. "Pick the heart three times in a row, and we'll say that's a win for you."

"And if I lose?"

"You die, of course," Lord Belmont said. "But since you're convinced you're going to die anyway, let's make it even more interesting."

"More interesting than being killed?"

The lich nodded as he idly danced a card around his fingers. "I'd planned on executing you quickly, painlessly," he said. "But to give you actual stakes that matter, if you play for Zoey and lose, I keelhaul you."

"What's that?"

"Strap you beneath my ship as we set sail so the barnacles on the hull tear your flesh to ribbons, and your blood attracts every shark around for a hundred miles," he said. "If you're lucky, you'll only last an hour."

Ethan cringed at the description. Despite the graphic images running through his mind, he knew he had to play, not only for a chance at freedom for himself, but for Zoey. He hadn't come this far only to die now. Sure, lots of people had probably said those words before and ended up not saying any more, but he was one damn lucky bastard. He had the stats to prove it.

What were the odds of picking three in a row, one in three, was it? That couldn't be too hard. No, wait. That wasn't right. Ethan closed his eyes and shook his head, trying to work out the math. All he succeeded in doing was giving himself a headache. Stupid eight intellect.

"Shall we play, then, Master Ethan?" the lich asked, shuffling the three cards with the grace and speed of a seasoned dealer. "Or do you wish to concede your argument to me and admit that a vampire is not worth the risk?"

Ethan steeled his spirit, sucked in a breath, and readied himself for the luckiest game he'd ever played. "Alright," he said. "Let's do it."

"Wonderful!" Lord Belmont said. He then turned to a skeletal guard and motioned toward one of the side halls. "Have the lovely Miss Zoey brought in. She'll want to see this."

The skeleton clacked all seven of his teeth together, after which Lord Belmont laughed and waved him off. "Of course, keep her in chains. Now go."

The next couple of minutes were spent in silence. Eventually, Zoey, shackled at the wrists and ankles and gagged with a dirty cloth, hobbled into the room. On each side of her stood creatures with pale skin, milky white eyes, and long claws that dripped a thick black substance. The moment the monsters saw Ethan, they lunged at him, hissing and spitting, only to be frozen in place by Lord Belmont's hand.

"Stay." When they did, he gave an exasperated sigh. "Ghasts. Terrible at basic manners, but fantastic at killing your enemies. What can you do?"

Zoey looked at Ethan with sorrow, but Ethan tried his best to return a look of confidence. "We're going to be okay," he said. "I promise."

"That's the spirit," Lord Belmont said. He then shuffled the three cards he had one more time before fanning them out to Ethan facedown. "Choose."

Ethan studied all three, trying to find some sort of clue as to which the heart was. To his dismay, he saw nothing that told him which card was which. After what felt like an eternity, Ethan shut his eyes and reminded himself to trust the luck. "The one on the left."

"My left or yours?"

"Mine."

The lich casually flipped the card over, and lo and behold, the heart popped up. "Well done, Master Ethan," he said. "I'll tell you what, to keep the point going: if you quit now, I'll let you go with my blessing, provided you never come back here again."

"And Zoey?"

"Why, she stays, of course," Lord Belmont said, dropping his hand on her head. "I wouldn't dream of giving her up so easily."

Ethan paused. He could walk away, and since he still had a ship, albeit a small one, he could potentially find a crew and win the race. It's not as if he knew her all that well, he told himself. It's not as if she hadn't backstabbed him.

Ethan snorted, disgusted with himself for even considering.

"No way," he said. "Zoey's coming with me. End of story."

"A compassionate lad, I see," he said. "Very commendable. Your loyalty, too, but as for your intelligence in the matter, I must say, I find it sorely lacking. The odds are not in your favor."

"Shuffle the damn cards, and let's get this over with."

"As you wish, Master Ethan."

The lich shuffled the cards once more, and once they were fanned out a second time, Ethan didn't bother looking at all. "Middle," he said. He then added with a chuckle. "My middle."

"The middle it is," Lord Belmont replied. After he flipped the card over, the lich whistled. "My, my, my. This has become quite the contest, has it not? Care to hear my next offer?"

"Only if it's about you letting Zoey go right now."

The lich patted Ethan on the shoulder before tousling his hair. "How you jest, Master Ethan!" he said. "No, I thought perhaps I'd sponsor you at the Grand Regatta."

"Say again?"

"The race," he said. "That is where you are headed, is it not? To race against Azrael and win a precious soul?"

Ethan cocked his head, and his mouth twisted. "How do you know about that?"

"I told you. I've been around a long, long time," he said. He then clapped Ethan heartily on the shoulder. "What do you say? You walk out of here right now, and I will send you with a skeletal crew as fine as any other out there. I'll even have my shipwright tend to your sails and rigging, so she'll cut through the water as if the gods themselves have blessed your ship. I'd wager even a fool asleep at the helm could win that race, then."

Zoey tried to speak, but the gag performed admirably and turned her words into unintelligible mush. Surprisingly, Lord Belmont gestured to one of his guards who promptly removed it.

"Would you like to add to this conversation, my dear?" he asked.

"Take the offer," she said with an unnatural calm. "One of us needs to get out of here."

"We're both getting out of here," Ethan said. "I win one more time, and we both get to leave."

"That you do," Lord Belmont chimed in. "Lose, however, and you both die."

"I know, but—"

Before Ethan could finish, Zoey quickly cut him off, her voice dripping with disgust. "Ethan, you're pathetic. You know that? Absolutely pathetic."

"What?" Ethan stammered, completely caught off guard.

"You're pathetic," she repeated. "Are you this stupid back home, too? A girl hints at some ass, and you become her bitch? I bet it doesn't even take that much, does it? A kiss? A smile? Hell, I bet if we were back home, I could get you to do whatever I wanted, whenever I wanted, and I wouldn't even need to get your stupid name right."

"Testy, testy," the lich said, shaking a finger at her. "Lover's quarrel?"

"I'd rather be drawn and quartered than have to kiss him again," she spat.

Ethan straightened, snapping himself out of the shock that had grabbed him. "Zoey, why are you being like this?"

"Don't, 'Zoey, why are you being like this?' to me," she said, mocking his tone. "There's no us, remember? I said that from the start. You were my toy. My useless, stupid toy that I should never have decided to play with."

"But—"

"But nothing, Ethan. I figured since we're both going to die, I wanted to die with a clear conscience, and that means not letting you toss your life away because you've got some white-knight complex."

The room fell silent, aside from the raspy breathing of the ghasts. In the light of Zoey's rant, Ethan had a lot to think about, a lot he didn't want to think about. He couldn't understand why she'd turned on him so viciously, and the more he tried to work it out, the more he felt his soul wilt and his shoulders fall.

"Perhaps you could make a decision before the oceans dry? Or am I the one being too optimistic thinking that might be something you could manage?"

"I'll play," Ethan whispered.

Lord Belmont snapped back as if he'd been cracked with a whip. "You will? Even after all that? Are you certain?"

Ethan bit on a knuckle as he made sure himself. "Yeah," he finally said. "It's the right thing to do."

"Very well, Master Ethan. Very well indeed," Lord Belmont said. He then smirked at Zoey and added, "Let the record show, Master Ethan is a far, far more noble being than you will ever be."

The lich shuffled the three cards one last time. Once finished, Ethan clasped his hands in front of his face and bounced lightly on the balls of his feet. This was it. All he had to do was win one more time.

"Left—No! Middle again!" he shouted.

Lord Belmont tilted his head as if he were a judge being asked to rule on a challenge. After a few seconds of thinking, he finally nodded to himself. "For the record," he said slowly. "State which one you want. I'll have none of this tomfoolery."

"Middle," Ethan said again confidently.

Lord Belmont flipped out the middle card. Two of clubs.

"No," Ethan said, gasping.

Even the lich seemed surprised. He revealed the other cards, and the five of hearts was indeed on the left. "And so the game ends," he said with a shrug. He then pulled out his pistol and gave Ethan a two-fingered salute. "You are a gentleman of the highest order, Master Ethan. I'll spare you the keelhaul."

With that, he pointed the weapon at Ethan's chest and pulled the trigger.

Chapter XVI
The Bone Room

THE SHOT STRUCK Ethan in the chest and blasted a hole out the back.

It hurt. A lot. But only for a second.

Ethan fell, striking his head on the cold floor. He could feel his skin grow warm and sticky. His vision dimmed, and the world seemed to stretch far away. He heard Zoey scream, and a moment later, she was kneeling at his side. Tears ran down her cheeks unabated, and she tried to cradle his face as best she could.

"Damnit, Ethan," she sobbed. "You were supposed to leave."

Everything faded to black, though his hearing lingered for a few more seconds. During that time, he heard Zoey struggle, and then Lord Belmont's commanding, though distant, voice. "Throw his body in the bone room. We'll raise him in the morning with the others."

Ethan wasn't sure how much time passed before his next conscious thought. Maybe it was only a couple of seconds. Or an hour. Hell, a century, for all he knew. What he was sure of, trapped in a void, was that death wasn't so bad. He'd always expected that if there were an afterlife, it would have more, well, stuff. Not any sort of stuff in particular, but at least some sort of stuff. Clouds. Angels. Trumpets. Ferrymen. Valkyries. Pitchforks, even.

But where he was had none of that. All that existed was him, or rather, his thoughts. He discovered that little bit when he tried holding his hand in front of his face, only to find out he had neither hand nor face. He simply was.

A tiny pinprick of light drew his attention, and he willed himself toward it. It grew rapidly, and then pain stabbed his chest. He tried to grab his torso, but nothing happened. Liquid filled his mouth. He sputtered at first, but when he realized how sweet it tasted and how wonderful it made him feel, he swallowed as much as he could.

His eyes fluttered open.

Ethan found himself on his back with Maii leaning over with a healing potion grasped in his jaws, pouring what was left of it into Ethan's mouth. "What's going on?" he asked. "Where's Zoey? And how did you get here?"

"You're in the pit. I'm not sure, and I figured you'd need my help after you refused to listen to me."

"Say again?"

"Right before you reached the top of the cliff, I picked up on Lord Belmont's scent and tried to warn you," he explained. "Liches have a peculiar odor, to say the least."

"Oh," Ethan said. "We heard you barking, or whatever, but honestly, couldn't make out the whole warning bit."

"Yes, I noticed."

"Where did you get the healing potion?" Ethan asked before he sat up with a groan. His whole body ached, and a splitting headache took hold of him as well.

"In the apothecary's room," he said, pointing his muzzle up and to the right. "All sorts of things there. Thought you might want one when I tracked you down here."

Ethan reached over and scratched Maii behind the ears. "Thanks."

Maii wiggled in place and smiled. "Do that again. That felt good."

Ethan obliged. While he indulged the jackal's request, he had a look around. He'd been tossed into a square room made from mossy stone that had an angled ceiling. A single oil lamp burned steadily at the entrance, and a light mist partially obscured the floor, which was good because it gave Ethan a moment to realize he wasn't in any immediate danger when he spied the corpse nearby. And then the twenty others scattered around. And then the piles of bodies crammed against the corners.

"Oh, damn," he said. "They're all dead, right?"

Maii snorted. "They're certainly not at the peak of their physique, are they?"

"No, I mean, they're not like zombies or skeletons or wraiths or whatever else Lord Belmont has around here," Ethan explained.

Maii shook his head and dropped to his haunches. "No, they're merely bodies at this point. Which is what the lich thought you were, I might add. I, on the other hand, knew you weren't dead at all."

"You did? How?"

"Gave you a nibble," Maii said. "You tasted very much alive."

"You ate me?"

"Nibbled."

"Why?"

"Why not?" Maii countered. "I've told you, I'm not beyond eating a former master, and I was hungry. I still have a lot of growing to do, and I wasn't about to eat one of these poor chaps. That would be disgusting."

Ethan sighed and rubbed the back of his head, trying to ease the headache that still plagued him. As he did, he noted that the jackal looked even bigger than before. "Speaking of, am I imagining things, or have you grown since this morning?"

"Flattery, my good man, will get you everywhere," Maii said with a bow.

"Is that a yes?"

"I can only hope."

Though he knew that Zoey wanted to approach the subject with caution, at this point, Ethan figured if Maii wanted to do him in, he would've already. And he certainly wouldn't have helped when he didn't have to. As such, he decided to be as straight-forward as possible and get right to the point. "What are you?"

Maii gave a devilish grin. "I'm not sure I know what you mean."

"Yes, you do," Ethan said. "Out with it. You're more than you pretend to be."

Maii took to all fours before launching into a giant downward dog and yawning bigger than Ethan ever thought possible. When he was done, he looked at Ethan with amusement in his eyes. "Wouldn't you rather enjoy the surprise later on?"

"No. Now, out with it. You have to obey me."

The jackal let loose a cackling laugh. "Not on that request, I don't," he said. "Sorry, your ring isn't that strong."

Ethan frowned. "If you don't tell me, I'm sure I can make things unpleasant for you in other ways."

Maii strolled around Ethan before sitting down in front of him. "Now, now," he said. "It's for your own good that you don't."

"Why?"

"Because if you're ever forced to tell someone, you won't be able to," Maii replied.

"I think I'd rather know."

Maii huffed and gave the length of his tail a few licks before replying. "Patience is a virtue," he said once he was done. "You're proving to be an exceptional companion, and so when I'm free of this ring—"

"Wait, free?"

"Yes, free," Maii said. "You didn't think I'd be compelled by it forever, did you?"

"Well, yes, I did."

Maii chuckled. "Then I'd suggest you adopt a different attitude, quickly. But as I was saying, being in your presence has certainly helped speed my growth along. I've dined on not only a man or two, but an ettin as well. And with fate on our side, I'm hoping to help myself to a few bites of lich." Maii paused a moment to shut his eyes and groan with pleasure. "I can only imagine what that will be like. But back to the point, keep feeding me, Ethan, and you won't regret it."

"Fine, but I want you to stop trying to eat me," Ethan said.

"Nibbled," Maii corrected yet again. "And I did stop."

Ethan nodded with a huff, conceding the point. "I suppose I can't be too mad, then, especially since you did bring me a healing potion."

"Precisely," Maii said. "I think that settles any debts owed to you for a sampling of your foot."

After a brief lull, Maii spoke up once more. "Might I ask you something?"

"Sure."

"How did you survive getting shot?"

"Nine lives," Ethan said with a sheepish grin.

"You're saying you're a cat?"

"No," Ethan replied with a laugh, realizing that not everyone or everything in this world knew about the mechanics of the place. "I only meant I guess I managed to cheat death."

With the healing potion now fully coursing through his veins, Ethan felt a ton better. Slowly, he took to his feet to find that almost all the pain had gone away. That lifted his spirits, but they shot far into the heavens when he inspected his chest to see only a faded scar existed where Lord Belmont had blasted him. "Damn, that stuff works."

"That's the whole point of the potion."

Ethan chuckled. "So it is," he said. He spent a moment thinking back to what he could remember, which wasn't a lot, but it ended up being enough. "Lord Belmont has Zoey in the ritual room," he said. "That's where we've got to go."

"To save her?"

"Yes, to save her," Ethan said, put off. "What else would we go there for?"

"Only clarifying your desires," Maii said. "No need to get testy."

"Sorry."

"Think nothing of it," Maii said. "But before you go smashing down every door in the place trying to find her, might I suggest something?"

"Sure. What's that?"

"Have a plan. Even if you get to Zoey and free her, Lord Belmont will tear you apart. You've got to get his amulet and destroy that ruby above all else."

"Right. That's a good point," Ethan replied. "What do we have to work with?"

"Aside from a lot of dead bodies and whatever paltry weapons and gear we can scrounge from around here? Not a lot," Maii said. "Everything I can see looks rusted beyond use. That said, I could probably turn you invisible once or twice, but that won't last long. Not against a lich, anyway."

Ethan perked. "You can? Since when?"

"Since I dined on that bounty hunter. You're not the only one around here that grows stronger, you know."

Ethan drummed his fingers on his side for a few moments, trying to come up with something. Sadly, he was at a loss. He also realized time was not something they could afford to squander. He was about to go ahead and wing it all when he noticed a small black pouch tied to a belt of a nearby corpse. "Is that a powder bag?" he asked.

Maii trotted over and gave it a sniff. "A full one, at that."

Ethan looked around and saw a few other corpses with one as well. "All right, Maii," he said. "I think I've got an idea."

"Is it a good one?"

"Probably not," Ethan said. "But it's the only one I have."

"Well, let's hear it," Maii said with a sigh. "Maybe I can help make it into something decent."

Chapter XVII
The Ritual

ATCHOULI, SANDALWOOD, and camphor.

Those were the oils and resins burning nearby. Zoey knew there were more, but she didn't know what. She'd been chained to a stone slab that rose four feet off the floor inside an octagonal room. Its walls rose thirty feet into the air and spanning half of them, enormous stained-glass windows stretched nearly from floor to ceiling.

Three stone columns helped hold the vaulted ceiling aloft, and from them hung threadbare red-and-gold banners with a prominent family crest displayed on each. Zoey didn't know whose family the crest belonged to, but she did think that whoever embroidered the basilisk had done an outstanding job. Normally, she'd have not even given a passing thought to such things, but focusing on them now turned out to be much more pleasant than thinking about the knife currently slicing through her forearm.

This was the third cut now, and as with the previous two, Lord Belmont picked up the blood she spilled with two fingers before using it to paint symbols on her forehead as well as his upper chest.

While this took place, the lich's skeletal minions stood in a wide circle, pounding ox-skin drums with heavy, rapid blows that seemed to ignite the very air around her with energy. Adding to the noise were a half dozen other creatures, chanting along with Lord Belmont. These, at first glance, appeared to be humans, but on closer inspection, they, too, were members of the undead, albeit their bodies were in much better shape than their skeletal cohorts.

They sported whole bodies with mostly intact skin that had been painted white. Their eyes, cloudy and gray, stared vacantly, and the foul odor wafting off them was enough to drop even the most seasoned undertaker.

Lord Belmont's thin black dagger flashed over her face, but this time, instead of it carving into one of her arms, she felt it open the side of her neck.

Zoey instinctively jerked away, but she didn't get far. The chains that held her were far too strong and far too tight. The side of her neck grew warm and sticky, and she sucked in a breath through clenched teeth and decided to have at her executioner one last time.

"There's something you should know before I die," she said, turning her head to face him.

Lord Belmont paused, dagger in hand, and looked down at her inquisitively. "And what would that be, my dear?"

"You've got something on your face," she said a split second before she spit on him.

The lich didn't flinch. He didn't even bother wiping it off. He looked at her with pity for a moment before gesturing to someone she couldn't see. "Light the brazier."

A ghast appeared near her feet, torch in hand. With it, it lit an iron brazier that was filled with oil-soaked coals. Flames immediately shot upward. Flames, Zoey noted, that were a brilliant white and gave off no heat whatsoever.

Lord Belmont dropped a withered hand on the top of Zoey's head and drummed his fingers there. "Pity, isn't it, that you'll not see what great things Master Ethan will accomplish for me?"

"Screw you," Zoey said, spitting on him once more.

Again, the lich ignored what she'd done, and instead of replying or retaliating, he rose his skull-tipped staff over her body and began swinging it in a circle, keeping in beat with the rhythm of the ritual. Words, ancient and powerful, rumbled from his mouth, sounding like mighty waves crashing against a rocky shore. "*Sorogn palumili imissim aberio!*"

A tingling sensation ran across her skin, and then suddenly the inside of her chest burst with agony as if sewer rats were trapped and trying to gnaw their way out. Zoey screamed as she arched her back, tugging violently against the chains.

"*Exeribin ostellae loninxia!*"

A dark, swirling cloud of greens and yellows took shape over her, and the lich quickly made a small incision in the middle of her chest and then cut some of her hair, dabbed it in the wound, and tossed it into the fire at her feet.

"*Sinien agio!*" Another cut into her body. More hair was taken and again dipped in her blood and tossed into the flames.

A crushing weight landed on Zoey's chest, and she struggled to breathe. Her lips went numb almost instantly, as did her fingers. Consciousness, she knew, was a luxury she wouldn't have much longer. Or perhaps, unconsciousness was a blessing she'd soon enjoy.

"Ethan," she gasped.

Lord Belmont smirked. "Will never be joining you again."

The lich pulled his ruby amulet from beneath his shirt and held it over her. The gem pulsed with energy, and if she concentrated on it as hard as she could, the vampire could've sworn she heard the sounds of hundreds, if not thousands, of voices screaming in terror.

The chanting came louder and more fervent, second only to the unrelenting beat of the drums. Black tendrils rose from the ground and snaked their way up the sides of the stone slab before entwining themselves around Zoey's arm. As each one touched her skin, the area around froze over, and her tissue withered.

"Miliec anti-tigelie!"

Zoey's heart stopped. Her mouth opened wider than it ever had before as she desperately tried to take in much-needed air that never seemed to fill her lungs. Cords in her neck and limbs bulged, and her muscles strained so hard that they nearly tore themselves apart.

Something sailed through the air. Something small, canister-like.

For whatever reason, Zoey's eyes snapped to it in her final moments. She watched it, mesmerized, as it fell into the brazier.

A split second later, the world erupted in fire and flying metal.

Chapter XVIII
The Ruby

THE SMOKE CLEARED, and Lord Belmont, full of shrapnel, roared when his amulet was no longer in his grasp.

He spun in place, swinging his skull-tipped scepter through the air as if it would connect with the head of whoever had done this. His wild attack struck nothing, and for a brief second, his furious eyes took in only the broken remains of skeletons torn apart by the blast.

But then the sounds of panicked footfalls drew his attention, and he spun one last time to see someone zipping out of the ritual room. The thief was fast, but not fast enough.

Lord Belmont leveled his staff, eager to watch the dark energies contained within and rip flesh from bone. *"Tollerium carne!"*

To his utmost frustration, while the skull's eye sockets glowed briefly, nothing else happened. The staff's energy was still drained, having been spent on the now-interrupted ritual, and it would need time to recharge.

The lich snarled. The power that usually flowed through him might have been diverted for a short while, but he was far from helpless, and the thief was about to find out how much the undead admiral was still capable of.

Lord Belmont rapped the bottom of his staff three times against the stone floor, and with each strike, he called upon words of power that had been embedded into the very stone of his fortress. "*Claudere. Portas. Statimae!*"

Off in the distance, faint but distinct, the sounds of rattling chain and the heavy crash of the portcullis slamming down filtered through the air. This was followed by the thunderous clapping of massive oak doors swinging shut throughout the castle, effectively cutting off all escape routes for the intruder.

"Stay here," Lord Belmont growled to a pair of ghasts nearby. He then pointed to Zoey, who was still breathing, but currently unconscious. "And she'd better be alive when I return. If I find a single toothmark on her skin, the two of you will have a new appreciation for eternal torment."

With that, Lord Belmont tore out of the room. As he raced down the hall and up the spiral stairs that led back to the main floor, the lich scolded himself for being so careless. Though he'd sent scouts to the vampire's ship to search for more crew, and he himself had made considerable effort to sniff out any other men or women who might have joined Zoey and her blood doll in their foolish crusade, he apparently had not been thorough enough.

No matter, he thought. He'd catch them soon enough, and he'd ensure that the tales of their upcoming torture wouldn't be forgotten for a thousand years by the time he was done. It was high time, he decided, that the world saw exactly what he was capable of and what the consequences would be for those who didn't kneel before him.

At the top of the stairs, he ran into the sunroom right as his quarry was leaving. He whipped his pistol from his belt and took a shot, but instead of taking the head off the thief, the bullet blew apart a marble bust by the doorway.

"Run, coward!" the lich yelled as he gave chase once more. "It'll only fuel my hatred of you."

On it went, through the debris-filled galley and then the ruined dining hall. Every time Lord Belmont thought he had him pinned or finally had a clear shot, luck interfered. As frustrating as that was, the lich knew luck only lasted for so long. More important, his guard would soon be reassembled, having healed the damage suffered by the explosion and thus would join the hunt.

The pursuit wound its way up to the second floor, and then the third, taking tours through the servant's quarters as well as what was once the library. However, once the lich realized that there was somewhat of a method to the thief's madness when it came to how he was taking his turns, he knew they would soon end up in the throne room.

Lord Belmont grinned to himself and instead of pursuing directly, ducked into a side hall before racing down a small spiral staircase that the cooks of old once used. Once back on the first floor, it was only a short race to the throne room. Right as he entered from one side, Ethan burst through a doorway on the other, his head turned over his shoulder.

"Master Ethan," the lich growled, though his tone did carry a hint of respect to it. "You're proving to be troublesome."

Ethan's eyes went wide with fright as he spun back around. Lord Belmont aimed and fired. Though his shot was not as lethal as he'd hoped, the lich still managed to score a hit. The bullet tore through Ethan's outer right hip, sending him sprawling behind a column.

"I must say, Master Ethan," the lich said, as he made a steady approach while his pistol magically reloaded itself. "You are indeed a loyal one, right to the end, aren't you?"

"I'm going to be your end if you don't let her go," he shot back.

The lich chuckled, and then he did a second time when a dozen armed skeletons came into the room from different entrances. "You'll serve as a good example to the rest of the world," he said. "I want you to know that your death will have a purpose."

"Sorry, I don't have any plans on dying," Ethan replied.

"We can't always get what we want," Lord Belmont said, rounding the column Ethan hid behind. "And now you die. For good, this time."

The lich raised his weapon, and Ethan threw the amulet with a sidearm toss. Seeing his prized possession sail through the air, Lord Belmont couldn't help but follow its arc across the throne room and into the jaws of an oversized jackal.

"Run, Maii!" Ethan shouted. "Just get it out of here!"

"What!" Lord Belmont spun around, only to find that Ethan had disappeared. Instinctively, he took a shot where the man had once been propped up, but his bullet hit nothing.

"Find him! Tear him apart the moment you do!" Lord Belmont screamed at his servants. "I'll take care of the dog."

The chase renewed, and his quarry this time was even faster than before. The jackal darted through the citadel with such speed and cunning, the lich was forced to admit that he nearly lost him twice. Soon, however, Lord Belmont began shutting doors and locking them with magical wards as he closed in on the animal. Sure, in the short term, he fell further and further behind, but it didn't take long for this proverbial noose he'd created to tighten. Eventually, he cornered the animal in the tearoom.

"Hand it over, pup," Lord Belmont said, marching steadily toward the creature who was currently hiding under a small, round table. When the jackal didn't move, the lich took out his pistol and fired. The bullet, aimed precisely where he'd intended, ripped through the tabletop and zipped by the animal's head, missing it by less than an inch.

"I know you can understand me," the lich said, narrowing his eyes. "Now bring me my amulet or things will get much, much worse."

The jackal tensed and glanced both left and right before sighing with resignation. He then eased out from beneath the table, amulet held firmly by its chain in his mouth. The animal barely took two steps before Lord Belmont's blood raged. He bolted forward, closing the distance between himself and the jackal in less than a second, tossing chairs and tables left and right in the process. He then swiped the amulet from the jackal's mouth with his clawed fingers and held it up to confirm what he'd already come to realize.

"A fake?" he muttered. "A fake! A FAKE!"

Whatever cheap illusion had been cast on the amulet faded. Now, instead of regaining his precious artifact made of gold and ruby, Lord Belmont had in hand a simple copper pendant on an even simpler chain. For several seconds, the lich stared at it in both horror and fury, but when he saw the jackal trying to slip away and realized his staff hummed with energy, he sprang into action.

"You're not going anywhere," he sneered. The lich whipped his staff overhead in a high arc with one hand and extended his other with fingers outstretched.

Shadowy tendrils sprang from the ground and wrapped themselves around the jackal's legs. The animal struggled and yelped, trying to break free, but the coils grew stronger and more numerous. In a few short breaths, they pulled him to the ground where he lay helpless.

"You think you're so clever, don't you?" Lord Belmont said, walking over to him. Initially, he'd planned on caving in the animal's skull with his staff, simply to release all of his frustrations, but when he got within a couple of feet of the creature, Lord Belmont paused and cocked his head to one side. "Well, well, well," he said slowly and with a devious smile. "Seems as if the amulet wasn't the only thing with an illusion around here."

The jackal lunged forward in a panic, vainly trying to break free, but went nowhere.

"Speak, pup," Lord Belmont said. "You can stop the charade. We both know what you are."

The jackal relaxed and slowly turned his head so that he was facing the lich directly. "I know you're without your ruby," he said. "And I know you won't last much longer."

Lord Belmont nodded but was unconcerned about any of it. "You may be right about the first part, at least for now," he said. "As for the latter? I'm afraid I'm going to live much, much longer than you think. Moreover, you can serve me for the rest of time as well."

The lich lowered his staff and pointed its head at the animal. He spoke softly, carefully intoning every syllable in the spell he was casting. After all, taking over a creature as powerful and magnificent as this one was, even if it was young, had to be done with the utmost care.

"*Ego dominum puppatae, etu perpetumas.*"

To the animal's credit, he resisted being dominated for longer than Lord Belmont had anticipated, but not by much.

Not by much at all.

The spell of invisibility finally wore off, and though it had lasted long enough for Ethan to avoid being shot—again—by Lord Belmont, Ethan would've loved for it to have lasted at least another five minutes. Hell, as long as he was wishing, an hour would've been nice.

As luck would have it, Ethan flickered back into plain sight as he rounded the corner to a long hall. It had dozens of decorative suits of armor flanking each side and beautiful tapestries depicting centuries' worth of history hanging from the walls. Some looked like religious scenes, with robed monks wearing looks of penance upon their faces and halos upon their heads, while others showed kings and queens throughout the ages sitting on thrones or leading vast armies. Ethan had always had a soft spot for medieval history, and he'd have liked to check them out a bit more if it hadn't been for the whole rescue-Zoey-from-the-lich thing. That, and two skeletal guards who'd just burst into the hall from a side passage, each with a cutlass in hand.

With at least a dozen of such things chasing him from behind, Ethan did the only thing that seemed smart: he charged.

Ethan's rusty sword, a weapon he'd lifted off an unfortunate soul in the bone room, flashed through the air. The skeleton nimbly shot to the right before issuing a thrust of his own that nicked Ethan's ear.

The skeleton dodges!
A skeleton grazes you!

Ethan bolted to the side, keeping the undead minion he was fighting between himself and the other, and attacked again, this time trying to anticipate where the skeleton might end up jumping. To his delight, he succeeded. His blade cut across the monster's forearms, hacking each one off a few inches below the elbow.

Skeleton hit!
Skeleton moderately wounded!
Critical failure!
Weapon dropped!

Ethan smiled. It was nice to hear that in reference to someone else for a change. The next exchange, which was very much lop-sided in Ethan's favor, saw him cleaving through the skeleton's head with a well-placed backhand.

Skeleton killed!

You feel slightly more experienced!

The remaining skeleton, now no longer having to deal with the other as an impromptu shield between it and Ethan, lunged forward. Its first attack sliced through nothing but air, and Narrator reported it as such, but the second managed to hit Ethan. Though he caught the creature's blade on his, as their two swords became locked together, the skeleton caught Ethan with a left cross that left his cheek bruised.

A skeleton lightly wounds you!

Ethan beat a hasty retreat, keeping his guard up, until the momentary daze wore off. The skeleton, however, pressed its advantage. Sadly for it, more than it should have. It tried to take Ethan with a low thrust to the gut, which Ethan knocked away before hacking it twice: one that chopped a limb at the shoulder and then a follow up that severed its spine between ribcage and pelvis.

Skeleton killed!
You feel slightly more experienced!

"You're damn skippy!" Ethan said, feeling quite good about himself. The words had no sooner left his mouth when the arm of the first began to drag itself back to its former body. "Oh, come on," Ethan moaned, backing away. "That's not fair at all."

Then more skeletons came from behind, six altogether, and after briefly glancing at their fallen comrades, spread out shoulder-to-shoulder, and marched toward Ethan.

"And that's really not fair," Ethan said before spinning on his heels and bolting away.

At the end of the hall, he hooked left and ran through an inner courtyard that had a large fountain in the middle before entering a door at the far side. There, he went left down another tapestry-laden hall before making a buttonhook and racing up a narrow spiral staircase and finding himself in a study.

"Hot damn," Ethan said, realizing where he was. Or rather, realizing where he was in accordance with Maii's instructions on how to get to the apothecary room.

He shot across the study and plowed through the door on the right. From there, he only had to make a short run down an L-shaped corridor with servant quarters on each side before he reached his destination.

The apothecary room looked about as big as a small shop at a busy strip mall. A couple of long tables stood in the middle with dozens of glass beakers, flasks, and distillation columns, along with burners, rubber tubing, and stands sitting on their tops. On all sides of the room were tall wooden shelves. Most had reagents carefully arranged in some method Ethan wasn't privy to. However, one side had a bookshelf filled with countless books and tomes. It also happened to be the shelf closest to the door.

Immediately, Ethan shut the door behind him, flipped the latch, and then toppled the bookshelf to create a makeshift barricade. When it crashed on to the floor, Ethan wondered if that wasn't the best of ideas. If every skeleton, creature, monster, and lich in this fortress didn't know where he was before, they certainly did now.

"No time to worry about that, Ethan," he said to himself. "Got to make some dragon's breath and melt this gem."

Focused on the task, Ethan pulled the amulet from under his shirt and set it inside one of the empty beakers on the table. He then raced to one of the shelves that stored powders and began sifting through all their names, looking for...for...

Crap, what *was* he looking for?

Ethan swore a few times as he shook his head, trying to remember what Maii had said. "It's very simple," Ethan mimicked in his best jackal voice. "All you need to do is mix...mix..."

His mind went blank, and then even blanker still when something slammed into the door.

"Come on! Think! Think! Think!" Ethan said, his heart pounding rapidly in his chest. He started snatching random jars filled with metallic powders. He knew he didn't need any of the roots or herbs on the other shelves, and he didn't need any of the liquids, either. Or did he?

The door rattled a few times before something hit it again and then a third time. Each blow reverberated loudly in Ethan's ears, and he had no doubt the door would be exploding into a hail of splinters in short order.

"You got this. You got this," Ethan said, bouncing on the balls of his feet. "You only need two things? Right? Yeah, that's it. 'All you need is something and something, Ethan.'"

His mind drifted further into the conversation he had had with the jackal, hoping it would spark his memory. "What if I get it wrong?"

"If you're lucky, nothing," he answered himself. "But seeing how you've no idea what you're doing, with all those reagents at your disposal, you could blow up half the castle for all I know. So, try and not be, well, you, and do something stupid."

Again, the door boomed. Ethan snapped his head up in time to see it split down one side. A half second later, another hit came. This time, however, it didn't seem as if it was done with a battering ram. It was an ax blade that cut into the wood, further splitting the door.

On the verge of panic, Ethan wished to God he'd specced a little more into his intellect from the start. Maybe then he'd have been able to remember what Maii had said, or at least have his memory spark when he read the labels to all the jars. Or hell, he could have turned out to be an expert in *Chemistry*, at which point he could've mixed a miniature neutron bomb with everything in the room.

But no, all he knew he was good for at this point was to do something dumb.

"Something dumb," Ethan repeated as a dumb, desperate plan sprung in his mind.

Immediately, Ethan bolted to one of the tables and snagged a hefty iron pot and slammed it down on the other table with the amulet. At that point, he tossed the amulet in, and as the door came under a renewed, relentless attack by both ram and ax, Ethan grabbed everything that he could that looked cool or smelled downright terrible (of which there was a lot) and tossed it into the pot.

He threw in powders that glinted in the light or looked as dark as a demon's heart. Potions that bubbled and churned were poured without a second thought (except for a small healing potion he found, which he promptly tucked away), and herbs that felt as if they wiggled in his fingers also found their way into the brew.

"Come on. Come on," he said, bouncing on the balls of his feet. "I just need one colossal, lethal fail, just this once."

The door burst, sending wood fragments flying in all directions. As the skeletons poured in, shoving each other forward as they stumbled through the narrow doorway and were tripped up by the overturned bookshelf, Ethan glanced at his homemade brew, hoping it was about to do something.

The surface, a dark swirl of browns and greens, bubbled. Wisps of gray smoke took to the air, and with them came a nearly overpowering acrid smell. In his heart, Ethan felt as if it were about to do something—or would if he had a few more minutes. Sadly, he knew there was no way he'd last that long.

A flicker of light caught his attention. A couple of feet away, an oil lamp burned steadily.

Ethan immediately snatched it up, and he sucked in a breath. "God, I hope all you need is a nudge."

The closest skeleton leaped toward him right as he threw the oil lamp into the pot and dove for cover.

Chapter XXIX
Released

THE GAST LEANED over Zoey.

It drew back its thin lips to reveal a maw of razor-sharp, crooked teeth. Putrid goo dripped from its mouth, splattering the vampire on the cheek. Though she teetered on the edge of death, thoroughly dazed, she realized she didn't have much time before the monster decided to make a snack out of her, despite Lord Belmont's orders not to.

"You really need a mint," she said, turning her head to the side and coughing.

The ghast answered with a snarl before grabbing her head and lunging toward her, jaw open. Its teeth bit down where her neck met her shoulder. Zoey screamed and tried to pull away, but the chains held fast. The ghast whipped its head to the side, tearing a large amount of flesh in the process and sending what little blood Zoey had left inside of her flying across the room.

Before the monster could take a second bite, a faraway explosion thundered, causing the room to shake and debris to fall from the ceiling. The ghost froze in place and trembled for a half second before screeching like a banshee and disintegrating into dust.

Zoey lost consciousness a few seconds later.

She awoke to being shaken by familiar hands. Her eyes opened, and though her vision was dark and blurry, and all she could see were the vague forms of stone columns in the ritual room as well as the lanterns that hung from them, she knew something was different. Not just with the room, but with herself. She felt whole again.

Weak, but whole. Her senses that had been dulled for so long had returned. If she concentrated, she could hear the sounds of another breathing nearby, and if she took in a slow, deep breath, she could pick up the unique scent of cedar from the ship she and Ethan had arrived on.

Had Ethan succeeded in destroying the ruby? Was she free of Lord Belmont's curse? She couldn't come up with any other explanation and thus dared to hope. But at the same time, she wondered if blood loss was taking its toll and all of this was a figment of her imagination.

If it was, it could be worse, she thought.

"Zoey, for the love of all, please be alive," Ethan said, suddenly appearing in her view. His form, like everything else around her, was hard to focus on, but there was no way she could ever mistake anyone else for him. She knew that adorkably sweet, panicked voice, and she definitely knew the soft touch his fingers gave as he stroked the sides of her face.

"I'm alive," she said. Though she managed the words, they took all she had, and she nearly passed out again just getting them into existence. "But how are you not dead?"

"Took *Nine Lives* Rank One," he said. "Then used all my luck to not die in that bomb I set off."

Zoey gave a pained laugh. "I can't believe you took that stupid perk," she said. "Check that. I can."

"That stupid perk is going to save your life, too," he said, taking her jab in stride.

"Does this mean you destroyed the gem?"

"Yeah," he replied, nodding. "And half the apothecary room, and the hall leading to it, and whatever was on the floor below. Now, hang on. I'm going to get you out of there."

Ethan kissed her lightly on the forehead before disappearing. Zoey tried smiling at the gesture but ended up wincing as a massive headache landed on her. She managed to lift her head off the stone slab long enough to look herself over. The flesh where the ghast had bitten her had been turned to ribbons, and both her arms still had deep cuts where her blood had been spilled. Chances were, she knew, even with the curse gone, she didn't have long to live. Vampires were tough, tougher than most, but they were far from immortal.

"I don't know where the key is," Ethan said. His eyes then scanned her body, and his face went pale. "You...I—I don't know what to do."

Zoey summoned what remaining strength she had. "It's okay," she said. "I'll be fine."

"No, you won't," Ethan said. "You're a mess."

"I know, but at least I'll die free of that curse."

Ethan grabbed her by the shoulders. "Don't you dare say that. No one's dying. I'm getting you out of here."

Zoey smiled at him, wishing he could know the peace that was now settling in her heart. "We all have to eventually," she said. "Trust me. I'm a nurse. I know. It'll be okay."

Ethan shook his head. "No, Zoey. I'm not leaving you."

"Knock that fairytale nonsense off right now," she said. "Just do me a favor after you've gone: When you beat Death in the race, have him agree to a double or nothing."

"What?"

"Tell him you'll play again," she explained. "For your dog and the kids I wasn't able to save."

Ethan intertwined his fingers with hers and squeezed. "You can't ask me to do that," he said. "Look how far we've made it together."

"I know," she said. "And thank you for reminding me what good people are capable of. But there's nothing you can do for me now. Even if you get me free, I'll only slow you down. Now get out of here while you still can."

"Correction, we've got to get out of here while we still can."

Zoey groaned, and she was about to continue to argue when Ethan leaned over and pressed his neck against her lips. The warmth of his skin sent a shiver through her body, and her mouth watered as she felt his blood pulsing through his arteries.

"No, Ethan. Don't," she said, fighting the urge to feast.

"It's the only way to heal you," he said.

"I won't be able to stop," she replied as she turned away. "It's not going to be like back on the ship."

"I know."

"I don't want to kill you."

Ethan clamped his fingers under her jaw and forced her head back toward him. "I know you want it."

"I—"

"Bite."

The voracious urge that had been building in her soul took over, and before Zoey could think, let alone say, anything else, she sank her fangs into his flesh. Her teeth easily cut into his neck and jugular.

She'd only managed a nick, but it was more than enough. Blood, sweet, satisfying, and most of all, rejuvenating, flowed into her mouth. With each gulp she took, the more ravenous she felt, and the harder and faster she drained the life from him.

Suddenly, Ethan threw an arm across her. To her surprise, it wasn't one that was trying to push himself away, but rather, he sent his hand under her shoulders and across her back, locking himself to her as his body convulsed and grew weaker.

Zoey's heart pounded against her chest, stronger and faster with each passing moment. Her breathing increased, too, but each breath she took carried a burning anger, a desire for revenge against Lord Belmont for all that he'd done to her. And now that his phylactery had been destroyed, she vowed to make him understand what a true creature of the night was capable of.

"Zoey," Ethan gasped. "Please."

She heard his words but didn't stop. She worked her jaws, scissoring her teeth so she opened up more of his veins. His blood flowed into her mouth faster than she could take it in, spilling out of her lips. She could feel it roll down her cheeks and hear it splatter on the stone slab beneath her.

Life radiated through her body. Her wounds closed, and she could feel strength she'd thought she'd lost forever return. As intoxicating as that power was, it didn't hold a candle to the euphoric feeling that intensified with every drop of Ethan's blood that she swallowed.

"Zoey." Ethan's voice barely came out as a whisper now. His other hand feebly clutched her chest as he tried to push himself free—instincts, she knew, driving his actions now. The instinct to survive at all costs. It would only grow stronger as his body grew weaker and drew closer to death.

It always did.

Ethan's struggles became more frantic, and Zoey locked her jaws, intent on feeding off every last drop of life he had to offer. The beast within needed it. Demanded it. And even when she was finished, and he was nothing but a desiccated husk, she'd still not be fully satiated.

Then he did something completely unexpected. He calmed, ceased his struggles, dropped his hand on her forehead before brushing back her hair exactly the same way he had the first time they'd shared a bed together, when she'd laid her head on his chest and fell into a blissful sleep listening to his heartbeat while thinking about how much she'd missed simply having someone to be close with.

At that moment, Zoey regained control and immediately let go of Ethan, who promptly collapsed backward in a heap.

"Ethan? Ethan!" she yelled, but he didn't answer or move.

Panicked, Zoey yanked against the chains, stronger than she ever had before, but despite her renewed strength, they still held. She forced herself to lower her head and relax. She needed to be at complete peace if she was going to shapeshift—assuming she could now. Whether she had regained that strength or if the lingering bits of Lord Belmont's curse still remained had yet to be seen.

Zoey shut her eyes as her mind freed itself from any ties to the physical world. Her body grew cold and distant, and a slight hissing noise filled her ears before she felt as if she were floating through the air. When she realized her transformation had been successful, and she was currently floating a few feet above the slab as a white mist, excitement got the better of her. Her body reformed, and she crashed back to the stone with the wind knocked out of her lungs.

"Kraken spit, that hurt," she said, gasping and laughing as she clutched her sides. A second later, she rolled off the slab and onto her feet, fully expecting to see Ethan's lifeless body sprawled across the floor. Instead, what she was greeted with was Ethan with his back propped up against the wall. His eyes were half open, and he had an open flask in hand.

"Potion of healing," he said, slurring his words and lifting it for her to see. "Not so stupid now, am I?"

Zoey laughed and cried at the same time as she darted over and knelt at his side. "No, Ethan, that was incredibly stupid," she said. "You're lucky I stopped."

Ethan sucked in a breath before polishing off what red liquid remained. "Luck, my lovely Zoey," he said, a little stronger and less drunkenly than before, "is my primary stat."

Zoey laughed and cleared her eyes before kissing him. "So it is," she said. She then smacked him on the top of the head. "But you're still as dumb as a sea cucumber."

"Yeah, maybe," he said with a shrug. "But I'm your sea cucumber."

Zoey raised an eyebrow and drew back one corner of her mouth. "You sure about that?"

"Since I just let you feast on me, I damn well better be," he said.

Zoey laughed again and helped him to his feet. "You are," she said, patting his chest. "But before we take a trip down lover's lane, what say we get out of here?"

"I say that's a damn fine idea."

Chapter XXX
The Duel

Moderately wounded.

THAT'S WHAT ETHAN'S character sheet said when he had checked his health status as they climbed the spiral staircase that led out of the ritual room. From what Zoey reminded him of, that wasn't remotely as bad as being gravely wounded when the ettin had smacked him, but he still hurt, a lot, despite the healing potion he'd chugged.

"The next addition to our party needs to be a healer," he said, wincing about halfway up the stairs.

"Most aren't too fond of vampires," she said. "You know, holy versus unholy and all."

"Most doesn't mean all," he countered. "I still think we should find one."

"Point taken," Zoey replied. When they reached the top of the stairs, she paused a few feet inside the throne room and looked around. "Where's Maii?"

"Maii is right here," came a cold, sinister voice. "Though, I'm not sure you'll recognize him now."

Ethan and Zoey pivoted. Standing a dozen yards away, leaning hunched on his staff, but looking thoroughly pissed off, was Lord Belmont. His left hand clutched his pistol at his side while the fingers on his right drummed on the staff's wooden shaft. The sparkle of light that had once been in his eyes was gone, and they now looked dull and cloudy. There seemed to be a hint of frailty to Lord Belmont's stature as well, as if he were an ancient plaster cast a single strike away from disintegrating. Yet despite that, the most worrisome thing aside from his confident demeanor was this monstrous thing at his side.

The creature stood nearly four feet at the shoulder and more than half of that wide. It sported a white coat of slick fur that held intermittent spots of teal with dozens of raven-black spikes sticking out along its back and limbs. A long tongue dangled from its mouth, snaking its way over a maw full of jagged teeth that looked like they could snap rods of iron with ease. Claws like daggers protruded from all four of its feet, and at the end of its elongated tail was another clawed hand that looked as deadly as the rest.

Zoey's eyes grew to the size of dreadnaughts. "Holy hell," she muttered. "He's an ahuizotl."

Ethan swallowed but was unable to rid himself of the hard lump in his throat. "Wasn't that one of the things you warned me about from the start?"

"Yeah," Zoey replied, her eyes never leaving Maii.

"And that's bad, right?"

Zoey nodded. "That's very, very bad."

"Worse than the lich?"

Zoey nodded again while Lord Belmont grinned broadly. "Seeing how he's with the lich, very much so."

Maii growled, saliva dripping from his mouth.

"So, um, what do we do?" Ethan asked.

"What you do, Master Ethan," Lord Belmont said, "is die."

The lich snapped his fingers, and Maii charged forward. Only a fraction of a second later, Zoey met the attack headlong and rammed their former friend with all of her vampiric might. The two became intertwined, a flurry, chaotic mess of fang and claw tearing at each other. As the bloody melee ensued, Zoey shouted at Ethan. "Kill the lich!"

Obeying more out of instinct than anything else, Ethan drew his sword, only to have to dive to the side when Lord Belmont took a shot at him with his pistol. The bullet caught Ethan right where his neck met his shoulder, carving out a painful chunk of flesh as it ripped through his body.

Lord Belmont hits!
You are seriously wounded!

Ethan rolled out of his dive, coming to rest behind a granite column. He spent a second clutching the wound with his hand. It bled profusely, and as much as it burned to the high heavens, he could tell it wasn't lethal.

"Master Ethan, well done!" Lord Belmont praised, much to Ethan's surprise. "I can't count how many people that shot would've felled!"

"Yeah, well, you're going to find out I'm full of surprises," Ethan shot back as he took to his feet. He glanced around each side of the column. On one side, he saw Lord Belmont starting his approach, and on the other, he saw Zoey and Maii still locked in a desperate struggle of dominance. As much as he wanted to delude himself into thinking Zoey had the upper hand, it only took a split second of watching to realize she was on the defensive.

"I have to commend you, Master Ethan," Lord Belmont said, drawing his attention. "It's been a while since someone has caught me unaware. I've grown sloppy over the centuries. You are a fantastic reminder that I should never underestimate an opponent."

Ethan didn't reply. Instead, he waited a few seconds until he was sure Lord Belmont was within striking distance and bolted around the column.

To Ethan's shock, dismay, and utter horror, the lich hadn't continued forward as he'd planned. Instead, Lord Belmont had retreated a few steps. Not only had he retreated, but he had his pistol up and ready, pointed squarely at Ethan's head.

"Well played, Master Ethan," the lich said. "But not well enough, I'm afraid."

Chapter XXXI
End of the Line

Lord Belmont shoots!
Lord Belmont misses!

AS NARRATOR NARRATED, debris flew in all directions as Lord Belmont's shot struck the marble column. Had Ethan not instinctively ducked a half second prior, it would've been his head that caught the bullet.

"A most splendid maneuver, Master Ethan," Lord Belmont praised. "I shall enjoy seeing what you're capable of when you reach your full potential—under my careful control, that is."

Ethan didn't reply. He glanced around the column to see Zoey now losing to Maii. Desperate to save her, Ethan flew out of his hiding spot, his legs driving him harder and faster than he had ever thought possible. Three strides into his run, out in the open and devoid of any and all cover, he prayed his luck would hold out long enough that Lord Belmont's next inevitable shot would miss, and he could reach Zoey in time to save her.

A couple of yards into it, Lord Belmont fired. His magically enchanted pistol belched smoke and flame, and Ethan's side exploded in agony. Blood sprayed across the room as his innards ruptured, and his legs gave out before he could take another step.

Ethan collapsed on the ground like a tossed rag doll. His eyes rolled up in his head, and the cords in his neck bulged. The world around him felt muted and distant, while everything he could see, from the carpet and stone tile that made up the floor to the oil lamps burning on the wall to the wooden rafters above, became blurry and surreal. In the back of his mind, he could hear Narrator saying something about being nearly dead, but that was just stating the obvious at this point, as far as he was concerned.

"Zoey," he gasped, refocusing his thoughts and rolling onto his stomach. He cried out in pain as he did, but onward he pushed, trying to reach her. His feet, however, lacked the strength to move him forward, and each time he moved even in the slightest, he swore his guts were spilling out of him.

The sounds of heavy footsteps grabbed his attention, and then one of Lord Belmont's dark leather boots appeared a few inches from Ethan's face, its salty odor assaulting his nose.

"And so the chase ends," Lord Belmont said with no small amount of satisfaction. "And it seems, as does the duel between vampire and ahuizotl."

Ethan squinted his eyes, trying to focus on what was going on, but he quickly realized he couldn't see anything anyway since Lord Belmont stood in the way.

"Ah, you want to see," the lich said, grabbing Ethan from behind with a skeletal hand, hoisted him up, and pressing a pistol against his head. "Now look, Master Ethan. I want you to witness this before you die. Even made anew, your vampire cannot prevail against your former pet."

Ethan groaned. His side and midsection felt as if someone had grabbed them with red-hot tongs and was now slowly tearing his flesh from his body. He could barely keep his head from falling, let alone raise it enough to see whatever was going on.

"Ethan. Ethan. Ethan," Lord Belmont said. "You're not going to be a poor sport about our duel, are you?"

Ethan shook his head as his eyelids grew heavy. It hurt to talk. It hurt to breathe. It hurt to be. Despite all of that, he managed a two-word, poignant reply. "Fuck. You."

Lord Belmont growled, and with one hand, he grabbed Ethan under the chin and lifted his head, all the while painfully digging his boney fingertips into Ethan's cheeks. "Watch, Ethan, as your pet chokes the life from your love," he said.

Ethan tried to shake his head, but the lich's grip was stronger than any vise, and he was forced to take in everything that was going on. Maii had Zoey pinned with his jaws clamped firmly around her throat. Zoey's mouth opened and closed as she gasped for air that she couldn't take in. Veins bulged in her head and neck, and her skin turned ashen.

"I could have her neck crushed in an instant, if I like," Lord Belmont said, leaning in close to Ethan's ear. "Do you think I should be merciful?"

"Let her go," Ethan said.

"Go?" Lord Belmont echoed. "My dear fellow, even you can't be as stupid as to believe I'd ever agree to such a demand."

Ethan opened his mouth to speak, but what little strength he had left him. His knees buckled, and Lord Belmont barely caught him before he smacked into the floor.

"Don't die on me yet, Master Ethan," Lord Belmont said, rapping Ethan lightly on the head with his pistol. "It'll only be a few more seconds before this is all over."

Ethan tried to speak again, to tell him to go to hell, but all he managed to do was roll his head to the side and nearly pass out in the process.

"Ethan!" the lich said, tone full of anger and frustration. "You're not being a good sport about this at all. Now stop dying and start watching!"

Ethan lacked the energy to do anything, but when Lord Belmont dug his pistol into Ethan's chest wound and gave it a twist, the lightning pain that shot through Ethan's body gave him a brief amount of strength and possible wit.

"You die first, asshole," Ethan muttered. In a flash, Ethan reached up, pressed the barrel of the gun into his chest with one hand, and with the other, he pulled the trigger.

The weapon fired, kicking like a rabid mule and sending a large ball of lead straight through one of Ethan's lungs and striking Lord Belmont directly in his black heart.

The lich wailed, relinquishing his grip on Ethan and falling backward. Green fire erupted from the gaping hole in his chest before fully engulfing him. As he burned, Maii lost his grip on Zoey's throat and staggered sideways. The ahuizotl's skin flared with white fire as the magical energy that compelled him to obey Lord Belmont vanished, and before Ethan could draw another breath, Maii fell over, unconscious.

At some point, Ethan realized he was on his stomach, face pressed into the cold stone floor. He took air in with ragged breaths and could feel his skin sticking to the ground. A coppery taste filled his mouth, and then the world spun as Zoey rolled him over.

"No, no, no," Zoey said as she feebly peeled back his shirt and inspected what he'd done to himself. Her fingers prodded the hole for a brief second before retracting. "Damn you, Ethan," she said, her voice cracking. "Why did you have to go do something stupid like that?"

Ethan spent what little energy he could muster into focusing on the vampire. "Seemed like a good idea at the time."

At the end of his sentence, he broke into a coughing fit that sent bright-red blood in all directions. It bubbled out of his mouth, ran down his neck, and even spattered Zoey across her frightened face.

"Come on," she said, trying to pull him upright. "We can get you to a bed. Maybe we can sew you up or find another potion."

Ethan grimaced and shook his head. "I'll never make it. We both know that."

"No! You're stronger than this!" Tears welled in her eyes and stained her cheeks. Zoey sat back on her haunches for a moment to wipe them away. "You've got a dog to save. You can't quit."

Ethan beckoned her closer with a wave of the hand. When she drew near, he grabbed her by the back of the head and pulled her down so he could kiss her one last time. As they pressed together, he shut his eyes and savored it all, while her alluring, albeit unnatural, scent reassured him everything was going to be just fine.

Dying, Ethan decided, wasn't so bad. Especially when it was in the arms of his vampire.

With his eyes still closed, he felt the tip of Zoey's tongue slide across his blood-tinged lips and then slip into his mouth. Her hands pushed against his chest, and her fingers tightened on his skin. Then she pulled away, and Ethan opened his eyes to find her staring back at him with her dark predatory gaze.

"Ethan," she said, her voice sounding full of so much power, it could send a kraken running. "I can save you, if you want."

Deep crevasses formed in his brow as Ethan tried to understand what she was saying. But with his head feeling light, and the world rapidly dissolving into a black mist, all he could do was mutter some nonsense about not quite following what she'd said.

"I can turn you," she explained. "Make you like me. But being like me isn't easy. Actually, it sucks a lot of the time, no pun intended. I don't want to you to feel like I condemned you to that sort of life. So, I need to know, right now: do you want me to save you?"

Though he was on the verge of losing consciousness, Ethan had a vague awareness of what she was offering. What the ramifications of such a gift were, however, he had no idea. On some level, he felt as if that was the last thing he'd ever want, but at the same time, staying alive didn't seem too bad either.

"Ethan? Ethan, I need you to answer me," Zoey said, stroking the top of his head. When he didn't respond, the woman sucked in a deep breath before kissing him one last time. "Please don't hate me for what I'm about to do," she said. "Some things I don't want to lose."

"Like?"

"You."

With that, Zoey held her wrist above his face so he could see and sank her fangs into it. Her blood flowed down her arm for a brief second before she pressed the wound against Ethan's mouth. "Drink and don't you dare stop."

The dark liquid poured into his mouth. It tasted like cherries as it coated his tongue and ran down his throat. A euphoric feeling started on the tips of his lips and quickly spread across his body. Goosebumps raised across his skin, and as every hair across his body stood on end, an insatiable thirst gripped his soul.

Ethan shot upright and clenched her arm with both of his hands. He sucked on her wrist as hard as he could. Her life force pumped into him with massive spurts. He longed to take it all, to make sure he didn't miss a drop, but it never felt enough. The pain in his gut and chest eased and then disappeared altogether.

His eyes regained focus, and the world seemed a thousand times sharper and more vibrant than it had ever before. His skin felt alive, and the hairs across his body alerted him to every microcurrent in the air. His nose filled with a thousand different scents that he could easily pick out. Some sweet. Some metallic. Some musty. Some he didn't even have a word for.

But when his hearing increased a hundredfold, that's what really got his attention. He could pick up the whistling of air as it rushed in and out of Zoey's nose. He could hear the oil lamps on the wall steadily burn, and the grunts of Maii, still unconscious. Most of all, however, he could hear not only his heartbeat, but Zoey's as well, and how they beat together in perfect synchronicity.

"This is incredible," Ethan said, tearing himself away from Zoey's wrist. "How—"

His words cut short as his stomach turned sour, and it felt as if a herd of elephants had decided to stomp on his chest. Ethan rolled on to his side and curled into a ball before screaming at the top of his lungs. Muscles throughout his body contracted violently, threatening to split themselves apart.

Then the heaving began. At first, nothing came from his mouth but vile curses and spit. But after a few seconds, dark, co-agulated goo flew out, spattering on the floor. Ethan clawed his shoulders and sides before reaching out to Zoey who had now backed away a few feet.

"There's a war going for your body," Zoey said. "The holy versus the unholy, if you will."

Ethan cried out in pain once again before retching a second time and then a third and fourth. That's when he stopped counting.

Finally, when he was thoroughly exhausted and had been long convinced that he had nothing left to defile the floor with, Ethan rolled onto his back and tried to catch his breath. "Is it over?"

"Yeah," Zoey said, straddling his thighs and sitting down. "It's over."

Several moments passed before Ethan dared to believe. When he did, he realized he could feel something new in his mouth. A quick run of his tongue across his teeth showed he now sported exceptionally sharp fangs. He wasn't sure what face he made when he found them, but it had to be something notable because Zoey giggled.

"Those are for biting, in case you were wondering," she teased.

"Thanks for the info," Ethan said as he pushed himself up to his elbows and looked himself over. His wounds, both the one in his chest and the one through his gut, were still open, but were no longer gushing blood. In fact, they even looked smaller. Likewise, the imperfections on his skin seemed to have all but disappeared. To all of that, he couldn't help but grin. "I guess being like you isn't so bad," he said.

"Glad to hear you say that," she said. "How do you feel?"

Ethan paused as he tried to put a word to it. "Godlike?"

Zoey laughed. "Don't let that get to your head. You're not immortal."

"Yeah, I know," he said. "I only wish I could move my legs at this point."

"Why can't you?"

Ethan flashed her a wry grin. "You're sitting on them."

"Ha. Ha," Zoey replied. She then stood and helped him to his feet. "There's probably some extra gear and weapons around here we could use, not to mention goods to sell. That'll come in handy. But there's something else I saw when he took me that you'll like."

Ethan perked. "What would that be?"

"His ship."

"Like a ship, ship?" Ethan asked. "Like one better than we had before?"

Zoey shrugged while grinning wryly at the same time. "I guess you'll have to be the judge of that yourself."

Chapter XXXII
Fin

ETHAN STEPPED ABOARD the late Lord Belmont's brig-sloop, the *Victory*, and whistled. She was a gorgeous ninety-eight-foot vessel with two masts and eighteen cannons, including a pair of light, six-pound chasers in the forecastle. Her dark wood seemed to hum the moment he stepped aboard, which convinced him that not only was this a sleek, powerful ship that could navigate high seas as well as punishing combat with ease, but that it had been imbued with powerful magics that had to be nothing short of insanely awesome.

"Holy crap, this is way better than what we had before," he said. "I mean like, way, way, way better."

"It is pretty nice," Zoey said, hopping off the gangplank, setting the still unconscious Maii down, and coming to Ethan's side. She snaked an arm inside his and gave him a squeeze. "But if you'd rather have the cutter we left back at the cliffs, I suppose we could leave this one here."

"Uh, no," Ethan said, laughing. "She's all mine."

Zoey tutted. "I believe the arrangement was you get a half share. You can have that section over there."

"I did save your life," Ethan pointed out. "Twice, in fact."

"And you'd never have made it out of Bartigua without me," she pointed out.

"You don't know that."

Zoey raised her eyebrow.

"I would've made it out eventually."

Zoey grinned and draped her arms around his neck before kissing him softly. "Of course, you would have, my adorkable little baby vampire."

"This baby vamp should still get an equal share of the ship."

"You can have it all," she said. "I just like messing with you. Besides, I'm not the captain type, you know?" When Ethan nodded with approval, she changed subjects completely. "Have you figured out how you want to spec, yet?"

"Yeah, well, sort of," Ethan said, pulling out his character sheet. There had been several notable changes since she'd turned him. First and foremost, obviously, under race, it no longer said...well, whatever it had said before. He hadn't paid attention. Or at least, he couldn't remember. It was probably human. Regardless, it said "vampire" now.

The other notable difference was the fact that his primary stats had enjoyed a sizeable boost of one point each, except for luck and intelligence, each of which had jumped a total of three. And while being stronger and faster than before was nice, not to mention now enjoying an insane amount of luck, Ethan was glad he also finally boasted a whopping eleven intelligence and could even do some multiplication in his head without causing an aneurysm.

The changes to his character sheet didn't end there. Beneath the increased primary stats were several potential new abilities he could pick from. He'd narrowed his choices down to three. "I'm thinking about *Mist Form, Call of the Night: Bats*, and *Paralytic Gaze*," he said. "What do you think of those?"

Zoey leaned over and looked at his sheet. "They're all useful," she said. "I mean, you're not exactly going to become the Lord of the Undead with your starting choices, but none of them are even remotely useless. I'd say pick whatever you think you'd enjoy the most."

"I kind of like the bats one," he said. "It says I can summon them three times a night, and the total number of bats coming scale with my level."

"True, but we've got Maii. Not sure summoning bats competes with having a pet ahuizotl. That would be the only drawback I can see to that."

"Good point," Ethan said. "What happens when he's big, though? I mean, we can't keep him forever. This ring only works for so long."

"True, but if you were to work those new vampiric charms on him and convince him to be a willing and valuable party member, he'd be great to have stick around."

"How do I do that?"

"Become a much more formidable lord of the night than you are," she said. "Ahuizotls are drawn to power. If you can pull that off, you're back to my original point: bat summoning will always play second fiddle to having a pocket ahuizotl."

Ethan mulled the thought over and eventually agreed to what she'd said. If he was going to have some ferocious monster at his side, anyway, the bats did seem pointless. Or at least not as useful as the other options could be. He didn't want to put all his talents into one tree, to speak. He was about to go with his second pick, mist form, on account of it was how Zoey had freed herself, when he noticed one more option he hadn't seen before.

"Oh, now, that's interesting."

"What is?" Zoey asked, leaning in for a better view.

"*Luck of the Devil*," he said. "Prerequisite: Twenty-one *Luck*. What's that do, I wonder?"

"It should say."

"It doesn't."

Zoey snorted with disbelief. "Then don't pick it for sure."

"Too late," Ethan said, stuffing his character sheet back into his pocket.

Zoey pulled away with shock splashed across her face. "You're joking, right?"

"Nope. Sounds cool, and let's face it, my luck saved our ass."

Burying her face in her hands for a moment, Zoey sighed before doing exactly what Ethan knew she had to: concede the point. "Fine," she said. "You're right. It did. But please, as you get stronger, don't make any rash decisions like that when it comes to abilities. There aren't any respecs here. You pick it. You live with it. Forever."

"It wasn't a rash decision," Ethan said. "It was a lucky one."

"Whatever."

Ethan smiled and kissed her on the cheek. "I'm kidding, by the way. It says what it does."

"Which is?"

"*Luck of the Devil*: Succeed all rolls for the next ten seconds. Cooldown: one week."

Zoey gave a pained expression. "That's situational."

Ethan nodded, knowing she was right. "True, but it also has to be stupidly overpowered if chained correctly."

"Maybe. Possibly."

"It will be. You'll see," he said. "Now then, I've got a question: even with my novice skills as a sailor, I know we're going to need more than the three of us to get this fine ship sailing properly. Where do we get a crew? I'm guessing we need like fifty."

"We could get by with thirty, but that's pretty bare-bones," Zoey said. "And we won't be able to fight worth a damn. We'll want a hundred or more."

"That sounds like a lot."

"It is, but we've got a few options," Zoey replied. "First, and easiest, we go back to Weynock, sell some of the loot we got, hire us a crew."

"Straightforward. Simple. I like it. What's the catch?"

"The crew will be dirty pirates and mercenaries for the most part who won't take kindly to us snacking on them," Zoey replied, chomping her teeth a few times for extra effect. "It'll be difficult to keep the feedings low-key. Not impossible, but difficult for certain. And if that cat gets out of the bag, we're going to have to be ruthless to put down whatever mutiny is guaranteed to follow."

"Okay, what else do we have?"

"Lord Belmont's ritual book and staff," she said. "We could potentially raise an undead crew."

"Potentially?"

Zoey nodded. "Yes, but I'm not exactly a spellcaster, and neither are you. We'll probably screw something up."

"Which means?"

"At best, we get an army of skeletal hamsters."

"And at worst?"

"We become skeletal hamsters."

Ethan snickered and rolled his eyes. "Okay, that one is definitely a no-go."

"The final option," Zoey said slowly, "is we go to Lenada—a small port on an island a few days away. Two people live there we'd be interested in."

"Who are they?" Ethan asked.

"The first one is a girl who won't mind us snacking on her, provided we stock up on healing potions so she can heal after each meal," Zoey replied.

"She sounds crazy."

"You're not too far off from that," Zoey said. "I had her as a blood doll for a while, but she quickly became annoying. Every day it was 'Zoey, make me a vampire.' And 'Zoey why won't you make me a vampire?' and 'Zoey, please! You know we'd make the cutest, most powerful unholy couple to sail the eleven seas.'"

"Couple?"

Zoey nodded. "She's a little infatuated with me."

"A little?"

"A lot. Still, we're going to need food. She'd be the easiest."

Ethan balked. "Eh."

"It's hardly ideal, I know, but if you want to keep what we are quiet—and believe me, we do—Lenada is going to be our best option, in my opinion. We'll just have to put up with the drama."

"I'm not a fan of drama."

"Me either," Zoey replied. "However, there's also one more guy there we might be able to hire on who would definitely come in handy, and he won't care if we're vamps at all, provided we leave him alone during meals."

"Who's that?"

"Marcus, a necromancer," Zoey said. "He might be able to raise us a crew with Lord Belmont's staff and ritual book. If that's the case, we wouldn't have to hire more people, and that means—"

"We don't have to worry about anyone else knowing who we are," Ethan finished.

"Exactly."

Ethan turned her suggestion over a bit. It sounded good, but a nag in his gut told him there was more to the story. "This seems too easy of a choice. What's the catch with this Marcus guy?"

"He's bullheaded and weird."

"Weird?"

"You'll have to see for yourself," she said with a shrug. "He also likes to try unconventional experiments, which don't always turn out well."

"Okay, well, that doesn't seem too bad as long as we aren't turned into skeletal hamsters," he said before mulling the options Zoey gave one last time. In the end, there wasn't a lot for Ethan to consider when he realized he didn't like the idea of snacking on an unwilling crew. In fact, he didn't like it so much, he figured whatever the future had in store for them at Lenada had to be a thousand times more agreeable than dining secretly on others.

"Alright, Lenada it is," he said, putting his hands on his hips and giving a curt nod. "Weigh anchor! Raise the sails! We make for the island this very moment!"

Zoey sucked in a breath before exhaling sharply and flashing a knowing smile. "Aye, aye, Captain," she said. "But I think I should say one last thing."

"What's that?"

"As I said, I honestly don't know how skilled Marcus is," she replied. "We could still wind up as skeletal hamsters."

Ethan shrugged, not wanting to dwell on all the ways this next leg of their adventure could go wrong. "Could be worse," he said. "But I've got *Luck of the Devil*. We'll be fine. You'll see."

THE END OF BOOK I

The Crew
Captains & Cannons Book II

It's hard to win a race without a crew... and Ethan's hope to obtain one before the Grand Regatta starts is dashed to pieces the moment he lays anchor at Lenada.

Her citizens are gone.

Her buildings razed, and mysteries abound.

What happens to him next continues the epic grand adventure across the high seas, one that's filled with more swords, cannons, pirates, and ships; not to mention a voracious ahuizotl with his own plans for Ethan's future.

Acknowledgements

My heartfelt thanks to my fantastic editor Crystal for working on this new series with me, as well as the Mrs. for all her hard work and motivation for getting it done. The littles, too, for offering a lot of great creative input as we tossed around early ideas for the storyline.

Of course, another heartfelt thanks to all of my beta readers who read early drafts and helped smooth things out.

And *another* heartfelt thanks to all of my readers and fans of this book. Here's to hoping you enjoy the next as much (if not more) as the first.

And, and...I definitely need to thank Bob Kehl for both his talent as an artist and the license on the amazing cover. The moment I saw it, I said to myself, "I don't know who she is, but she needs a story." And thus, the quest for *The Pirate* was born.

About the Author

When not writing, Galen Surlak-Ramsey has been known to throw himself out of an airplane, teach others how to throw themselves out of an airplane, take pictures of the deep space, and wrangle his four children somewhere in Southwest Florida.

He's also recently taken up murder yoga, and thus discovered a passion for choking friends out. Thanks to his long legs, he tends to favor triangles, but won't pass up a good cross-collar.

Drop by his website https://galensurlak.com/ to see what other books he has out, what's coming soon, and check out the newsletter. (Well, sign up for the newsletter and get access to awesome goodies, contests, exclusive content, etc.)

About the Publisher

Tiny Fox Press LLC
5020 Kingsley Road
North Port, FL 34287

www.tinyfoxpress.com